APRONS & VEILS
BOOK FOUR

I0561558

The Vanishing of
Miss Victoria

GRACE HITCHCOCK

VALMONT
HOUSE PUBLISHERS

Published by Valmont House Publishers

GraceHitchcock.com

Names: Hitchcock, Grace, author.

Title: The Vanishing of Miss Victoria / Grace Hitchcock

Other Titles: the vanishing of miss victoria

Series: Aprons and Veils; book 4

Identifiers: 979-8-9912707-9-3 Large Print | 979-8-9869570-7-4 Paperback | 979-8-9869570-6-7 Ebook

Subjects: Christian Romantic suspense fiction

All scripture quotations, unless otherwise noted, are taken from the King James Version of the Bible.

Cover design by *Carpe Librum Book Design*

Editor Chantelle Mills

Author is represented by The Steve Laube Agency

For Dakota,
always & forever
my heart is yours

"I will extol you, O Lord, for you have drawn me up and have not let my foes rejoice over me. O Lord my God, I cried to you for help, and you have healed me. O Lord, you have brought up my soul from Sheol; you restored me to life from among those who go down to the pit. You have turned for me my mourning into dancing; you have loosed my sackcloth and clothed me with gladness, that my glory may sing your praise and not be silent. O Lord my God, I will give thanks to you forever!"

PSALMS 30: 1-3 & 11-12 ESV

CHAPTER 1

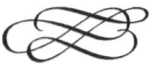

L *as Vegas, New Mexico*
November 1898

CORINNA IGNORED the fresh blister on her right heel as she served another plate of flank steak and potatoes to a dusty rancher. Her black skirts swished over the crimson and white tiles as she wove about the Harvey House's pristine tables, begging the busyness to keep the haunting memories at bay. But no matter how many extra shifts she took on, the ache in her chest from her mistakes was ever present.

"Miss Corinna!" The rowdy man from

her table shouted, lifting his china cup in the air and sending her jumping and nearly knocking over the pot of hot coffee on the lunch counter. His friends shook their heads at his outburst, one elbowing him.

She smiled apologetically to the Harvey Girl working the counter. Corinna grabbed the heavy pot to refill the man's cup, commanding her racing heart to slow. After months of working as a Harvey Girl, Corinna had hoped that she would cease jumping at every shout of her name, but with her past chasing her very shadows, it was difficult not to fear the reckoning seeking her.

"How about you finally stop teasing me and agree to step out with me, Miss Corinna?" The lanky cowboy grinned up at her as his friends dug into their lunches of beef stroganoff and tenderloin tips of beef picante.

Buck Bridger was a handsome enough man, but Corinna couldn't afford to be distracted—distractions could end with her becoming too comfortable and her wrists in irons. "Mr. Bridger, I sincerely thank you for your daily invitation, but I work every day."

"They give you off every Sunday morning for church and a full day off every ten days, don't they? I've been coming here long enough to know the rules." He lifted his fried chicken leg in a salute and took a bite.

"Some girls get days off, but *I* am always working," she returned with a smile and filled the other men's cups as she dodged Buck's questions. It was becoming harder and harder to avoid telling falsehoods to shield herself. She returned the pot to the counter as one table of guests in her section vacated.

She smiled at the young family leaving and tucked the tip into her apron pocket. A quarter had seemed so paltry a sum not too long ago, but now, every coin was precious, and she was grateful for anything extra. She piled the dessert dishes and cups in such a way to only make one trip to the dirty dish bin. Sweat dripped from the golden curls framing her face, but she did not heed them. She couldn't afford to take a break while

Buck Bridger was near the Harvey House. If Buck caught her on the back porch taking a breath of fresh air, he'd talk her ear off and try to get her to talk too—and that was something she could never allow.

Life on the run was exhausting, especially when one was innocent, but did her thieving in-laws care? No. They only wanted her to pay for her husband's murder with her life and her fortune. . . if one could even call that rat of a man a husband. But the marriage certificate that Corinna Victoria Alistair-Roberts kept hidden in the box under her Harvey House dormitory bed said William Roberts had been *her* rat.

She moved behind the potted palm that marked the staff's area, set the dishes in the dirty bin on the shelf, and reached for the rag and bucket to clean off the table and draped a fresh tablecloth over her arm.

Corinna scrubbed the table and tossed the linen into the air, watching it settle over the wood like a discarded wedding veil. She ran her hands over it, smoothing out the wrinkles. She hadn't even had a veil when she'd married—even though she had kept her mother's wedding gown in a trunk in the attic for such a purpose. She and William had eloped too suddenly to even retrieve it.

She collected the cutlery and set them atop the table, aligning the silverware perfectly. Order out of chaos brought her a sense of control—something she desperately wished for after her world tumbled everything out of place. *Will anything be set to right again?*

After their hasty elopement last Thanksgiving, William had discovered she didn't get a dime of her inheritance until her father's death. He only remained long enough to take all her cash, gold, and any jewels she had brought with her. If that rat had stayed, he would have been overjoyed to know that Corinna had come into her inheritance quickly after all. She may not have killed her late husband, but she had certainly killed her father. Father's death had been at her hand as sure as she was waitressing in this quaint, dusty little town—not from any weapon, but from a broken heart at her deceit and choices.

She hated giving up her father's surname of Alistair, almost as much as she hated that Roberts had legally replaced it. Thankfully, no one here knew about either surname. The lies by omission and forced silence made for a rather lonely existence and it didn't help her loneliness when her only friend in the Harvey House, Lorna Elliot, married yesterday.

The other waitresses were friendly enough. It was her past that was the problem. Any questions about her past from others left her breathless, tongue-tied, and anxious, which resulted in her being very difficult to befriend . . . apparently.

"He's back," Freya Lacy sang under her breath.

Corinna turned to the blonde waitress at her elbow, balancing the coffee cups and saucers as she finished setting the table. "Who?"

"That gorgeous friend of Lorna's husband, Tanner Sterling!" Freya fanned her cheeks with her hand. "Now, that's a man that could make a girl give up her position as a Harvey Girl."

"Maybe for you," Corinna muttered. "I'd much rather an apron than a veil."

"And he's staring at you again," Freya whispered.

"A-always stare," Corinna aligned the chairs about the table and nodded. *Perfection.*

Freya wrinkled her brow. "Pardon?"

Corinna forced the full sentence out and grabbed the full pot of coffee in anticipation of the guests' needs. "They always stare. Not unusual."

"Yes, but usually our guests are not quite as handsome as that one. Whew." She flapped her handkerchief and dabbed her cheek. "Gentlemanly with perfect manners, tall and broad as they come, with dangerous, piercing blue eyes under golden hair and sun-kissed skin? How could you *not* notice that he's a dream come to life? Why, he's fairly walked out of the pages of those dime novels I see you reading in our Rawlins dormitory parlor." Freya procured the coffee pot from Corinna. "I'll serve him."

"My section." Corinna ground out. She could not afford for the head waitress to catch her passing off her duties on another waitress after last week's warning. Corinna had attempted to give away Buck Bridger's table to Pernilla and, of course, Dolly Matthews had caught her in the act. Dolly never seemed to catch Corinna doing all the extra tasks for the rest of the girls though.

"Oh, don't worry about that. I know it makes you uncomfortable to serve any good-looking man." Freya swished away, smiling down on the broad-shouldered Mr. Sterling before Corinna could explain that neither his stares, nor his good looks, unsettled her. Serving never unsettled her.

She was used to working in a restaurant from a young age and was used to stares, but it was *conversing* that was the issue. At the clearing throat behind her, she started again. She sucked in a breath as the white linen cloth between her hand and the silver coffee pot slipped. Her fingertips burned against the scalding side. She plunked the pot down on a nearby vacant table and gritted her teeth at the smattering of coffee seeping into the white tablecloth. She adjusted her grip and closed her eyes, bracing herself at the tell-tale *tap tap* of heels approaching her. *Blast.*

"I've held my tongue for weeks now, Corinna Victoria, but I cannot continue to allow you to push all your tables onto others when you encounter an *enthusiastic* guest. It isn't fair, and if you cannot perform your job, there are twenty others who will do so."

Corinna didn't have to turn around to know who chided her, but she forced her chin down and turned, curtsying. "I'm sorry, Miss Dolly, b-but—"

"But nothing." Dolly Matthews held up her hand to stop the flow of excuses and fished around the little basket she had draped on her arm. "I had planned on waiting to announce this at the meeting before the evening shift. However, it seems you need to know now. I've decided more advanced methods are needed to encourage you all to improve your work." She lifted the shining bronze badge from the basket and turned it over in her palm. "I just picked these up at the post office. I heard about this method at another house and decided it was time to adopt it here at the Castañeda. As you can see, the badges have numbers. The waitresses will all be numbered from one to fourteen." She motioned to the tiny circular bronze pin with an engraved "1" in the center that Corinna hadn't noticed on Dolly's bodice. "As head waitress, I'm, of course, number one, and always will be, unless the house manager decides otherwise." She dropped the pin the size of a penny in Corinna's palm.

Corinna gritted her teeth against the gleaming "14." She wanted to protest that she was a wonderful waitress. Corinna knew it. But when she didn't stand up to the others and keep her sections, no matter how handsome the guest sitting in it happened to be, Corinna would of course *appear* the weakest link in the Harvey House chain of fresh-faced waitresses. "Miss Dolly, I didn't give—"

"Go on. Pin it on your bodice. It's a reminder that we waitresses value hard work at the Harvey House. However, if anyone should retain position of fourteen for longer than two weeks, they will be dismissed."

"Yes, Miss Dolly," she murmured. "I'll set this table again—"

"Oh no." Dolly planted a fist on her hip. "I think you are overdue for your break. Take some time and think long and hard about your position here."

She eyed the watch pin on Dolly's bodice. "I still have an hour left of my shift, though."

"I know. I have an errand for you while you think. Take this and move out of the way, please." Dolly Matthews fished an envelope from her pocket and shoved it into Corinna's hands. In following of the Fred Harvey standards, Dolly snatched a clean dish and began stacking the plates and silverware, grabbing the now-spotted tablecloth, and draping it over her arm. It all had to be cleaned and replaced.

"Let me help, and then I can post it for you." Corinna tucked the mysterious envelope into her apron pocket, removed the coffee pot, and reached for the clean stack of dishes. "It's my fault that we have to reset the—"

"No, thank you, Miss Corinna." She dismissed her with a wave. "Your shift is almost over, and we need to take a breath from each other. Bring that letter out to Queen Ranch. It's Lorna Elliot *Reid's* final pay. She forgot to pick it up before her wedding."

"This is highly unorthodox," Corinna whispered as her fingers grasped the sealed envelope even as the idea of visiting the peaceful ranch called to her. Lorna *had* asked her to drop by the ranch to check on her stallion, Bunny, while she was on her honeymoon in Colorado Springs.

"So is handing off every table that makes you uncomfortable," Dolly retorted.

Corinna glanced over to Tanner Sterling's table. He downed his cup as Freya brought him a plate of pasta. Corinna swallowed her protest.

"The carnival for raising money to build the new children's home is in two days," Dolly continued, "which is hosted by the Harvey House, as you very well know, and you haven't even signed up for a booth yet. I suggest you think on it too while you walk, or else you'll be stuck with a booth that no one wanted." Dolly nodded toward the door. "You better get a move on it if you want to be home by dark. I do not want to be held responsible if you twist your ankle in a gopher hole if you tarry and are stuck finding your way home at night."

Corinna bit back another protest that it was Freya who had *taken* her table without asking, but as that would take some explaining and draw more attention to herself, she nodded and sped for the kitchen's swinging door while Freya giggled at Mr. Sterling's table again as she lingered with her pot of coffee, but, of course, Dolly ignored the breech of etiquette.

Corinna wove about the bustling kitchen staff, tugged off her apron, and tossed it in the dirty laundry basket in the back corner of the kitchen. She slipped out the back door, drawing deep breaths of fresh air, cleansing her anger of Freya's stealing her table and Dolly's unfair treatment. If only she was free to stand up for herself—to unleash her tongue. *No. Do not wish for things to be different. You are lucky you have avoided a jail cell thus far with those Roberts after you, especially with only changing your surname to your middle name. Head down and work hard.*

She unbuttoned the top of her high collared black gown and tucked the envelope inside before buttoning the stifling collar once more. Her feet ached at the thought of the long walk ahead of her with her already throbbing blisters, but she didn't dare remove her shoes and risk getting the cuts filled with dirt and making the situation worse. Avoiding the main street, and therefore avoid any chance of meeting Mr. Bridger, who seemed to be everywhere these days, she strode behind the hotel toward the ranch.

At the cut through to Queen Ranch, she found a raging river in the place of the quiet creek she had encountered merely two weeks ago when she had walked down here with Lorna to visit her friend's future home. Corinna squinted up at the blue sky and the position of the sun as Lorna might do. She sighed. She had no idea how to tell the hour by it, but as the walk likely took up the last bit of her shift, she knew it was getting too late in the afternoon to take the long way around to the wooden bridge leading to Queen Ranch. If she didn't complete this task, Dolly would most certainly come up with another horrid chore to make Corinna regret her choices all the more.

She strode along the bank, watching for any spots where the waters quieted, but it only raged. At last, she found a spot with a trio of staggered boulders that created almost a natural bridge if one leapt. She sank down on the muddy bank and tugged off her black half boots, sighing in relief as the leather and hose came off, allowing her poor aching feet the chance to breathe, if only for a few moments.

She withdrew from the bank and bouncing on the balls of her feet, she charged forward and leapt from the bank. She laughed as she landed atop the first stone easily, despite her feet slipping a tad. She gauged the distance to the second. With the furious water beneath her, this boulder seemed a little further away than it had from the bank, and a hint of doubt curled around her heart. "Lorna could do it. Can't be too hard."

She crouched and sprang forward. Her soles slipped on the smooth surface of the second boulder, and she stumbled, the stone striking her knees through her skirts. "Ow!"

She sat back and rubbed the agonizing spot, blinking back her tears and questioning her abilities again, but she was almost to the other side, and the funds had to be delivered by *her* for some reason and not wait until Lorna returned. Corinna winced as she stood and swung her arms back and forth. "Come on, you frightened rabbit. Remember the stories you read with Father of daring women and brave bounty hunters. This is nothing to daring, dead-shot Drake. Nothing!" She simply needed to try hard enough.

She tossed aside the last of her inhibitions and leapt. Her foot met not the solid rock, but the freezing water as she plunged, the river engulfing her and sweeping her away.

CHAPTER 2

A faint cry rolling across the long grass caught his ear. Tanner Sterling whistled short and sharp, signaling his palomino to halt in their return to Queen Ranch. Silver snorted hard. "Hush, boy. Listen." Tanner stood in his stirrups and searched the direction of the cry. "Hello?" He shouted. "Hello, can you hear me?"

"Help!" A strangled cry reached him.

It was a woman's scream. He kicked Silver into a gallop and charged toward the river, racing along the bank as close as he dared, searching. He jerked back the reins when he heard the cry again. He spun in his saddle. There, clutching on a fallen log, was a heap of black skirts and streaming blonde hair. The river was raging. He didn't dare lead Silver into waters like that. He dismounted and tested the strength of the fallen trunk with a few good *thunks* of his boot's heel to the wood. It was solid enough. He spread his arms and carefully crossed the narrow log, watching for patches of slime that might cause him to slip, the corner of his eye always on that heap of black and blonde. "Are you hurt, Miss?"

The woman whimpered. "H-help me, please."

She had a genteel voice. What was a lady doing out here? Alone? How did she come to fall in the river? He knelt, the wet wood seeping into his leather chaps as his hand found purchase and encircled her wrist. With a single heave, he hoisted her up. She was a little thing and, despite her sodden skirts, didn't weigh much more than a sack of feed. Tanner set her on the log beside him, her hair still obscuring her features. "You all right there, Miss?"

"Thank you." She threw her arms about his neck.

His hand slipped at her unexpected launch. "Whoa!"

She gasped as he fumbled back, and with his arm about her, they fell head over heels back into the churning river. She nearly slid from his grasp as the water whirled them about.

He gripped her skirts and kept a hold on her. He wasn't taking the risk that she could swim. "Stay with me!" He shouted as the river turned into rapids. Keeping her in tow behind him and his feet aimed downstream to brace himself if needed, Tanner kept an eye out for any logs that might have been jammed up in the creek from the last storm. Silver raced along the bank, following them and releasing a concerned whinny.

The woman's head went beneath the water. He heaved his hold on her skirts, slamming her body into his as he wrapped his arm about her waist, tugging her above the water.

"Hold on! We are almost to the falls. It will spit us out soon enough," Tanner shouted above the roar.

"Falls?" she cried out, fear cracking her voice.

He tightened his arm about her tiny waist as he kept them above water with his legs and free arm. He reached for any boulder and shoved off those that threatened to knock them senseless. The falls were mild, but it could still bash them if they were not prepared. His boots were heavy now from being waterlogged, but at least he was able to protect the lady from the worst of the boulders. To the lady's credit, she did not cry out again or drag him under in her fear.

"Falls!" Tanner shouted as the water sped and then, they were in the air. Plummeting, he curled his upper body around the woman, positioning so his feet would hit the water first, protecting the woman from the brunt of it. The water slammed into his legs and they plunged to depths of the river. In the stillness of the fall's base, he shoved off a rock with her in his arm and swam for the shore. At last, the water turned calm. Slime coated the river rocks and made dragging her onto the bank difficult as his boots slipped.

In the shallows, he released his hold on her as he flopped on his back, coughing up the river. If he was this winded, how did the lady fair? He turned his head slightly so he could observe her while gathering his own strength.

She crawled to her hands and knees, mud up to her wrists. She coughed and drew in shaky breaths. Her soaking hair cascaded over her shoulders, shielding her face from view.

Should he push back her hair and see if she was injured? Would she consider it forward? He hadn't dealt with many ladies in his time. He was used to doing what needed to be done. "Miss?"

She shook her head, the movement giving him a glimpse of her face. Why, she was the same stunning Harvey Girl he'd spotted in the dining room getting in trouble from Miss Dolly while Miss Freya preened over him.

She shoved back her hair, leaving streaks of mud and crimson at her temples and cheeks. She panted, lifting her gaze heavenward with a whisper of thanks.

"You are bleeding." He jerked up, sweeping his gaze over her exposed skin.

She sat back on her heels and lifted her hands, pink water dripping from her fingers. She had multiple slices on her palms. They didn't look deep, but they had to be painful.

He grasped her elbow and helped her to the grassy bank. He released a shrill whistle for Silver, shaking his head at her wounds that gushed red. Her stunning hazel eyes widened, and a soft smile appeared in the corner of her lips as Silver trotted to them and knelt so Tanner could reach the saddle packs.

Grabbing his canteen from the saddle horn, Tanner dug through the packs for the emergency kit he kept handy. He fished out the leather pouch and withdrew the linen wrap and squatted beside her, gently taking her right hand in his. The cuts appeared clean, but with the river water and mud, they might get infected. He opened the canteen and poured clean water into the wounds. She didn't even make a hiss. She was a strong one.

"You'll want the doctor in town to clean these proper when you return, but this should stop the bleeding." He wrapped the linens over her palms, pressing to halt the blood as he wound the fabric in confident, secure motions until it looked like she wore a fingerless glove.

She turned her hand, studying it as he worked on her left hand. "H-how?"

"Pardon?"

She swallowed, and her brows furrowed as if she were focusing on her words. "H-how did you know? How did you keep us from bashing into the rocks, and how did you know how to wrap wounds?"

"I spend a lot of time on the trail and knowing how to tend to an injury can be the difference between life and death. And this ain't my first time falling into a river."

She studied him, not in the way Miss Freya had, as if he had been a steak on the Harvey House menu, but rather with interest, as if trying to figure him out. "You're a rancher?"

"I'm a bounty hunter." Or *was*, more accurately, but he was having a hard time remembering that it was his first day on the job as a foreman for Gaston Reid on *Queen Ranch*, but he didn't think explaining that would mean much to the lady in the state she was in.

Her eyes brightened and a smile bloomed so brilliantly that he blinked. Did she hear him correctly? Most everyone grew wary the moment he mentioned his occupation that involved criminals and weapons.

"A bounty hunter? Oh, how delightful!" She clapped her hands and winced as if she had forgotten about her wounds. "I've never met one before."

"I've been called many things in my life, but *delightful* has never been one of them." He chuckled, tugging at the red bead that held his tan Stetson in place during the river and adjusted the brim of his hat, studying the lady for signs of sun sickness. It was a mite cold for that, but with a newcomer, and a soft lady turned Harvey Girl, one couldn't be too careful. Her cheeks were flushed, and her pulse had been elevated when he had been wrapping her hand. He lifted the back of his hand to her forehead. "You feeling alright? No nausea?"

"My pa *adored* reading dime novels about bounty hunters in the Wild West." She ignored his questions and pushed the hair from her eyes, smiling up at him. "He would have been beyond excited to know that I've actually met one after we've read about you so extensively!"

"They have novels about bounty hunters?" He reached for her wrist. *Her pulse is still fast.* "How about dizziness? You feel dizzy? Or feel a fit coming on?"

"No dizziness. But, yes, you are fairly popular reading material in Chicago. My pa and I had a whole shelf of books dedicated to bounty hunters."

"Chicago? Is that where you are from?" He hadn't missed the past tense when she spoke of her father. *Likely he passed, and that's why she's a Harvey Girl now.* He reached for his canteen again, handing it to her with a little shake, hoping that it would bring her coloring to a normal hue.

Her eyes widened as if she realized how much she was talking. She accepted the canteen and turned it in her hands as if it were strange to her. "I grew up in the city and only recently came to New Mexico after training in Topeka with Lorna Elliot."

He bit back a smile and uncorked it for her, tapping the rim. "Drink."

She drew a long pull of the fresh well water and nodded her thanks, handing it back to him. "Delicious. What about you? The novels said your kind were men without a home and justice was your compass. Is that true?"

He snorted. "That's some flowery language, but it's true that I tend to roam wherever my job takes me, but I have a cabin with my brothers in the mountains not too far from Las Vegas. It's been our home for a long while now."

"How lovely." She turned to the partial view of the Gallinas Mountains, mostly hidden behind the foothills at this distance. "I worked briefly at the Montezuma Resort. The panoramic view every morning from my bedroom window would take my breath away. So, what are you doing on Queen Ranch then? Is there a criminal about?" She sat up, looking about as if a man in a scarlet bandana might appear behind a cedar, brandishing a pair of Colts.

"Not that I know of, but I am turning over a new leaf and becoming a foreman for my friend Reid. He owns the place."

"Gaston Reid? My best friend married him yesterday." She tilted her head. "Were you at the wedding? I don't remember seeing you."

He certainly would have remembered seeing her last night. He might have even broken his rule and danced with the stunning woman if he had, given he'd purposefully sat in her section of the dining room twice since coming to town. *Which is why it is a good thing you didn't see her. Women are a distraction.* "Briefly. I wanted to return to Queen Ranch to set up my room and get familiar with everything before I started as the foreman."

"Foreman? But do you have any experience with cattle being a bounty hunter?" She laughed. "Reid is a Texas Ranger, but he had a little experience from all his time spent on the Elliot Ranch in his boyhood. Did you work on a ranch before becoming a seeker?"

"I don't know much about cattle, but I know a lot about taking charge and getting results." He shrugged. "And more importantly, Reid owed me a favor after I saved his and Lorna's lives."

"You did? Was it with that ghastly gang, the Death Riders? I nearly lost Lorna because of them, but she's safe now. . . because of you?"

"Just doing my job." He nodded as if it were no big deal even though the wonder in her eyes made his chest swell a fraction at her admiration. "As for my new job, I was just in town ordering fresh supplies and taking a meal at the Harvey House before making my way back." He frowned. "But why are you out here if you know that Lorna Reid is on her honeymoon?"

"Punishment." She laughed at his expression. "Dolly Matthews insisted that I drop off Lorna's final payment before dark as I was not being as helpful as she wished."

His brows shot up. All of this because she had given away his table? But she was so friendly that he couldn't understand *why* she would try to avoid serving him. "And you came out all this way on foot because of Miss Dolly's punishment? But it's too late for you to be out alone."

She nodded. "Which is why I tried to save time by crossing the river."

"The river is far too high." He slapped his Stetson against his thigh. "If I hadn't come along—"

"I know that *now*." She studied her hands. "I only didn't want to be walking in the dark."

What he wanted to do was have a word with Dolly Matthews, but that was not his place. He could, however, save her the walk. "I can take it for you."

"That would be wonderful as I have a long, wet hike back into town." She pushed herself to her feet, eyeing the bank with a shiver. "There is no way I will attempt to cross *that* again, so I'll be going the long way back . . . once I find the road. Can you per-haps point me in the right direction?"

"After taking the time to fish you out, I'm not going to allow you to walk all the way back with soaked skirts slapping your limbs and slowing you down with the sunset approaching and cause you to potentially catch your death." He rose and beckoned his horse, helping her up with his other hand. "Silver can take us back in a quarter of the time."

She reached her hand out to the horse's nose, allowing him to catch her scent. "I don't want to put you out. You're soaked too, and I am sure you had things to do before you rescued me."

He wasn't going to take no for an answer, even if he had to ride behind her while she walked to ensure her safe return to town. Just because the Death Riders were locked away didn't mean there weren't still dangerous people about. Las Vegas had become civilized, but it hadn't been so many years since it was as wild as Dodge. He grinned. "I'm a *former* bounty hunter—riding in a different direction in a moment's notice to help a damsel is what we do."

She laughed and slapped away bits of

grass that clung to her skirts. "I'm certain that is in fact *not* at all what you do, but if we were in a novel, yes, it would be."

"Then we best not disappoint your expectations." He chuckled and lifted her into the saddle to sit sidesaddle. He climbed up behind her and wrapped his arms in front of her to guide Silver forward. "Back to town, boy. There's a carrot in it for you."

Silver threw up his head in agreement and trotted.

"I haven't spent much time with horses . . . they frighten me, really, but I have never seen a horse so intelligent."

"My brother Wade is a horse breeder." He patted the palomino's neck. "Silver is one of the best Wade has ever trained. Silver and I took a liking to one another since he was a foal. He's been with me a long time and is a better friend than any dog."

"Can he do other tricks too?"

Tanner grinned. "He can dance better than most men—myself included."

She whipped around to face him, bringing their lips impossibly close. "I'd like to see him dance sometime. I saw a dancing horse at the White City years ago, and it was," her gaze dropped to his lips for a half a breath, "magical."

Too soon, they approached the massive red brick Harvey House in a Mission Revival style with two wings jutting forward on the north and south sides of the main building with a slate roof over adjoining arches leading to a covered porch. Between the wings there was a courtyard with a single live oak in the middle and beyond it, adjoining the north and south sides of the building, there rose a bell tower with a good-sized black sign with green trim. The sign's painted gold letters read, *Hotel Castañeda, 1898.* "Well, it was a real pleasure, Miss."

"I hope you aren't planning on dropping me at the lobby," she giggled.

"Oh." He blinked. "I got lost in thought." He redirected Silver toward the Rawlins dormitory building behind the hotel where the Harvey Girls slept. He hopped down and instantly felt bereft of her warmth on the chilly evening. He lifted his hands to her waist, helping her down when he caught sight of a few waitresses peeking through the parlor window's lace curtain, whispering to each other.

"Seems we have quite the audience," Tanner said, smiling at the pretty Harvey Girl.

Her cheeks flushed, and she stepped away from his hands. "I thank you for the ride."

She turned to go, but he caught her hand, gently, so as to not disturb her wounds. "Do you have something for me?"

She tilted her head.

"The money for Lorna Reid?" He prompted.

"Oh!" She turned her back to him and fished out the wet letter from the top of her gown and handed it to him, her cheeks scarlet now. "I-I didn't have a pocket."

He tucked the limp envelope into his vest pocket with a nod. "Think nothing of it, Miss—I didn't catch your name."

"I didn't throw it." She smiled up at him.

"It would be most helpful should I ever wish to find you again." He patted his horse's neck and leaned toward her a hint. "Please?"

"Corinna."

He swiped off his hat and bowed his head. "It is lovely to meet you, Miss Corinna. I'm Tanner Sterling."

"It's an honor to meet you, Mr. Sterling. Now, I better change and see to my cuts before the whole town starts talking." She smiled at him once more and disappeared inside.

He tugged on his hat and swung into the saddle. One thing was for sure, he would be coming back to the Harvey House tomorrow during her shift to get himself one of those smiles again.

CHAPTER 3

*D*olly had been slightly gentler with Corinna today and had even apologized for sending her on an errand that ended with her soaked and hands in bandages. Dolly even offered for Corinna to take the morning shift off. She refused and had managed to move up to position twelve relatively quickly, thanks to another girl's mistake in calling a guest by his first name and another pouring tea in a guest's cup instead of coffee.

Corinna finished wiping down the lunch counter and chucked the rag into the bin under the counter. She lifted the top of the coffee urn and peered inside. *Empty*. The breakfast rush had turned into a lunch rush, but the urn was always to be kept filled for any cowpoke who ambled inside and wanted a decent cup of coffee. Dolly would be livid if she discovered it empty on Corinna's watch.

And as the kitchen staff took much needed breaks after lunch, the task was left to the Harvey Girls. The other two waitresses, numbers thirteen and fourteen, were busy serving families in their sections. She glanced at the only table still occupied in her section. The old banker was digging into his pie with gusto. She had time. She bustled into to the kitchen and prepared the first few pots. Corinna paused to peek out once more, but the banker had snapped open his newspaper and was contentedly sipping his tea.

When the first two pots were brewed, she gripped one in each hand and backed into the swinging door and set the heavy coffee pots beside the urn. She shook out her arms and collected one pot. She climbed on the stool and poured the coffee in the top of the urn, sweat gathering on her forehead as her arms strained with the effort of holding the pot aloft and tilted so any splashing coffee wouldn't burn her.

"Good to see you again, Miss Corinna." His voice made her gasp, and her hand slipped from the rag to the spout.

Tears sprang to her eyes.

"I am so sorry!"

She hastened down the stool and plopped the half-filled pot on the counter. She gritted her teeth against the second burning in the same spot in two days. It was already blistering. She would be fortunate if it did not scar. "Mr. Sterling," she managed and forced a smile to hide her pain.

"I should have waited for you to step down." Mr. Sterling twisted the brim of his hat in both his hands.

"It's fine." She smiled again, but the pain only increased. She needed some butter, or a hunk of ice. Anything to dull the smarting.

"Seems that I will have to fetch my medical kit again. Good thing Silver is out front." He gave a short sharp whistle, with a playful wink.

The guests in the Harvey House sent him a scowl.

A giggle burst within her. "Shh! What would Miss Dolly say?" Corinna refrained from cradling her hand, thankful that Mr. Sterling did not realize how much it hurt. She must be getting better at hiding her emotions after William crushed her spirit after a single hour of marriage. "I'm not so pathetic that I must be bandaged every day."

"Please, call me Tanner." He leaned over the counter, staring at the exposed angry, red skin between her thumb and forefinger. "Well, I'm a nincompoop for teasing. You really do *need*—"

A scream followed by shrieks coming from the lobby drew their attention to the dining room door just as a massive palomino's head appeared and Silver clomped into the dining room, his gaze on Mr. Sterling. The children in the dining room squealed with laughter and Corinna couldn't help keep her own laughter from bubbling out, even as she knew Dolly's wrath would be following if they did not fix the situation at once.

Tanner leapt from his stool. "Silver! I didn't actually call you, boy."

He reached for Silver's reins as Dolly Matthews strode through the doors, her gaze landing on the horse and Corinna, gasping as she nearly dropped her stack of clean china plates.

"I leave Corinna in charge of the dining room for *one* hour so I could eat, and *this* is what I get? A horse in the dining room?" Dolly hissed and set down her plates and motioned Corinna over. "Help me!" She lifted her hands to the palomino.

Tanner rested a staying hand on Corinna's forearm for half a moment and strode in front of them both. "I can't believe Silver heard me. I accidentally called my horse and—"

"I believe explanations can wait!" Dolly pointed toward the door. "Please, see to your horse, Mr. Sterling."

He grasped Silver's reins, muttering something to his mount under his breath and sent Corinna an apologetic grimace as he led out his horse, which made the laughter inconveniently bubble up again. She managed to turn it into a heavy cough, even though Dolly stared at her suspiciously.

The house manager raced into the dining room. "Miss Dolly! What is the meaning of this?"

"I am so sorry, Mr. Perkins. I was only taking my break."

"And yet, this has never happened on another head waitress's luncheon break. I don't know how I am to write that recommendation letter for you at this point." Mr. Perkins twisted the end of his greased mustache, tsking and shaking his head.

Corinna stepped forward. "M-my fault, sir. I was in charge."

"You allowed this to happen?" Mr. Perkins narrowed his beady eyes at Corinna. "There is a mound of dishes in the kitchen. Release the dish boy, and you get to work scrubbing until there is nothing left to scrub."

Dolly shook her head. "Sir, I don't think—"

"Please, Miss Dolly." He pinched the bridge of his nose and slowly exhaled. "If we didn't have Preacher Martin's charity carnival for the new children's home this week, I'd be sending for Miss Corinna's replacement, but there's no reason innocents should suffer because you—" He seemed to gather his temper as he drew in a sharp breath. "Most girls would never get a second chance after the stunts Miss Corinna has pulled."

"I was only expressing my concerns and seeking your opinion on how to help her become a better waitress, sir. I didn't think you were taking notes on Miss Corinna's performance based on what I said."

"Of course I did." He snapped his fingers at Corinna. "Miss Corinna, switch your badge with the number fourteen girl the minute you see her!"

Maura, the current last place badge holder, smiled up at Corinna from where she was scrubbing the table in the corner.

"You didn't have to do that for me," Dolly whispered as Corinna unpinned her badge.

Maura pranced over and switched numbers with Corinna.

"I know. It's all right, Miss Dolly." Corinna headed for the kitchen, any humor over the horse in the dining room immediately dying down at the sight of the dish boy's mountain range of dishes. "Break."

Ezra lifted his brows and pointed a sudsy finger to his ear. "What did you say, Miss Corinna? Can't hear much over the clank of the dishes."

"T-take a break, Ezra." She shoved out the words and motioned to the dishes.

"You get punished again?" He grinned, rubbing his hands together. "Alrighty! I wish more Harvey Girls would get in as much trouble as you. I ain't never had so many breaks until you showed up. Thank you!"

"Happy to help." Corinna bit back her smile. If she oversaw the dishes, she would probably dance a jig herself if someone came to relieve her in the middle of her shift. She checked her bandages at her palms. They were clean enough, but she'd have to change them afterwards. She reached for the top dish, grimacing at the cold gravy meeting her touch . . . at least, she hoped it was gravy and not the residue from one cowpoke's phlegmy cough.

Ezra plunked on his hat, chuckling. "Just wait until I tell William. He's going to be so mad he traded shifts with me today."

Her entire body went ridged at the name, her fingers curling around the cutlery. *William is a popular name. It's not your William. It's not him.* At the hand on her shoulder, she returned to the present and the young man's concerned gaze.

"You okay, Miss Corinna? If you are feeling poorly, I can stay."

"No. I'm fine. Thank you. I-I was lost in my own thoughts." She scooted out from his touch and gave him a convincing smile, motioning him to the door. She couldn't change the past, or control her future, but she could control these dishes. She rolled up her black sleeves and set to cleaning with renewed vigor. She was almost finished scrubbing the first stack when laughter caught her attention, and a group of Harvey

Girls strode past the sink after their luncheon.

"You seem mighty comfortable talking with Tanner Sterling." Pernilla Margot crossed her arms, her deep brown eyes narrowing on Corinna, one hand gripping a half-eaten puff pastry.

"He's a bounty hunter." Corinna focused on the rim of a cup stained with a woman's lip rouge. If she fixated on work, she could talk, but the minute she was not preoccupied, her tongue would get tangled again as it always did when non-work conversations began. She had never had this problem working in her father's restaurants where everyone was like family. Of course, she hadn't been hiding half herself away either.

"He is? But he said he was a foreman on Queen Ranch?" Pernilla shrugged and bit into her pastry, the raspberry filling catching on her bottom lip. She scraped her fingertip along the filling and sucked it off her nail. "I saw him first. Just thought you would like to know."

"Pardon?"

"I waited on Tanner Sterling when he

first came to the Harvey House weeks ago, and I put my claim on him with all the other girls." She tilted her head. "You weren't still employed at the Montezuma Harvey Hotel then. You certainly must have heard of my claim on him."

"Claim?" She reached for another dish. She hadn't paid much attention to the other girls' conversations during meals, or in the walks to church. She had been too busy looking over her shoulder.

"Yes." Pernilla frowned. "Have you never been around other women? When one has the first claim, it is courtesy to allow that woman to try to win the man in question first, and as I plan on succeeding, he is my future husband, and I would appreciate it if you kept your beaming smiles to yourself and not distract him." She tossed the corner of the pastry into the waste bin. She smoothed down her pristine white apron and tugged at the black high collar. She gave her cheeks a pinch as she headed toward the dining room entrance.

"I don't beam at anyone," Corinna muttered, even as she recalled him saving her from the creek. A man had never quite caught her attention before like him . . . not even William. With William, he had gradually begun to glow in her vision until he was a star in her heavens whose light warmed the corners of her heart. But Tanner Sterling was more than simply a glow in her line of sight, he was as warm as the sun bursting through the clouds on a winter's day when he walked into a room, but she supposed that reaction had more to do with his former occupation and how it reminded her of Father and the sweet times they shared over those dime novels.

Pernilla paused to plant her hands on her hips and glare at Corinna. "Yes, you do, which is why we are having this conversation in the first place. You have never shown interest in any man before, and I thought I'd warn you off, especially after I saw you in front of the Rawlins dormitory on his horse, all soaked, with his hands about your waist as he helped you down. I almost confronted you last night, but I was about to go out with Freya, and I didn't want to make her late meeting with her beau, or make an ill impression in front of my future husband—no man wants a jealous wife."

"That is ridiculous." Corinna swung around to face her, the water on the dinner plate soaking Pernilla's apron. "Sorry!"

"You did that on purpose!" Pernilla gasped, grabbing a clean rag, and wiping at it. "You are lucky it's just water as my shift starts in five minutes. Dolly hates any delay."

"I only wanted to convey that I am not interested in Mr. Sterling like that. He merely helped me."

"I'll give you the benefit of the doubt." Pernilla sighed and untied her apron. "I am sorry I snapped. It's only water, but I'll have to change. Just promise me that you won't steal him away?"

"Of course." It was an easy promise.

"Thank you, Corinna." Pernilla rewarded Corinna with a smile. "And if you are ever interested in a gentleman, just let me know, and I'll do my best to help you catch him. We Harvey Girls must stick together!"

Corinna nodded and returned to scrubbing as Pernilla hurried away to change. She had no interest in men. Not after William broke her heart. However, explaining that would mean confessing that she had been married—as short of a marriage it was with him signing the certificate, asking about her inheritance clause, and then walking out the door with her money and every piece of fine jewelry she had on her person at the time.

She had planned a life with William, given up everything to elope with him, and all he had wanted from her was money. She had dreamed of building a family with him, a life with him. Her heart still twinged when she thought of when she returned home to her father the morning after the wedding. His eyes had been swollen from weeping over her note from the night before, but when he saw her, he did not chide her. He wrapped her in his arms, kissing her tear-stained cheeks, saying that he forgave her and begged her to come home. William had abandoned her and so, she stayed and worked alongside her father until his heart gave out.

She only wished she could forgive herself as easily as Father had that day. But the damage from her elopement had been done. She knew he had a weak heart, and the strain of that night and the days that had followed, though forgiven, had done its work. And when that first threat from her husband's family arrived, nine months after William had left her, Father's heart gave out completely.

She had been warned about William's family from her father. He had sensed her getting close to William and told her, under no uncertain terms, that even though William had cut ties with them and Father had agreed to William being an investor, Father did not consider William a worthy suitor. His family was too dangerous and had close connections to some powerful crime families, but had she listened? She had considered herself in love and above such nonsense as the consequences of leaping too quickly. The fall had broken her as surely as the consequences of her actions had killed her father, and she had not stopped running since.

If she were smiling too much at Tanner, Corinna would dampen her smiles. Love had gotten her into this mess—never loving again would get her out.

TANNER RODE along the border of Queen Ranch, dodging cedar trees and scraggly bushes. There were prettier parts of the land, but this one was far from the river and didn't provide the brush enough water to thrive. He rode along the fence line, searching for weakness to prevent cows getting out and rustlers from getting in, when a form appeared on the hill. From the way the rider held himself, Tanner recognized him at once. What was Noah doing this far from the Sanctuary? *Trouble.* Tanner gritted his teeth and kicked Silver into a gallop to meet his youngest brother. Was someone hurt? Was that banker making trouble again? Tanner had sent in the overdue payment last week to Mr. Bradshaw with his earnings from the Death Riders' capture. After Mr. Bradshaw had come to the ranch to check on his holdings and seen the work the brothers had put into the land, he had become determined to call in the loan and in two years, Mr. Bradshaw legally could. *Did Bradshaw find a loophole that lets him call it in sooner?*

Noah lifted his hat, flipped it, and settled it on his head. Tanner sagged back into his saddle, slowing his horse at the signal that all was well.

"Good to see you, Noah. Why are you here if there's no trouble?" Tanner rested the reins on his thigh.

Noah reined in his horse, leaned on his saddle horn, and flicked up the brim of his hat. He looked the most like Tanner with his gold hair and blue eyes, but his personality was playful while Tanner's was all business. He supposed it helped that Noah had been shielded from the burden of supporting the family at thirteen, but even the youngest of them remembered and possessed scars, seen and not, from the train that had brought them West.

"Came to check in on you, Tanner. We got your letter from old man Morris, on his way back up the mountains, about quitting bounty hunting, and we wanted to make sure you were okay, given we knew how good you are at it. Something must have happened to make you quit. So, we drew straws on who would come to town, and I won." Noah stood in his stirrups, stretching, and plopped back into the saddle, making his mount dance to the side in protest.

"Should've explained more in my letter." Tanner shook his head over worrying his brothers, but the fur trader, old man Morris, had been about to leave the Harvey House for the mountains, and Tanner hadn't much time to write a note. "There was no need for you to check on me, especially given the rain. Did you get caught in it?"

"Got rained in at the mid-point last night and ate my provisions. I'm powerful hungry. I've been thinking of that Harvey House cookin' every minute. You wouldn't believe how hard it was to pass up the Montezuma turn in the trail to head over here, but thoughts of the Castañeda helped."

"You showed great fortitude." Tanner

grinned. "But you could have just sent a letter back with the fur trader in a few weeks. I wanted to learn the newest tricks to the trade from Reid's ranch and see if I could help our cabin become sustainable without my hunting for bounties. I want to raise cattle. I don't like being away from you all for so long, but that banker still needs to be paid." *Thief that he is.*

"We aren't a bunch of helpless kids anymore, Tanner. We haven't been for a long while." Noah patted his horse's neck. "You don't have to give up your job to be near us anymore to protect us."

"And yet, while none of you are married, I feel as if you are still counting on me."

Noah lifted his gaze at Tanner, a slow smirk spreading. "Fine words coming from a *single* man nearing thirty years. I'm only eighteen. I got plenty of time to find me a pretty wife. You, on the other hand, don't have time to mess around worrying about us anymore. If you want to be a bounty hunter, do it. If you want to become a rancher, I understand, and will gladly help you build a fence, but don't use us as an excuse for giving up the job we all know you are the best at and love."

"My motives are twofold." Tanner dug into his saddle pack for his leather pouch of beef jerky and tossed it to his brother. He could deal with the hunger pangs until he returned to the ranch. "It's time for a change. I feel like my luck might run out one of these days, and I've worked too hard to keep our family together to get myself shot and miss out on all the future days with you all."

"Only the Lord knows the number of our days, but I agree with you on your luck, brother. Ever thought of marrying? I heard there were women aplenty in the area with the new Castañeda in town." Noah grinned at him as he dug out a chunk jerky and clenched it between his teeth, tearing off a piece. "Sure would be nice to have a sister on the ranch with little ones runnin' about. It would liven up the place."

Tanner hadn't given marriage much thought until he had fished out that lovely Harvey Girl with a sense of humor to boot. "I'll admit, it's crossed my mind."

Noah hooted and spun his horse in a circle and walloped Tanner on the shoulder. "And *there* is the reason for you grinning more times in the past few minutes than I have seen you smile in months."

"To be fair, I haven't been home long enough lately for you to notice."

Noah settled back in his saddle, adjusting the leather strap beneath his chin holding his Stetson in place. "So, I'm guessing with your new position, you won't be back to the cabin for Thanksgiving next week?"

"Not sure yet. The boss will be back next week from his honeymoon, and we can discuss it then. I think he might be open to me riding out to the ranch for the day and night, given as he still owes me for saving his life." He chuckled. "But, even without that reminder, I doubt he'd object. Reid is a good man."

"Reid? No wonder you got the job as foreman with *no* experience." He snorted. "Reid will probably be glad to have you out of his hair for the day."

"Even though I will likely be giving up my Harvey Girl served Thanksgiving meal."

Noah shrugged and tore off another piece. "Clint's cooking has improved since you mailed us that cookbook."

"Improved could mean a great many things," Tanner chuckled.

"Well, given we are always short or missing ingredients, it's getting better than edible."

"That's quite the offer to pass up a Castañeda meal." Tanner wheeled his horse around. "Come on, let's get you some food."

"Food? But town is in the opposite direction!" Noah protested, pointing toward Las Vegas. "I've been thinking of the Castañeda's apple pie, which I haven't had since they opened, for the whole of the journey."

"You'll get plenty. I just don't have time to go today. Tomorrow there will be quite the shindig at the Harvey House, and with the way you smell, you'll want to take a bath in the creek before you dine at the Castañeda, because who knows, maybe the baby of the family will find his wife first."

"You sure are putting a lot of stock into a

bar of soap," Noah mumbled and nudged his horse to follow Tanner's. "I'm thinking it's more likely *you* who wants to smell like a prairie wildflower for the lady that has your grinning. But, if that's what it takes for you to settle down at the Sanctuary, I'll even wash my hair."

CHAPTER 4

*I*t had taken nearly the entirety of the next morning to prepare the wraparound porch and courtyard of the Castañeda with fall decorations for the carnival to raise money for building the children's home. From what Corinna overheard from the Harvey Girls, Preacher Martin and his wife had felt called to provide a home for orphans for years and the church had already purchased land in town to build the home. This carnival would be the final push to raise funds to begin building. If she had her funds, Corinna would donate more than enough to build it, but with her assets locked away, all she had was time and an able body to help.

The Harvey Girls had draped the arched colonnades with every fall wildflower they could find—purple coneflowers, cheery sunbursts of black-eyed Susan, purple aster, and fireweed.

The men on staff had hauled the tables from the dining room to the corners of the porch where the Harvey Girls dressed them in fine linens trimmed with the brilliant yellow boughs of the quaking aspen trees and the fiery branches of the eastern redbud tree.

And now that the event was beginning in a quarter of an hour, Corinna and the girls brought out trays of refreshments, sandwiches, and pastries, spreading them at each table. After placing her last tray and making certain the netted dome was secure atop the food to keep the flies away, Corinna glanced about the porch to see where she might help with last minute preparations. Thankfully, she didn't need to take time to change out of her uniform as the Harvey Girls were running the event and wanted to be easy to spot should any need arise.

The Harvey Girls had different booths set up for the town folk to come play, and all the proceeds would go to helping the cause. The main event was the raffle where a year of dinners could be won—a prize that already had every bachelor in town signing up, and at fifty cents an entry, it was the most lucrative of all the booths . . . and as it had been Corinna's idea, she had hoped she would be working there, but seeing all the men flocking the booth, she was grateful that Pernilla had elbowed her way to the front to the volunteer sign-up sheet this morning.

Corinna paused by a booth with a broad table with ten different cones holding various turquoise jewelry prizes and a stack of three tossing rings. A silver bracelet with a turquoise stone was in the hardest location to capture in the ring toss. It was quite stunning and must be worth a pretty penny.

Laughter reached her, and she glanced up to find the townsfolk appearing, and the fiddler picked up his bow and played a lively tune that pulled guests from the ornate lobby into the makeshift carnival. His music set Corinna's toes to tapping. She dearly loved to dance, but to do so, meant to let her guard down.

"You need to be at your booth." Dolly paused at her side.

"I was never assigned." She motioned to the booths. "All have Harvey Girls running them, and it seems all are in working order. I was about to find you."

"Good. There's one more—one of the girls got sick and it needs to be manned. Follow me." Dolly wove through the guests already meandering the wide porch and around the corner to a booth that already had a swarm of boys pointing at glass jars and tanks.

"Ah, here's the booth." Dolly stopped in front of a pet-the-reptile booth. "No one else would sign up after Jenny took ill this morning."

Corinna's stomach dropped. "I-I don't think I can do this."

"It's just frogs, turtles, and a few harmless snakes." Dolly shrugged. "I would run it myself, but I have to oversee the whole event."

To Corinna's surprise, Dolly actually seemed genuine in her remorse. "A-are your certain that there aren't any other booths?"

Dolly flipped open her notebook, turning the page and running her finger down the line. She grimaced. "It's not better than this. You might wish to stay here."

If Dolly can face a booth full of reptiles and not grimace, what on earth has her frowning like that? "Dare I ask?"

She sent Corinna a pitiful smile. "There's an opening for the kissing booth. But even *I* would never ask you to do that." She shuddered. "Some girls have no shame when it comes to testing out future husbands. Certainly, the thought of marriage passed my mind two or three times, but never seriously. I love my position too much to give it up for any man, unless he has a fortune, but even then."

"A k-kissing booth?" Corinna's lips parted. "That was *approved*?" She had heard a flock of girls giggling over the idea in the parlor when they had collected ideas for booths, but never did she think such an out-landish idea would be permitted, especially given the high standards Fred Harvey re-quired of his waitresses.

"I was just as surprised as you, but ap-parently, kissing booths are becoming rather popular, even in the East. They are scandalous, but the board thought it would raise a significant portion." She rested her hand on Corinna's shoulder. "I know we haven't exactly gotten along for nearly the entirety of your time here, but I truly do not want to see you miserable. I can take the reptiles for fifteen minutes if you want to wander about the booths and find one that needs another girl. I know there is one male on staff who can be spared soon and can take over the reptile booth so I can return to my duties."

Everything in her wanted to question Dolly's gesture, but she decided it was worth the risk to accept the offer at face value. "Thank you, Miss Dolly." She darted away, moving through the booths.

She nodded to a Harvey Girl as she sold her sock puppets to a group of children, wove around the confectionary booth, and dodged the line at the dart throwing booth, until she reached the three-legged race where a child and her father were ready to go but were waiting on challengers. She smiled to Vera Ward who appeared to be running the event. "I can run if someone needs a teammate for the race, Vera."

"Oh, would you? I haven't even had a single race yet, and they have been waiting nearly five minutes, and I fear they will leave." Vera Ward sighed. "I can't win if no one joins the three-legged race! I need to win booth with the most entries! That reward is too good. Can you imagine getting twenty dollars to spend while on vacation at *any* Harvey House for a weekend? But I can't even begin to fantasize what it would be like because no one will run. We need to find you a partner and quick!"

"I can join her." Tanner Sterling held out his ticket to Vera and smiled at Corinna. He was clean shaven, with his thick, blond hair combed back with a single curl that refused to be tamed. His blue shirt made his eyes piercing, forming a lethal combination.

"Thank you!" Vera beamed up at the giant man.

"I hardly think we would be a fair match against a father and child." Corinna glanced up at Tanner. The man was impossibly tall beside her. The top of her head didn't even come up to his shoulder. "But I suppose we are such a mismatch, we might fall straight away."

"I never fall, but I can pretend to," Tanner grinned down at her.

"I hate to correct you, but I recall you falling into the river." She reached for the short length of rope and bent to bond their ankles. His boots were well worn but polished as if he had made a special effort for the day. *Did he do so for me?*

"Extenuating circumstances." He held his hand down to her and helped her to standing.

As she righted herself, a mother and son joined the race. Her cheeks burned at what Dolly would say if she saw her racing now that there was another team, and they didn't need Corinna to compete with Tanner.

Dolly wouldn't even wait to hear the truth before she sent her packing.

"On your mark, get set, *annd* go!" Vera waved her little red flag, giggling at the racers all stumbling at her tricky start.

Tanner's hand wrapped about Corinna's waist, securing her to him. They surged down the makeshift track, but when they came to the line of potato sacks to hop over, she jumped before Tanner was ready, and he tripped forward, bringing her down with him.

She braced herself for impact, but his arms wrapped about her, and he pulled her against his chest as he crashed into the earth, shoulder first, grunting and laughing. The others hopped over without a problem. She pulled him to his feet. "Hurry!" She laughed as they hobbled forward and placed dead last. "Good job!" She called to the little girl who had won with her father as Vera handed her the prize of a stuffed bear.

She turned to Tanner and, forgetting they were still attached, smacked into his chest.

Tanner chuckled and reached out to her,

brushing her hair from her face, and running his thumb over her cheek. "The Harvey Girl police will be coming for you with such dirt on your cheek." He winked.

She caught sight of Pernilla scowling at her from under the live oak where she was still selling raffle tickets in the courtyard. *That will not do.* She had to get away from him. They bent at the same time to untie the knot and knocked heads, sending her falling to her backside. She swallowed back a grunt.

"You are the most accident-prone woman I've ever met." He rubbed his forehead. "I might need that shining white armor around you that you seem to think I wear from all that reading."

"I wouldn't object. I'm not usually this clumsy, so I think it must be *you* who is causing all these mishaps," Corinna protested with a laugh, her cheeks warming under his smiles.

"I'd hope not. Otherwise, I'd probably be dead already from my former line of work." He freed the knot and helped her to standing once more. "There, you are free now. I'll let you get back to your booth. Or, are you planning on racing again?"

"Oh, no. I'm moving about and seeing which booth needs help." She dusted off her apron and ran her hands over her hair, hoping to tame any stray hairs.

"I'll come with you then if you don't mind. My brother is here with me, and he got a mite consumed with winning a prize knife from the throwing knife booth. It could be a while, and you'd be doing me a favor to allow me to wander with you."

Corinna motioned him to join her and trailed along the booths, picking up her pace when she reached the kissing booth, intent on skirting right past it, especially with Tanner at her side. She didn't know what she would do if Tanner stopped, or worse, if Jean May needed her help.

"Corinna!" Jean May waved her over to the scandalous booth that the girls had arranged to look like the side of a tiny, vine covered house with a painted cut out made to look like an open window where the girls could stand behind and lean out. "Corinna! Corinna, please come. I need a break."

Corinna's lips parted, and she felt heat rush to her cheeks as she glanced at Tanner and back to Jean May. "I-I can't possibly!"

"Just for a moment. No one is at the booth now. I only need five minutes!" Jean May tsked, grabbed Corinna's wrist, and pulled her away from Tanner's side to stand behind the booth, whispering, "I need to use the necessary."

"No, Jean May, please, I—"

"I won't be long. And if you keep scowling like you just ate a raisin, I am sure no one will want to kiss you anyway." Jean May giggled and darted away to the hotel.

Corinna didn't dare glance up at Tanner and instead, focused on the woodgrain of the makeshift windowsill. A ticket slid across to meet her fingertips. Her heart skipped. She had put kissing behind her forever, but the thought of kissing Tanner . . . well, he could make a girl come out of retirement. She lifted her lashes and found the cuff not to be blue as she had hoped. It was red. *Who is wanting to kiss me?* Her stomach somersaulted, and she forced herself to look up. It was a fellow she had never seen before but bore a striking resemblance to Tanner Sterling. Behind him, Tanner didn't look very pleased. In fact, if one could see steam bursting out of ears, she believed she could see Tanner's.

"I didn't know you'd be the one I'd be kissing, but I guess I can kiss you before I wait for Miss Jean May to return," he drawled, grinning broadly. "A fellow doesn't get the chance every day to kiss such a lovely lady, much less two in a single day. I should come to town more often!"

TANNER DIDN'T KNOW he could crack from anger, but Corinna obviously didn't even want to be at the booth in the first place. *What is Noah thinking? How does flashing a ticket entitle him to a kiss?*

"I-I am not s-supposed to be here," Corinna whispered.

She never stuttered when she spoke with him. Tanner stood in front of Corinna's booth, arms crossed, staring down Noah. "I'm afraid it's not your turn. It's mine."

Corinna gasped from behind him.

"I don't see your ticket, Tanner." Noah grinned at him, mirroring his gesture, and flicking up the brim of his hat.

"They are in my pocket. I was here first." If he stalled long enough, perhaps Miss Jean May would be back. He glanced over his shoulder, but in the sea of black and white skirts and aprons, it would be as difficult to spot her as a rattlesnake in the sand.

"Then put your ticket down and get to it. One kiss don't take long . . . unless you do it right. And I *know* you don't get no practice." He winked at Tanner.

Tanner clenched his fists. The boy needed to be taught some manners. Maybe he should just quit Queen Ranch, go right back to the Sanctuary, and make certain his brothers learned right from wrong, because it was obvious something had gone wrong with Noah. Tanner turned to Corinna who was twisting her hands. He leaned toward her, catching hints of vanilla and honey. Man alive, she smelled divine. *Focus!* "You don't have to work this booth, Miss Corinna. Close the booth until Miss Jean

May returns. No woman should give her first kiss away like this."

"I've been kissed before." She mumbled.

His brows lifted, but it wasn't the time, or, more importantly, his place to find out *who* she had kissed, even though he desperately wanted to clobber whoever had kissed her. *And why are you even thinking you are entitled to that information? You are as bad as Noah.* "You want to close the booth? I can help you."

She shook her head. "I promised Miss Dolly that I'd help out *any* booth in exchange for her working the reptile booth . . . I suppose I merely changed out reptiles." Her gaze flicked to Noah and back to him, a soft smile materializing and making her appear all the more innocent and vulnerable. "And it's just a little kiss, and if freely given for the sake of charity, there is no risk of feeling sullied."

Noah elbowed him and grinned at Tanner. Noah tapped his ticket with his fingertip. "Well, then. You best not stand in the way of charity, bro—"

Not on my watch. "Hold your horses, boy."

Tanner dug into his pocket and withdrew his remaining tickets, laying them on the counter. "I'm taking my turn." He looked over his shoulder to Noah with a smirk as he leaned on the booth's sill. "It may take a while. You best get on with you and try to win that prize knife."

Miss Corinna's ears blazed, but she had, at least, stopped twisting her hands.

"Nah, I'll wait." Noah crossed his arms, a smirk playing at the corner of his lips. "You go ahead, Tanner."

Noah was wicked. *What kind of game is he playing?* Well, whatever it was, Noah was going to lose out on kissing Miss Corinna. Tanner slid all the tickets to her.

Her lips parted. "Y-you wish to use all *four* tickets?"

"Is that against the rules?" He lifted his palms up. "Because if it is, I apologize for the assumption."

"I don't know the rules, but it seems above board." She twitched her forefinger, beckoning him closer, her cheeks blossoming. Another man joined the queue, and she dipped her head, mumbling something under her breath about it all being for charity.

"All above board for sure." He lifted her hand and gently pressed a kiss atop her hand. "That's one." Tanner slid the ticket across to her.

A laugh bubbled out of her, and her smile brightened her eyes as she pocketed the ticket. "That must be the most expensive kiss on the hand ever given."

"Seems like a steal of a deal to me," he whispered, still holding her hand. He turned her hand and lifted the cuff a hint and kissed her wrist.

Her laughter melted away.

The rest of the carnival faded for a moment as he slid the next ticket to her. "That's two."

"Two," she whispered.

Tanner leaned toward her, gauging her reaction before closing the distance, and brushed a kiss at her cheek, drawing a gasp from her. "That's three, little lady."

"Only one ticket left now," she whispered and lifted her long lashes up to him, her cheeks brilliant.

His gaze rested on her full lips. He didn't want any other cowboy kissing her. Jean May needed to get down here *now*. He leaned in, waiting for Corinna to come claim it. Ticket, or not, he wasn't going to kiss any woman unless she asked for it.

"I'm back!" Jean May sang, her eyes widening at Tanner standing at her booth. "Oh, you run along, Miss Corinna, I'll be doing the kissing now. I must say, I have impeccable timing to return with two handsome men awaiting kisses."

Tanner pocketed the remaining ticket, ducked away, and spun on his heel. "Already got my kisses from Miss Corinna, Miss Jean May. Noah here has plenty of tickets to spend, though." He trotted in the opposite direction of Corinna, weaving around tables laden with lemonade and treats, desperate to cool the heat from his neck. Those newfangled kissing booths should be outlawed.

CHAPTER 5

anner had kissed her! Corinna's fingertips rested on her cheek. He had been so sweet and impossibly tender for such a rough bounty hunter. He was a man who chased dangerous criminals, leapt into raging rivers for complete strangers, and yet, he cared enough for a lady's feelings that he didn't take advantage of the situation like Buck Bridger would have. She shivered at the thought of Buck spotting her at the booth. He certainly would not have stopped at kissing her hand and cheek. But Tanner's chaste kisses were enough to send her knees to wobbling for the first time in a year. *If a simple kiss to the cheek causes this reaction, what would a real kiss from him be like?*

She missed the step down the porch at the thought and nearly tumbled. She grabbed at the railing, righting herself before anyone could spot her. "No more kissing," she whispered. "Or thoughts of kissing."

"I'll second that! I cannot believe it. I heard you were running the kissing booth with Tanner Sterling as your customer?" Pernilla hissed, grasping Corinna's elbow, and dragging her around the wing of the Castañeda's porch. "I told the girls that it couldn't be true after what you promised me yesterday." She crossed her arms and lifted a single brow. "I said that you wouldn't want to damage your relationship with a Harvey sister."

"I didn't mean to—"

"So, you did then." She huffed, eyes welling with tears. "Well, none of the girls will believe a word you say now. I told you I *claimed* him, and you agreed to let me have him and then, there you were, kissing him like some sort of soiled dove from the saloon!"

Corinna drew in a sharp breath and stilled her hands from striking the girl. "How dare you say such a thing. I am no soiled dove, and he kissed me on the hand, wrist, and cheek."

"The wrist?" Pernilla gaped at her.

"It was hardly indecent for a kissing booth. Besides, the booth was *your* idea in the first place! You can't blame me when you didn't even volunteer to run it for the first hour."

"None of the handsome customers were supposed to be free until later. I checked. And I don't care to hear your excuses." She flipped her hand to Corinna, palm up. "It should have been *me* kissing Tanner Sterling. You are going to regret this, Corinna Victoria. I am going to make you regret it."

She was about to say she already did, but then, that wouldn't have been the truth. Having Tanner kiss her was the best moment she had since her world imploded. No, that sweet memory would be cherished until she died a maiden widow.

She lifted her chin, daring Pernilla's ire further.

"Take over the lemonade stand. I have a kissing booth to take over from Jean May. I don't know how, or when, but you *will* pay." Pernilla cast over her shoulder as she stormed off, mumbling something about the booth idea being no good anymore since Tanner had already visited and spent his tickets.

That's exactly what my in-laws said right before I ran away. For someone who simply wished to blend into the shadows for the whole of her life, she was getting an awful lot of threats, and all because of a sham of a marriage and kissing booths. She smoothed her hair and plastered on the calm de-meanor that the staff in her father's restau-rant had expected of her for years—before she had scandalized them all, including her father's widening social class, by eloping with a dangerous Roberts man. But she was no longer that careless girl from twelve months ago. One innocent kiss would not be the end of her—or really *three* chaste kisses.

The rest of the afternoon passed without her seeing Tanner again, as if he were just as embarrassed by the whole kissing booth as she, but embarrassment and the bounty hunter didn't seem to go together. The man exuded confidence, charm, and above all, character. Any other man in that line would have kissed her lips three times and not thought a thing about it. But she had a feeling he was unlike any other man she had ever met. *I wonder what his lips would—* She shook that thought right out of her head for the tenth time and filled the fresh punch glasses the dish boy brought her with cold lemonade.

"Miss Corinna, help me out and try to do something that gets you in trouble in the next few minutes," Erza whispered with a wink. "The dishes are piling up."

"I do not envy your dish load at the end of the night! You best believe that I will not risk stepping a single toe out of line," she returned.

"That's William's worry. *My* shift ends at five, and I will miss the dinner crowd," Ezra hooted.

"I heard a rumor that you were at the kissing booth," Buck Bridger leaned against the bark of the live oak beside her lemonade table. "I asked you if you'd be there, and I recall that you said no and were most insistent about it."

"I wasn't planning on working the booth." Corinna lifted a clean glass to the afternoon sun peeking through the narrow leaves, pretending to find a smudge simply to give herself somewhere to look other than Buck's green eyes that seemed to never leave her face.

"I'll never be late for nothing again for the rest of my life after missing my chance at catching you at the kissing booth for the first shift." He leaned on his knuckles over her table. "You sure I can't convince you to take a turn at the booth again? It would give you just the right excuse to kiss me."

She polished the glass even more with the corner of her apron. "I would never take kissing a man lightly."

"And yet you let that bounty hunter steal a kiss." He smiled down on her. "I suppose you like your beaus dangerous?"

"He's not my beau, and he did not *steal* anything from me."

"Not your beau, and yet you allowed him a kiss? Seems like my theory is correct. What if I told you that I've done a little bounty hunting myself? Would that spark your interest?"

She made the mistake of meeting his gaze in her surprise.

He chuckled. "See? I knew that would pique your curiosity. Yes, I've caught a few criminals. I did so to line my pockets enough to set up my ranch a few years ago. Every now and then, when a particularly large bounty appears on the post office wall, I ride again. It would be a crime not to when I am naturally so adept at it."

"I am sure the public appreciates your service." Her hip knocked into the lemonade bowl and the pale-yellow beverage splashed on her apron. "Oh dear, you must excuse me. Miss Dolly would be vexed if I did not change my apron right away." She glanced about, and sure enough, Dolly stood at the edge of the square.

She excused herself and went to Dolly.

"Would you mind taking over the stand?" She gestured to her apron.

"It's always something with you, Corinna."

"It's only lemonade. Buck Bridger was pestering me."

Miss Dolly's eyes narrowed over Corinna's shoulder. "And he is still watching you. Some men don't know how to take a hint. Do you want me to send him away? I can if you want me to."

"If you do, he'll just find me later." She gestured to her apron. "Which is why I took desperate measures to escape."

Dolly shook her head, tsking under her breath. "I'll speak to him. None of my girls should feel unsafe while on my watch." She motioned her toward the dormitory. "You've been up helping me before the rest of the girls. Take off the rest of the evening —go rest, or change out of your uniform and enjoy the carnival."

"Really? I thought you'd be angry with me for soiling another apron."

"Of course not. I simply like the women under my command to work hard, or else the failings come back to me as head waitress and that would affect my ability to one day become a house manager." She waved her forward again. "Go rest before the staff dinner. You've earned it. And if you see number four, switch badges with her. I believe Pernilla possesses that badge at the moment. She has been all too concerned with kissing today, and that is not how we Harvey Girls conduct ourselves, even when a kissing booth is involved."

With a smile of thanks, Corinna left the crowd and crossed the back street toward Rawlins dormitory, a brick two-story building with three French doors lining the first level. She entered through the middle set that gave her access to the stairs. At the top of the landing, she paused in the hall of doors and found the door to her room ajar. Her senses bloomed, and her heart pounded. The Harvey Girls *always* closed their doors when unoccupied to keep out any critters that snuck through windows, or holes in the bottom floor.

Had the Roberts family found her at last? She should have kept her derringer handgun hidden under her skirts. *Why did I allow myself to grow so comfortable?* She had even carried at the Montezuma, but here, with the townsfolk about and the constant milling of Harvey Girls and staff, she'd felt shielded.

Foolish. Foolish girl. She swallowed as the more recent threats resurfaced. The Roberts had warned her after Father's untimely death to give them everything, or else. When she had refused, they named her as the murderess of William and cast about lies and rumors that she might have even had a hand in Victor Alistair's death too. At the time, she hadn't thought anyone would believe the Chicago crime family's claim—and then the policemen came questioning about William, and the threats had become all too real. She had underestimated her husband's people one too many times, and she would not do so again.

Spying a taper on the hall table, she grasped it and removed the candlestick. The heavy iron gave her the courage to tiptoe forward. A woman stood over an empty trunk with her hands on her hips, muttering as she bent and tossed a few garments across her shoulder.

Corinna took in the room, all was normal. Nothing was ransacked, no one was hiding under her bed. Her heart squeezed at her momentary panic. She was safe. She tucked the candlestick behind her skirt and called, "Hello there."

The woman started, her cheeks pink as she curtsied. "Oh, hello there! You must be my new roommate! I'm Summer Hyacinthe."

Corinna curtsied as well. "And I am Corinna Victoria, your roommate. What a lovely name you have."

"My parents are a pair of romantics. I'm certain my mother partly said yes to my father's proposal because of his surname and her other beau's name was Mudd, which was not romantic at all, but please don't mind me while I make myself at home in the closet. You have so many pretty dresses! I don't think I have a quarter as many as you do. Are you a town girl? Or is your family rich? But if you were from a rich family, I doubt you would be working as a Harvey

Girl, unless you are a poor relation?" She gasped. "Or you are refusing to marry someone equally rich and powerful and therefore are on the run? I heard a similar story about a girl who used to work here earlier this year, a Sophia Fairfield. But, come to find out, she ended up marrying the man that was going to be her future stepson instead!" She flapped her hands before her flushed cheeks. "I have to say, it is all so thrilling, and I am hopeful for my future here. I've heard there are so many men to choose from that some girls turn down proposals weekly! How many proposals have you turned down? Or are you focusing on your career like Miss Violet Trent, the House Mother? I met her an hour ago when she let me inside, and she seems ever so nice."

Corinna smiled. She wouldn't have to worry about filling the silence with Summer for a roommate. "That's right."

"Which part?"

Corinna moved to the closet and pushed her dresses as far onto one side as she could manage. "Please, take your half of the closet.

I would have moved my things earlier, but I didn't think anyone would be arriving today, but it was a rather busy morning and afternoon."

"I didn't know I'd be here until this morning when I received my placement. I could hardly believe my good fortune to be placed at such a prestigious establishment. Even though the hotel hasn't been open long, it has garnered a lot of interest across the states, but of course, you know that!"

Corinna wondered who she was replacing. Perhaps Dolly simply required another on staff to help with the influx of guests now that the Castañeda was gaining a reputation. "Did you come alone?"

"I came with two other girls, but they are rooming with a Miss Pernilla."

Corinna's heart surged. Was Dolly going to replace her with new recruits even though Dolly had seemed almost nice to her only moments before? *Mayhap she sent for them earlier and will change her mind about firing me.* Her badge placement *had* improved, so surely, she was in no imminent danger of being released from her position.

"I heard that the Castañeda is one of the best Harvey Houses to be placed with since so many girls make wonderful matches here. Miss Jean May was running into the dormitory to use the necessary and change her apron and showed me to my room. She was the one who told me about Miss Fairfield, and then proceeded to tell me about a Miss Parish, who was Miss Fairfield's maid, that married a wealthy rancher, and a Miss Elliot who married the town sheriff, a former Texas *Ranger*, who gave up his position as sheriff after marrying Miss Elliot and took up ranching instead." She gave her dress a good flap and hung it up in the closet. "A lot of people ranch out here, don't they?"

"Yes." Corinna held out her hand for the last dress from Summer's trunk.

"How kind!" Summer gave her a beaming smile and handed it over. She withdrew some lace doilies and shoved the trunk to the foot of her bed. "I'm from St. Petersburg, over in Florida. My dad was a sailor, but when he died during a hurricane, my ma said I had to go find work, and as nothing in St. Petersburg suited me, I decided to come out West to find me a husband. They say your heart is either with the waves, or with the mountains, and I'm hoping to find my heart here, as I never much had the stomach for all the storms that roll in every summer. Do you have a lot of storms out here?"

"I wouldn't know." She drew the curtains, daring to glance below and see if Buck had been distracted, or if he had followed her to the dormitory.

"Oh? You are new here too? Or transferred from another House?"

"That's right." Corinna spied the keepsake box under her bed peeking out. She hardly kept her gasp from escaping. She kept the box tucked in the corner of the wall and bed. It shouldn't even be visible. Corinna sank to her knees and flung it open, taking note of all her belongings. The stack of letters was still bound with a scarlet ribbon, the bit of lace from her mother's wedding veil, and . . . She shifted through the items. Her gold bracelet with the heart-shaped diamond was missing. She closed the box and slowly rose. "Did you see anyone in here when you arrived?"

Summer spread one of the doilies atop her pillow and one on the shared night-stand. "Oh, lots of girls have been popping in to speak with me since I've arrived. You all are a friendly lot, but I'm not sure why I expected you all to be any different. It will be nice to have friends after years of scraping by in Florida and no time for so-cial events. Why, I think I'll feel guilty at first for having any time at all for myself, but I suppose after ten days of hard work, I will be too tired to feel guilty for resting."

Corinna swallowed back her panic. Anyone could have taken it . . . and Pernilla had promised revenge. *But how could I ask Pernilla if she went through my things without revealing the item and its value?* She nearly jumped at Summer's hand on her shoulder.

"You seem upset. Is something missing from your box? I promise, I never even knew it was under there."

"A sentimental piece is missing," she breathed. If anyone stole that bracelet with the intent to sell it, her in-laws *would* find out. They had so many under their thumb, by blackmail mostly, and at their command. They most likely had connections in the law offices across the states. She groaned. She had been so careful to only use the cash she had earned from her position and never sold any of her items of value that she had managed to hide from William. This bracelet had belonged to her mother. William had been quite vexed with her when he didn't find it. The diamond was the largest she owned, but when she suspected his duplicity in their marriage, she had hidden it away in the chamber pot under the hotel bed. He never thought to look there. *Why didn't I hide it more carefully?*

Corinna rested her head on the mattress. She had been foolish to use her middle name as a surname to sign up for this job, but she couldn't give it up too, not when it was the last thing that linked her to Father. She had taken care in every other area to make herself as small as possible, keeping her mouth shut and head down so as not to draw attention. The Roberts had connections—powerful connections, that could end with her in a noose.

It had to have been Pernilla. Panic shot her to her feet. She raced to Pernilla's shared room. She banged on the door. No answer. She turned the knob, surveying the room from the threshold. She narrowed her eyes at Pernilla's trunk. She raced to open the lid—her fingers stilling. Everyone in Chicago had decided that Corinna had been guilty of William's death. No one had listened to her pleas that she was being framed. By deciding to rummage through Pernilla's things without proof, wasn't Corinna doing the same? She sagged back on her heels. If she was wrong, she could lose her position. Before she could change her mind, she hurried down the stairs to search for the House Mother, Violet Trent. She would know what to do. The parlor was vacant and so was Miss Trent's little study. *Perhaps she is still at the carnival.* Corinna gathered her black skirts and bolted across the street as a fiddler played a merry tune.

She grabbed the first Harvey Girl she saw. "Jean May? Have you seen Miss Trent?"

"No, is everything well, Corinna?" Jean May frowned and grasped Corinna's forearm. "You look like you are about to be ill. Can I fetch you some tea? Or send for the doctor?"

I'll be dead soon if I don't find her. She shook her head and stumbled to grasp the arm of a passing Harvey Girl, Maura Carr. "Miss Trent?"

"I saw her go for a walk with her friend from the mountains."

"Thank you," Corinna muttered and spun toward the sidewalk. She peered each way down the street and didn't see her.

Fear clawed at her throat and swirled her senses. Should she dare confide in the house manager? But Mr. Perkins was looking for a way to let her go. She twisted her hands. She had to do something! The bracelet could be being sold even as she searched. She needed to find someone who could help her track down something lost. *Lord, help me! Send me someone who*—A figure in blue guided a palomino down the street. *Tanner.* If the West's best bounty hunter could not help her, no one else on earth could either.

CHAPTER 6

Silver nickered and pranced to the side as a gentle hand brushed against Tanner's arm. He turned to the petite Harvey Girl behind him, the setting sun betraying the distress lining her pretty hazel eyes. "Miss Corinna? Is something wrong?" He glanced over her shoulder for Buck Bridger, an occasional bounty hunter, that always seemed to be present these days. He didn't particularly care for the man who swooped in and stole away his bounties and didn't like that Buck had set his eyes on Corinna. *He probably did because he knows she caught my eye.*

"Yes. I need your help." She twisted her hands, tears filling her eyes. "You find lost things, yes?"

Thoughts of Buck Bridger and his yellow-bellied ways disappeared. "I can." He flicked up the brim of his Stetson. He hated seeing her so upset. His fingers itched to enclose her hands, to offer whatever comfort he could. "What did you lose? Was there a pickpocket here tonight?"

"I can't speak on that score, but—" She pressed her hand to her mouth, and turned away to swipe her lashes, and clear her throat. "No. I shouldn't have even asked you. Forgive me."

He grasped her hand. It was smooth and seemed unused to hard labor. He reached into his pocket and withdrew his oversized handkerchief that he had thankfully replaced this morning. "There is nothing to forgive yet, unless you are planning on putting something in my food next time I come in?"

But even his poor attempt at bringing a smile did not lighten her features. She blew her nose into the handkerchief and rumpled the cloth in her hand. "When I returned to my room, a bracelet was missing from my box under the bed."

He frowned. "Is it valuable?"

She nodded, pulling her hand from his.

He missed the contact, which was beyond foolish. Tanner hadn't known her long enough to miss her. He crossed his arms. "What does it look like?"

"It's a gold band with a diamond pendent in the shape of a heart."

"How big is the diamond?"

She worried her bottom lip. "The heart is four carats."

He released a low whistle. If she possessed such an item, why on earth was she working as a waitress? It explained the soft hands. But he supposed many of these Harvey Girls had pasts they'd rather keep hidden. Heaven knew he had memories and secrets he'd rather keep tucked away in a box in the corner of his heart for the rest of his life than bring them to light, shake out, and examine. No, he kept that lid nailed down, and it would stay that way until he died. He couldn't blame her for keeping silent on that score.

"It is quite sentimental. It was my mother's. My father gave it to me on my tenth birthday, and he passed away three months ago."

Not too long ago at all. His gut twisted. He well remembered the pain of losing his parents. "I am so sorry for your loss, Miss Corinna."

Her bottom lip trembled again. "Thank you. I-I miss him every day. I need to find this bracelet, Tanner."

Her trust in him was humbling, and he could only pray that he could locate it for her, but finding jewelry was a far cry from finding criminals. "I'll do my best. Now, do you have anyone in this town that would want to steal from you? Or were other girls missing items too?"

"No one else mentioned anything missing." She dipped her head.

"So, that leaves someone taking something just from you . . . someone who either knew about the bracelet or had easy access to your room to search your things to take the most valuable item. Does one of the girls hold a grudge against you?"

"I doubt they would take such an obviously expensive piece. They would more likely gossip and speculate about it."

"Forgive me for hazarding a guess, but Miss Pernilla seemed quite put out with you after the, um, booth." He rubbed his ear and glanced away. He could guess what the woman had to say after seeing him with Corinna, but he was not interested in Miss Pernilla. He had been polite to her, but Tanner could offer Miss Pernilla nothing but kind words. *And there is only one woman who has caught my eye in my lifetime.*

"She was."

"I wish I could help you, Miss Corinna, but my ways are usually unorthodox, and I do not think the House Mother would look kindly on my going up in the women's dormitory to search for a missing piece, and if I asked, then it would give the thief a chance to hide it outside of the Rawlins building. I can keep an eye out for it in town and see if anyone tries to pawn it, but likely, if it is such an expensive piece, they will either wait you out before selling it, which could take months, or years, or more likely, they will mail it out of town to pawn it in the East."

"The post!" She clutched his arm, alarm lacing her voice. "It will be going out any minute on the last train out. They might have mailed it, and if they did—"

She was spiraling. He grasped her hand again, attempting to keep her lassoed to the present. "Let's go check it now." At her nod, he pulled her toward the post office where a single lamp flickered in the window. Through the window, he could spy the postmaster leaning over the counter, scribbling something.

Tanner knocked on the door twice, and the postmaster looked up from his writing, scowling, and pointing to the sign hanging in the window.

Closed

Tanner knocked again, holding up his

forefinger, hoping the postmaster would give them one minute.

The postmaster clomped round the counter to the door, unbolting it and opening it an inch. "We are closed for the day and have been for a quarter of an hour! You will have to wait like everyone else in this town until morning."

"We don't want to mail anything. We only have a question."

"Well, ask it! I am missing most of the carnival as is!"

Tanner crossed his arms. "Did anyone mail anything in the last hour?"

"That's confidential." He pinched lips together in a show of disgust.

"Please, Mr. Cole, it's important," Corinna whispered, blinking her long lashes at the man.

No one alive could resist those wide hazel eyes of an angel for long, especially when she called a man by name.

Mr. Cole huffed. "Well, I suppose it would be ethical enough to admit that *yes*, a man mailed a small package for the last train out."

She sagged against the doorframe. Tanner could practically smell the fear rolling off her shoulders. He knew she was attached to the piece, but this seemed like there was far more to the story than she had told him.

"Is it too late to fetch it?" Tanner asked.

"Yes!" The postmaster motioned them out and slammed the door, barely missing their heels.

Tanner placed a hand on her arm and pulled her down the boardwalk and away from the post office. "Miss Corinna, I will keep looking."

"It's too late." She wiped at her lashes. "It's gone."

"No, it could've been anyone mailing a small package. It didn't have to be our thief. That was only one idea. If you ensure the dormitory is empty, with every lady still at the carnival, I can go through their things."

Her cheeks turned bright. "I would be hard pressed to forgive another Harvey Girl for allowing a man to go through my private things. I'll think of something else, even if I must question every girl in that building for some nugget of truth."

"Why are you so afraid of it being mailed? A piece so unique should be fairly easy to identify as stolen once I mail out a description."

"Mail out a description?"

How did her cheeks go from bright one moment to pale the next? He rested his hand on her shoulder, giving her a little pat. "Yes, I have contacts across the states and can have them be on the lookout."

"Oh, no, please, do not trouble yourself. It is gone," Corinna repeated and shook her head. "I shouldn't have been so foolish as to keep it in my room. I should have locked it in the hotel safe, but I didn't want questions about—"

At her shoulder trembling beneath his hand, his stomach clenched at who was causing such a reaction. "And why would that be a problem?"

"I don't like being questioned when I've done nothing wrong." She shrugged his hand off, taking a step away from him. "This was a mistake."

"Is someone looking for you?" He side-stepped in front of her to keep her from bolting. "Are you in danger, Miss Corinna?"

She wrung her hands and moved to step around him. "I-I shouldn't have asked you to find it. You are retired after all, and it is only a bracelet."

"A *diamond* bracelet that is worth a fortune," he corrected her.

"A stone, not something living and breathing," she whispered and rested her hand on her heart. "I can remember my father and mother in here. Thank you for your help, Mr. Sterling. Goodnight."

"At least allow me to walk you back to the dormitory?" He glanced over his shoulder toward the revelry spilling out of the saloon. "I wouldn't feel right about letting you go back alone when you have to pass the saloon."

She gave him a sad smile. "There are far more frightening things than a walk in the sunset through a sleepy western town, Mr. Sterling."

"Things like Miss Pernilla?" *Or worse?* He

rested his hands on his gun belt as his mind raced with possibilities.

"Have a good night," she whispered and darted away.

"Goodnight, Miss Corinna," he replied, but she was already across the street and running. She must be truly afraid to dismiss such a loss, and only a woman in danger would run like her skirts were on fire.

CHAPTER 7

"Unacceptable." Mr. Perkins huffed, seizing the corner of the tablecloth, and ripping it from the table, sending the china shattering on the dining room's red and white checkered floor. "Miss Corinna, clean this up before the dinner guests arrive, and when I come back, I expect a table worthy of the Fred Harvey House! Then, you'll give your station to Miss Pernilla." Mr. Perkins spun away from Corinna to glare at Dolly. "Get control of your staff, Miss Dolly, or I will find someone who can."

Dolly nodded and waited for the manager to leave the dining room. "He's worse than usual. I'm sorry Corinna, but you'll be pouring the coffee tonight, and while you're at it, switch your badge number with Summer."

From position four to seventeen. Corinna gritted her teeth, forcing her face into a resemblance of compliant acceptance.

"He would expect nothing less as a punishment." Dolly bent to pick up the pieces. "Sorry."

Dolly's momentary friendliness had grown after the carnival, even though her stress level seemed to rise. Corinna suspected it half had to do with a conversation Dolly had with the house manager after the carnival that had ended with Dolly in tears. For the rest of the week, the manager had been taking Corinna to task, and Dolly had been defending her. . . but honestly, Corinna *had* been making far too many mistakes thanks to the anxiety gnawing at her belly. She couldn't eat, and sleep alluded her, leading to mistakes. If she were Dolly, she would seriously consider firing herself. "Yes, Miss Dolly."

"And Corinna?" She whispered from the

floor where she gathered the broken bits of china into her apron. "Please, do not disappoint me again. I am running out of excuses to keep you on—all I have left now is that Thanksgiving is in a few days, but beyond that, it's up to you."

"The house manager wants me gone so badly? But, why?"

Dolly glanced over her shoulder, and seeing that they were alone, she replied, "Apparently, his sister's daughter has her eye on Tanner Sterling, and you were seen kissing him at the booth. I, of course, saw right through it, but any mistakes will be used against you, which is why I've been so hard as of late."

"Pernilla is his niece?" Corinna groaned. No wonder Mr. Perkins was being so hard on the pair of them. "I-I am sorry I have made this difficult and will attempt to do better."

Dolly rose and patted Corinna's arm and flitted away to repair the table.

Corinna poured her anxiety into sweeping away the remaining pieces of china and setting the most perfect table known to man. After days of her stomach being tied in knots and nothing happening, perhaps she could dare to hope that she might not need to run after all. If they did know Corinna's location, the Roberts family would have sent her a telegram, letting her know she was a dead woman—they enjoyed playing with their prey all too much not to alert her. Perhaps she could unpack the small carpetbag she had stowed her meager funds and two dresses and a few items she would need if she had to leave in the night. She'd have to burn the letter she penned to Lorna Reid explaining her departure too in the event she needed to run. Maybe she could allow herself to rest tonight?

Noticing a stain on a white tile under the table, she grabbed a bucket and scrub brush. Thankfully, the bounty hunter was too busy with Queen Ranch to return to the Harvey House and question her further. Corinna had never been good at spinning tales, which is why she kept her mouth shut most of the time around the other Harvey Girls . . . but with the bounty hunter,

Corinna felt far too comfortable with Tanner. He reminded her of happy times sitting beside her father at the fireplace in their parlor on East Erie Drive, reading dime novels that offered no education but plenty of entertainment. Their library had been filled with them. It had been a happy time.

And Tanner made her happy. She paused in her scrubbing the coffee and milk stain that spread from the white tile onto the crimson. She had felt twinges of admiration for William long before he paid attention to her, but with Tanner, it was no twinge. His smile was enough to knock her off her feet.

The gong sounded nearby, which meant a flood of guests would be arriving soon, along with the mail train. She wiped the tiles with her clean rag and dropped it, along with the scrub brush, in the bucket and stowed the bucket behind the oversized fern that separated the Harvey Girl's work area and the dining room. She turned to catch a glimpse of the crowd pouring out onto the platform across the courtyard.

Her stomach twisted again at the thought of *who* might be arriving on the train with the mail, but she focused on filling the coffee pots as Pernilla whipped about the room, checking tables, a smug smile in place. She stood at attention beside Corinna's previous station, Pernilla's number three badge gleaming in the remaining rays of the sunset streaming through the window. Corinna tried to ignore the girl's gloating and draped a linen cloth in her hand and grabbed the coffee pot, her designated duty as number seventeen, which received no tips.

The final gong sounded in the dining room and the fifty-three people that wired their orders ahead poured into the dining room behind the house manager manning the gong. She smiled to the new arrivals even as she felt a trail of sweat trickle from her hairline. But she did not recognize a soul among the passengers. Perhaps all her worrying was for naught and she could enjoy her work once more. The guests took their seats, and Dolly surged into motion, the rest of the Harvey Girls following suit.

Show time! She joined the dance of the Harvey Girls with her pot of coffee. As the designated coffee girl, the task of filling and refilling *all* the cups that remained upright in the saucers fell to her. It was an exhausting job as the pot was heavy and every passenger's cup would need to be kept full at all times, which meant she would not stop moving for the entire thirty minutes of the passenger's meal.

In the corner of her eye, she spied Tanner at the threshold of the dining room, hat in hand, her heart skipping a beat from excitement and fear. She did not have time to even smile at him, though, as the cups were already in the correct position for coffee, upright in saucers, given the guests had wired ahead. She ignored all the cups upside down in the saucer, which meant they had requested tea, and should be left for the designated tea pot girl, number sixteen. She filled all the coffee cups, keeping in mind the guests that were intent on gulping the brew down in one gulp, which meant she needed to see to them directly after her first round.

Shouts filled the dining room as fine ladies dropped their coffee cups, screaming, and a few gentlemen leapt back so quickly, their chairs toppled over. Corinna spun toward the mayhem, trying to find the source.

Dolly scrambled from table to table, her face pale as her lips parted in shock. She lifted her hands, calling out, "Everyone, please be seated, we will replace all your coffee cups and brew!"

Coffee? Corinna's limbs quaked and she peered into the nearest table's coffee cups, a little horned toad was belly up in one cup, while another scrambled to the rim, and yet another leapt out onto the fine linen tablecloth. She started and nearly dropped her pot as a squeal escaped her lips.

"Hush! It's just a harmless toad!" Pernilla removed the pot from Corinna's hands and set it on a vacant table. "We need to be calm and fix this situation." She scooped up a frog and plunked him deftly into her apron pocket. "They won't hurt you—well, not really if you know what you are doing." Pernilla bent to catch another toad.

The Harvey House staff flew about the room, catching toads from tables, and

Corinna stared down the fiend in front of her. Using the saucer, she attempted to scoop him into a milk glass when the creature fixed his eyes on her and squirted blood from its eyes straight at her. She screamed, falling to her derriere as she scrambled back.

Strong arms lifted her to her feet. "I'll get him." Buck Bridger grinned down at her. "Seeing a toad squirt blood from his eyes for the first time can make even the bravest rattled." He lifted the horned toad and ran his thumb over its back. "They are actually kind of cute creatures once you get used to them."

"And don't mind the shooting blood." She shuddered. "Thank you for helping me up, but please get him out of here." She pointed him to the door.

"Anything for you, Miss Corinna." Buck cast her a grin over his shoulder as he scooped up a second toad in his Stetson on his way out the door.

Dolly seized her arm and spun her around. "What on *earth* was that? Corinna? Where did they come from?"

"I-I don't know! I was just hurrying and pouring cups of coffee!"

"And you didn't see the cups housed horned toads?" Dolly asked in disbelief, rubbing her forehead with one hand.

"The cups are set so far up on the table, and I was rushing, and the guests didn't see them either. Oh!" Corinna flapped her hands as another toad appeared on her table. "I didn't stop to look inside each cup—I never do!"

"The house manager is going to eat you *alive,* Corinna. I tried to get Miss Violet Trent to plead your case, but as the dining room falls under his rule, I doubt I can save you this time."

"B-but, I didn't do it."

"I never thought you did for a moment, especially given your reaction with the reptile booth." Dolly scowled and picked up another toad, plopping it in her apron pocket. "I believe you would have been the first to scream if you beheld them. However, there will be a thorough investigation of the staff. Whoever did this is going to be fired." Dolly waved Corinna onward. "I won't make you catch toads, but you best fetch fresh coffee cups and order the kitchen staff to brew new pots of coffee. We will have to clean the urn too before we re-fill it. Though, I doubt the urn is the source given the spout size. Tell any guest that you see that their meal is free."

Guests continued to pour out of the large dining room while a few good-na-tured cowpokes and ranchers joined in the hunt. Within a few minutes, every toad had been caught and the tables given fresh cups.

Corinna blocked an exiting family. "Please! Won't you stay? The meal will be on the house."

"You couldn't *pay* me to dine here! Come children, let's get you back onto the train where it is safe." The mother turned her nose up as the father ushered his children out, most of the other guests following.

Only one or two tables of guests from the train remained, but only because of the promise of a free meal as they inspected anything placed before them with the greatest of apprehension. The locals, how-ever, thought it a great joke and returned to their tables. The house manager followed the train passengers out the door with vouchers for another free meal in hand, but no amount of coaxing would pull them from the safety of their train car.

Corinna inspected each cup carefully before filling it, even though it delayed her speed and would probably get her into trouble with the house manager. But now was not the time to throw caution to the wind.

Tanner sat at the table that would have been hers if she hadn't unjustly been given coffee duty, and an odd sensation of jealousy and relief swirled within her. She needed to avoid Tanner, given that he knew too much, but Corinna did miss the strength his company offered and their ease of conversation. Tanner lifted his cup, summoning her with a winning grin. She pressed her lips into a thin smile and filled it, feeling Pernilla's glare burn into the back of her dress.

"Miss Corinna, I trust that your coffee doesn't include any horned toads?" He winked at her. "Not that I mind the little creatures, but I doubt they make for a good cup of coffee."

"Hopefully not. I'm lucky Mr. Perkins didn't fire me on the spot." She murmured.

"You're in the last position?" His gaze flicked to the number on her badge. "Seventeen? I thought the badges went up to fourteen?"

"We added three new girls. And you should know that I was four not too long ago." She dipped her head. "I must go."

"You seem tired, Corinna."

"Just what every girl longs to hear." She laughed and lifted the coffee pot. "Excuse me, but I really need to see to—"

"Every guest who refuses to have coffee?" He smirked before softening his features. "I only meant that you usually don't have dark circles under your eyes." He leaned toward her over his coffee cup. "Is it the bracelet? I have put notices with all of my contacts throughout the country."

"N-notices?" Her heart sank. *Even after I told him he didn't have to?* Her in-laws had too many people under their thumb to allow that seed of hope to grow that they wouldn't find her. She swallowed. She would have to run again . . . she just had to be ready at a moment's notice. She could only pray that she had a few months left of working at the Harvey House before they came calling. She desperately needed the funds so she could disappear once and for all. "That really wasn't necessary, Mr. Sterling," she replied with a little laugh that possessed a hint of desperate wheeze as she blinked back the dots swirling in her vision. "I hope I didn't bother you too much by asking, but really, you have much more important things to do than to look for a little piece of jewelry." She lifted her pot again. "Duty calls. Enjoy your meal. It's on the house."

Thankfully, he simply pressed his lips together and leaned back in his chair, but she had the sinking feeling that he was not going to release the matter until he had answers. *I suppose that is why bounty hunters are so good at their job.* She dared a glance back at his table. Pernilla was already there, fairly cooing over him, but his gaze was on Corinna.

She ducked behind the lunch counter and traded her pot for a freshly brewed one from the kitchen. With renewed vigor, Corinna saw every single guest's cup filled to brimming and did not receive a single complaint from any of the tables, though she did receive a jest from every table. She forced herself to laugh over each teasing comment again and again. Dolly even gave her one of her signature solemn, slow nods of approval and tapped her finger on her watch pin. Well, at least Corinna would not be fired with the new batch of relief girls that arrived the night of the carnival.

She nodded in passing to Dolly and wove about the kitchen staff to the small dining hall in the rear of the hotel to take her lunch. Instead of taking a seat at the staff table and risking Pernilla cleaning the tables quickly and joining her, Corinna stepped out to the small back porch and sank down on the wooden steps in a heap of skirts with her plate of fresh salad and glass of lemonade as crows cawed in the aspen tree with its blaze of golden leaves.

A rope was fixed to one tree's white bark

and strung to another where drying laundry fluttered on the line in a rainbow of colors. While the Harvey House sent out their uniforms, the girls still had to take care of their own things. Corinna gritted her teeth at her own looming laundry day. She had only washed clothes a handful of times, and her first few attempts had ruined a blouse and the whole process would take nearly her entire day off. *Maybe I can hire a lady in town with my earnings while I still can?* It would be an expense she couldn't afford, but she needed her clothes cleaned and ready for when she took flight. She took a giant bite of salad, allowing the tension in her shoulders to ease as the nourishment bolstered her courage when the back door slammed open.

Corinna started and knocked over her glass of lemonade onto her cuff, glancing up to find a frowning Harvey Girl. "Pernilla!" She moaned and shook off the sticky drops from her hand. "This will be a mess to clean."

"I know your secret." Pernilla hissed. "And the lie you have been living is over."

CHAPTER 8

"*S*ecret?" Her heart stuttered. She had far too many secrets and any one of them might be the end of her façade.

"You are no Harvey Girl." Pernilla crossed her arms, victory in her gaze as she called over her shoulder. "I found her, Dolly. Someone inform Mr. Perkins!"

"I beg to differ. I've been a Harvey Girl for months." Corinna gestured to her uniform as she rose and shook out the dust from her hem. Thankfully, the lemonade had only spilled on her hand and the porch, and she wouldn't need to change.

Dolly joined Pernilla, a frown plastered

on her pretty face as she slowly closed the door. Her eyes seemed sad.

Alarm flittered through Corinna's body at the head waitress's expression, her stomach churning. "Dolly?"

"Pernilla seems to have discovered some distressing news." She frowned at Pernilla. "News, which I hope you will refute once and for all."

This was it. They knew Corinna had been married and her reputation ruined by those Roberts and if they knew that, there was little doubt that they didn't know about the warrant out for her arrest too. Would her one decision to elope never cease haunting her?

"Are you Corinna *Victoria* Alistair, the daughter of the owner of the famous *Victor's Steakhouse?*" Pernilla held her chin up, victory gleaming in her eyes.

Corinna's heart staggered. "W-what?"

Pernilla lifted a letter from her pocket, the seal broken. "I picked up the mail from the front desk today for all of the Harvey Girls, intent on distributing it during our staff meal."

"That's addressed to me!" Corinna reached for it, but Pernilla lifted it out of reach.

"Yes, but you see, I usually get so many letters from all over the country that I accidentally opened your letter from a Chicago manager at a Victor's Steakhouse. Now, I had to ask myself, why would the manager from a famous steakhouse be writing you? Then, I thought of your surname and *who* your father must be and why you have all them fancy dresses in your closet. You are Victor Alistair's daughter, the parvenu heiress to the Victor Restaurant empire."

Corinna sputtered. In all of her scenarios, the idea that her father's dear, trusted manager, and her godfather, finding and contacting her had not been a risk. Leo Murphy knew the risks of such an act, especially to write her full name on the address. Why did he take such a chance? She gulped. She had to discover the contents of the letter. "I-I can explain."

"Oh, Corinna, so it is true." Dolly rested her head on the porch column and sighed.

"You want to expand your restaurant empire along the rail, don't you?"

It had been one of her father's pet dreams, but there was no way that she could fulfill it, not with the Roberts on her trail and her funds tied up in their hands. "I- I did not come here to spy. I promise." *If they know about my father, does Pernilla know about the warrants?* She twisted her hands. The story had been kept from the papers, no doubt, for one reason only—money. Her godfather would have tried to protect her, to buy her time.

"Oh, please! Why else would a woman of means work here?" Pernilla challenged, crossing her arms.

"I honestly feared what you were hiding. No Harvey Girl comes to us so well trained," Dolly massaged her temples, groaning.

"If I'm so well trained, why did you constantly push me?" Corinna pressed a hand to her stomach. If she lost her job, she didn't know what she'd do.

"Because you had so much potential that you reminded me of myself." Dolly pinched the bridge of her nose. "I feel like such the fool. This is why I do not allow myself to become so involved."

"Well, I knew her parentage had to have been true. I've spoken with the manager, and Mr. Perkins said you were to be terminated at once when you confirmed it. You are no doubt behind the appearance of the toads as well." Pernilla lifted her pert little nose in the air.

"That was not your place," Dolly hissed at Pernilla, planting her fists on her hips. "How dare you go over my head like that."

Pernilla shrugged. "Well, it's done. Now, will you terminate her, or shall I go inform the manager that you are allowing a spy in our midst? It seems that would be the decision of a traitor. It would risk your future plans of becoming a house manager—a position that is already hard enough for a woman to obtain, but a woman with such a mark against her? Impossible."

Corinna twisted her hands. "Please, Dolly, I have nowhere else to go. You must believe me."

"Says the heiress with the tongue of a serpent!" Pernilla scoffed.

"Unlike Pernilla, I do not feel my job is at risk if I keep you." Dolly folded her hands in front of her skirts. "However, I'm afraid, with the manager being informed of the situation and already making his decision, I cannot give you another chance." She reached for Corinna's hand. "Please understand that this gives me no joy. I must release you from your position, effective immediately. I will collect your remaining pay, as well as a rail pass, while you pack your things. You have one hour to vacate the Rawlins building and say your goodbyes."

"Though, you've always been so aloof, I doubt you have any friends in the first place." Pernilla interjected. "I guess now we know why you were so snooty. You thought yourself too good for the likes of us. I believe this is yours." Pernilla shoved the open letter in Corinna's hands and disappeared inside.

Dolly patted Corinna's arm. "I wish I could keep you on, Corinna."

"I understand. If I were in your position, I'd fire me too." Corinna sagged against the column as Dolly left her. *Lord, I need You to guide my next steps and protect me from the foolish past of my youth.* She looked heavenward and forced the tears clogging her throat back with a determined swallow, shoved off the porch steps, and ran toward the Rawlins dormitory.

She glanced over her shoulder down the street of the little town and sighed. Of course, it was time to leave when Las Vegas was finally beginning to feel like home. It would cut her to the core to bid Lorna farewell via a letter. Their friendship had not been long, but Lorna was closer to Corinna than any other girl she had known for years. And then there was Tanner. He had reminded her so much of happy times with her father, it would be a shame to lose that connection . . . and that handsome smile. *But I suppose when I start to think about a man's smile, it's for the best that I leave.*

She knocked on the front door of the dormitory and waited for the lock to turn.

Jean May smiled her greeting and

checked the grandfather clock. "You are off early. Is it your break?"

"Something like that," she muttered, unwilling to explain when her hopes had been shattered again. She climbed the stairs and opened her door, gasping at the sight of all her drawers thrown open and her dresses in a heap on the floor, as if someone had ripped each from the hanger as they searched each gown and dumped them. She whipped the letter from her pocket, her fingers trembling as she opened it, expecting the worst.

Dearest Inna,

I have been searching for you for months. Imagine my surprise when I spotted a wanted poster with your diamond bracelet come through my friend's jewelry store with a location to wire any news. Victor's Steakhouse is in dire straits. We need you to return to see that your father's legacy is not destroyed by your in-laws' greed. There is hardly any money left in the restaurant's account to even order the famous beef for the restaurants. I know you fear returning with the false warrants out for your arrest. However, if you do not return of your own volitation, I fear what may become of you and your father's legacy. I implore you to return and face the spurious charges against you. I will stand with you at the trial and see that you have justice.

Your friend and godfather,
Leo Murphy

She shoved the letter into her pocket and threw a few more of her belongings into the carpet bag, only taking her plainest day gowns, tossing the rest of her fine gowns into her medium and large trunks. She jotted down Leo Murphy's address and slapped the paper atop one of the trunks so that they could be sent to him. What use were fancy gowns if she were dead at the hands of her relatives? Pernilla could have been the one behind the room being tossed, but she did not dare wait to confront the girl. Not even bothering to change from her Harvey uniform, she seized the handles of her bag and charged out her door and slammed into Dolly.

"Corinna!" The head waitress grabbed her by the shoulders. "I didn't mean for you to leave in such haste. I brought you your funds." She held out a stack of bills that was far more than Corinna expected. "I gave you my portion of tips today since I made you wait the tables with coffee. It's not much, I suppose, to an heiress, but I didn't know if you had any funds at your disposal, and we didn't give you any time to wire for more."

"That is very kind of you. I don't have much left in my savings."

Dolly nodded. "I hope you don't think ill of me for this termination. Honestly, if Pernilla hadn't acted on her own, I would have simply put you on probation. After all your hard work, you have proved yourself devoted to this job. I think this termination is premature at best."

"Thank you, Dolly." She tucked the money into the top of her carpetbag. "I-I don't know what to say."

"Say that you'll take care of yourself. It is not a kind world out there for a desperate woman." Dolly frowned, a spark of anger in her voice.

"You speak as if from experience."

Something flashed in Dolly's eyes. "Yes. Yes, I am. But that life is behind me, and it will *never* be a part of my story again, as long as I am able to work, and I intend on dying as a Harvey Girl, or marrying a man of means. But, unlike me, you have options." She handed Corinna a slip of paper. "Here's your rail pass. It will take you anywhere on the line that you wish to go, but I suppose there's no reason for you not to return to Chicago. Take care of yourself, Corinna Victoria. I wish you well."

———

TANNER COUNTED out his coins and deposited them beside his half-eaten plate at the Castañeda. Corinna's behavior had stirred something in Tanner's belly—and it wasn't the butterflies from the carnival. She had acted afeared, akin to someone who had a secret, and in his former line of work, secrets meant skeletons, or more likely ghosts bent on revenge. So, he had kept an eye on the jumpy Harvey Girl throughout lunch, and when she had disappeared in the kitchen, he reckoned it was time to ask the postmaster about the bracelet again.

Diamonds and questioning usually led to one of two things—shock, or silence. And all he received was shock about town. He had sent wires to his contacts across the Atchison, Topeka, and Santa Fe railroads and to the major cities, but as he hadn't received any telegrams out on Queen Ranch, it couldn't hurt to check in with the post office before he headed back.

Leaving his palomino at the Harvey House hitching post, he trotted down the street to the post office and pushed open the door. The same postmaster from the night of the carnival eyed him as before. But, instead of a frown, the postmaster put aside the stack of mail and offered Tanner a nod as he reached for his cup of steaming coffee at the counter.

"Glad you came by, Mr. Sterling. Have a stack of mail set aside for you, but no telegram. Otherwise, I would have had my boy bring it out to you on the ranch." Mr. Cole turned to the floor-to-ceiling shelving on the wall behind the counter, bent, and with a grunt, lifted a small crate to the counter. "Got to be too much for your little mail slot to handle. You've got more mail than anyone else in town, besides Buck Bridger."

Tanner nodded his thanks and filtered through the mail, which were mostly re-quests from would-be clients and a thick envelope. He cut the envelope open with his hunting knife and found a stack of posters. He had made a point of having all wanted posters sent to him over the years and had neglected to contact the sheriffs across the states regarding his recent retirement.

Out of curiosity, and habit, he flipped through the stack in case he had seen a suspect. He eyed some of the higher rewards and clenched his teeth as temptation swirled. Being a foreman meant gaining experience around cattle, which he hoped to pivot to after hanging up his gun belts, but the pay as a foreman was a fraction of what he used to send home to his brothers. He flipped the page to the final poster. A pair of familiar wide eyes and full lips met his gaze. He staggered and gripped the counter. He rubbed his palm over his eyes and read the poster again.

Wanted for the murder of her husband, Corinna Victoria Alistair-Roberts.

He could not reconcile the words and picture with the woman he had come to know. He didn't want to believe it, but everything was falling into place. Her evasive answers, her spotty history, and the way she avoided any topic of her past, besides her father. The mention of that moment at the scandalous kissing booth not being her *first* kiss . . . as if she were *experienced. Experienced in murdering her husband.* He crumpled the poster in hand. He tossed the rest into the bin. He should alert the town sheriff. He should confront Corinna. He should—

"You okay there, son? You want a cup of coffee or something?" Mr. Cole lifted a brow as if expecting him to keel over.

Tanner shook his head and smoothed the poster out again and eyed the bounty. *Two thousand dollars?* He gaped. Such an amount would draw every low life and dishonorable bounty hunter for hundreds of miles. Tanner could not only return to Sanctuary Ranch and his brothers but purchase the place outright and set it up for years with such a sum. And he knew right where the woman lived, and soon, so would every bounty hunter in the West.

Tanner shoved the crate to Mr. Cole but kept the poster of Corinna. "You can toss it."

"You can't—"

Tanner slammed the door and marched across the street toward the Harvey House. He stormed into the lobby.

He paused on the stained hardwood floors long enough to nod to the startled clerk behind the carved front desk and swipe off his Stetson. He drew a deep breath outside the dining room doors, the poster gripped in his hand as his disbelief turned to anger.

How dare that woman lie to this town? How dare she wear the Harvey Girl uniform? It stood for propriety, purity, and hope. Corinna Victoria had lied to all of them. He didn't know if he was blinded with rage because he had allowed himself to dream of her, or because he wanted to believe that she was falsely accused despite the evidence right in front of him. Of course, she would say she was innocent—they all did.

He couldn't rightly stride up to her and demand to know if she was a murderess—

poster, or not. He strode inside and watched the Harvey Girls buzzing about the room, but the petite golden-haired beauty was not among them, even though it was still her shift.

The head waitress approached him with a strained smile, Miss Dolly's gaze lingering on his shirt. "Mr. Sterling, back so soon? Would you like a cup of coffee at the counter? As you can see, all our tables are filled at the moment. And you will need to don a guest jacket provided from our coat-room again if you wish to enter."

He ran his fingers over the brim of his Stetson. "No, thank you, Miss Dolly. Where is Miss Corinna? I believe she's supposed to be working."

"I'm not certain." Miss Dolly's countenance fell. "But I suppose she is on her way to the station and heading back to Chicago."

His heart pounded in his ears. "What do you mean?"

"She's been terminated and rightfully so. She is a liar and a spy." Miss Pernilla interjected, one hand gripping the coffee pot and her other on her hip, the badge number sixteen glistening on her bib apron. "I just came from the dormitory to see if she departed without doing my room harm or taking anything. It seems all was in order, but you should know that she has deceived us *all.*"

"We do not know that yet, Miss Pernilla, and won't unless a Victor's Steakhouse appears along the line in the next few months," Miss Dolly chided. "Go see to your tables, or you risk getting another shift to make up for your meddling today. Remember, you have two weeks to raise above sixteen before you too are terminated."

His attention snagged on the word *steakhouse.* Corinna *Victoria* Alistair-Roberts sounded even more familiar now, but he couldn't quite place it.

Pernilla smirked. "Yes, Miss Dolly, but I stand by what I did, and Tanner deserves to know."

"You mean, *Mr. Sterling* deserves to know," Dolly corrected her. "And while he may deserve to know, perhaps not the entire dining room." Miss Dolly narrowed her gaze at the Harvey Girl.

"And what does she have to do with Victor's Steakhouse? I've eaten there a few times while in Chicago."

Dolly shook her head. "I won't gossip about Miss Corinna. Excuse me. Miss Pernilla, I suggest you get a move on it."

Miss Pernilla nodded to Dolly and rested her hand on Tanner's forearm in passing, whispering, "Corinna Victoria is no poor working girl. She is an heiress to one of the largest restaurant chains in America, next to Fred Harvey Houses. She only joined because she wanted to gather information on opening her own chain of restaurants along the railroad. It is little wonder she was so good at her job. Her father's training of his daughter and raising them both from the middle class to the upper crust, was so legendary that even I heard about it in the papers, but it was her little doe-eyed, mumbling act that distracted us all from the truth. She is Corinna Victoria Alistair. She is the daughter of the owner of Victor's Steakhouse."

The chasm between what he thought he knew about Corinna and the truth was growing, and with it, the belief that she was innocent shriveled, placing her firmly in the category with the criminals, the enemy of everything he stood for in his career, which earned him that ridiculous title as the Angel of Justice.

CHAPTER 9

Tanner jogged to the Las Vegas train station, anger boiling over. He slowed at the platform. He clutched his fists and pulled his hat down to hide his expression. People gave Tanner wide berth on the platform as his spurs *clinked* with every stride toward the woman in black standing at the edge, gripping a carpetbag. "Just where do you think you are going, *Miss Corinna?*" The truth of her name itched his tongue.

She blinked, a soft smile appearing. "I didn't expect to see you again, Tanner. Though, I must say that I am happy to say goodbye instead of leaving without speaking."

He needed to play this out for just a minute, give her a chance to tell him before he jumped to the final conclusion. He eyed her flushed skin. *Sweatin' like a sinner in church.* "Is someone ill?"

She worried her bottom lip. "Someone will be if I don't leave."

"What's that supposed to mean?" He flicked up the brim of his hat and looped his thumbs on his gun belt. "Are you in trouble?"

The train released a shrill whistle, making her jump. "It means there is too much to explain before I need to leave. I-I wish I could tell you everything, but—"

"But you are up to your old games." He gritted out. Tanner couldn't believe he had been taken in by the siren. How many times had his very own father been taken in by a beautiful woman? Tanner had prided himself on never falling for one, and here, he had let his guard down because of the façade of purity the Harvey Girl had projected.

"Pardon?" She shifted her carpetbag to her opposite hip with a little laugh. "The carnival is over, Mr. Sterling, and this is no game."

"And yet, you are still playing the innocent lady. Drop the act, Miss Corinna, or should I address you as *Mrs. Roberts?*"

She paled at the name and glanced furtively at the massive steam engine and the line of passenger cars it pulled. "I-I need to board. I don't have time to explain everything to you."

He seized her elbow but kept his grip light. While she may be a liar, she was still a lady, and he would never harm a woman. "Stop right there, Mrs. Roberts. You aren't going anywhere."

"Do *not* call me by that name." She scowled up at him.

"Why? Because it fills you with guilt over the murder of your husband? 'Cause it certainly isn't remorse I read in your eyes."

"I can explain, Tanner," she whispered, her gaze flitting from his hand and back to his eyes.

"They always can." He ground out.

"No, listen. Before you cart me off to prison to claim whatever fanatical amount of bounty my in-laws have placed on my head, you *must* listen." She grasped his free hand with hers, her grip ironclad as she tugged him away from the front of the platform to the corner where they could not be overheard by the other passengers.

He tugged himself free, and knowing she could not outrun him, Tanner crossed his arms to keep the siren from touching him with such familiarity again. "You have one minute before I see your sorry hide in jail."

"*Hide?* I am a lady, sir, and you will address me with respect." She lifted her pretty chin in the air, allowing him to catch a glance at the haughty heiress turned unfeeling murderess. "Refrain from speaking with such vulgarity in my presence, especially about me."

He snorted. She was well versed in her act. "I will show you respect when you have earned it, not before."

Tears filled her eyes. "I never should have trusted you to find that bracelet. It has turned into such a debacle." She dashed her fingers under her lashes. "Every man has turned out to be such a disappointment."

He flicked open his dull silver pocket watch. "Forty-five seconds."

"You're impossible." She set the carpetbag on the platform and crossed her arms. "Fine. A year ago, I married a man with ties to a crime organization in Chicago."

"Roberts . . . You mean to say you married into *the* Roberts crime family?" His brows shot up.

"The very one." She nodded. "I was introduced to him as an investor in my father's restaurant."

"Your father brought an investor into your home—from a *crime* family?"

"We didn't know at the time that William Roberts was still connected with his family. He had vowed that he had disowned them and wished to carve his own path. My father believed that William spoke the truth and invited him into our lives. I first met him while I was working in the restaurant. My father wanted me to know every part of the business. I was the one who made William's first steak at the restaurant." She dipped her head. "He was kind to me, and I was attracted to him, so, of course, we talked when he came over to our home to meet with my father every Friday evening. I fell in love with his personality."

"So, he charmed you?" He snorted. Seemed women could be just as gullible as his father had been with that mistress that destroyed their family.

"Like a snake." She glanced over her shoulder toward the Castañeda on the other side of the tracks and the foothills of the Gallinas Mountains beyond. "William took a spinster who had no value in society's eyes, apart from wealth, and made her come alive. When I discovered who his family was, I had already fallen in love with him. William assured me that he left his family behind years ago, and I believed him." She shook her head. "I had been stuck in my schedules and patterns before him. He was always so spontaneous and made me act in ways I never thought, and it excited me—his past excited me."

"And influenced you in becoming a murderess." He rested his hands on his gun belt again.

She lifted her hand. "No. I have never done anything illegal, besides omit the truth of my surname on my Harvey contract. And even then, I do not consider Roberts my real surname."

Because you murdered your husband. "And yet, you were married to him."

"If you can call it a marriage. William convinced me to *elope* even though I had the perfect home and a loving father. I knew my father would never approve of him because of William's past."

"And yet, he invested with the man."

"Money and marriage are two very different things."

"They go hand in hand in the circle you belonged to." Tanner may not have grown up in those circles, but he had traveled enough and read extensively.

"It was a *new* circle to us. Growing up, I spent my days in my father's restaurants and never had time to fall in love . . . until William. And then, for the first time in my life, I believed a man desired me for me and not for a connection with my father, or his money."

"You would have me believe you were that naïve?" Tanner scoffed.

"Yes. William assured me that he didn't care about my fortune, but the moment we were wed, he asked about my trust fund becoming his. The problem was that I didn't have any trust fund until my father's death as he saw to my every need and paid me for my work in the restaurant. However, everything, including my future fortune, was tied up in his restaurants and house, which William had not accounted for when he asked me to marry him. So, on our honeymoon night, William took all my money, gold, and jewels, besides that bracelet, which I hid in the chamber pot when I discovered what he was about. He abandoned me in a hotel room. I was devastated."

Despite Tanner's resentment toward the woman, he couldn't help but feel a twinge of pity for her. He well knew what it was like to be taken. *Like she did to you and the whole town of Las Vegas. Remember, she's a liar, and therefore, your enemy. Feelings equal weakness, and weakness is death to a bounty hunter.* "So, you, a woman scorned, followed William Roberts and killed him for his sin against you."

"No! I am a woman of faith. I would never take vengeance into my hands like that, no matter how much I enjoy reading about bounty hunter justice. I was hurt. I had believed I was loved beyond measure by William, and it turned out that belief was unfounded. He measured my worth by the amount of money in my bank account, which was hardly anything. I didn't have need to hoard money. Father gave me pin money every month, along with the funds I earned from training in the restaurant, but everything else was in Father's name."

"Very convincing. Let's get you to the sheriff's station." He seized her elbow. "This will be the easiest bounty I've ever hunted."

"Do you despise me so that you would wish me dead?" She jerked away from him, breathless.

"I wish to see you in prison where you will wait until you get a fair trial, and the jury will decide your fate." He swallowed at what that entailed—even if she did lie, a life behind bars would hardly be living. "But I doubt you need to fear the worst."

"Don't you see? It's because of William's ties to the crime family that I will never see a trial—much less a fair one. I do not know how William died, but he must have had a lot of enemies if he could treat the woman he professed to love with such disgust. How can I expect his family to treat me when he thought I was worthless?" Her tears welled, spilling over onto her cheeks.

Despite his hurt, his thumb itched to wipe them away. "He does sound like the lowest kind of varmint."

"He was. Please, please at least try to investigate on your own to determine I'm innocent. The moment you bring me to a jail cell, I'm a dead woman. The Roberts family have connections *everywhere*. I ran as far as I could from Chicago, determined to be free, even though it meant sacrificing my father's legacy. Don't you see how frightened I must be to leave all that I know and my home?

Please, won't you be the angel of justice I've prayed for the Lord to send me?"

His grip tightened. No. He would not allow her to sweet talk him into releasing her. She was an enemy of the law and needed to be treated as such. "Why should I believe you when you have been deceiving everyone since the day you arrived?"

She swiped away her tears. "I didn't want to deceive anyone. I never told a lie—really. I just never answered anyone directly and omitted my married name, which hardly counts since—" Her cheeks brightened. "Well, it hardly counts."

"Still a lie. Let's go."

At his words, her tears grew into sobs and folks about the platform and even in the passengers peering through the windows of the train cars were watching them.

He tugged her off the platform, waving away people. "Nothing to see here folks. I'm on the side of the law."

Murmurs over a Harvey Girl being unlawful filled the platform but were soon drowned out by the release of bursts of steam and a warning whistle, sending the nosy passengers into their seats.

"Tanner! Please," she whimpered, but did not fight his hauling her away from the platform onto the boardwalk toward town.

"Do not call me by that name," Tanner echoed her words and guided her between two buildings for privacy. "To my prisoners, I'm Sterling."

"I thought we were friends!"

And I thought we were more—I thought you would be the one that would be different. No. He was not going to be like his pa and fall in love with a woman who would only bring heartbreak and ruin to his entire family. He shook his head. "I don't think I can ever trust you again, Corinna, not when you lied. I don't abide by liars."

"I am *not* a liar." She grabbed his arm. "Yes, I told a lie. I didn't *want* to lie to you, but you must understand. No one has ever been on my side since my father died. No one—except Lorna, and I didn't even tell *her* the truth." Her bottom lip trembled. "I didn't want to lose her, just like I didn't want to lose you. Everyone I become close to is ripped away, by life, or by threats."

"What does that mean?" Tanner pulled away from her, his heart tearing at the distance he was being forced to create.

"Even from the grave, William is still ruining my life."

"Well, you can't lose me when you didn't even have me to begin with."

Corinna flinched at his words. "I should have never married that rat of a man. I've regretted my rashness the moment we returned to that hotel room. I was not treated as a bride, but as a woman deceived." She rested her free hand on his chest, gazing up at him. "But I never would have harmed William, no matter what he did to me." She shook her head. "God help me, I believed I loved him. Even after he left me, I mourned that I gave him my heart and wept bitterly for the future that was never really ours."

"Then why did you run?" He pulled away from her small hand that was scorching a hole through his vest. She was not the woman he thought she was, so why did her touch still affect him? "Only the guilty run."

"I told you!" She flung her hands in the air. "Because I would never receive a fair trial, not with the Roberts' thumbs tipping the scale to guilty. There was too much I had to prove about my whereabouts the night William was murdered. But I swear to you that I had nothing to do with his death. I was at home reading my father's favorite dime novel."

"Was anyone home to verify your whereabouts?"

"I dismissed the servants so I could read and mourn my father's death in my own way and in peace. But I fear the Roberts family planned around my mourning period, waiting to frame me."

Tanner leaned against *Rudy's Mercantile* wall. As angry as he was with her, he well recognized the tone of pain and loss. He had heard it too often on the orphan train that brought him and his brothers West. He had heard it in each of his younger brothers' cries as people along the line kept them for free farm labor. The worst had been young Noah's screams as a childless couple coaxed his tears to cease with lollipops and a stuffed horse. "And how is that supposed to help your story?" He questioned softly.

"Exactly. They will see me hung and my fortune turned over to them as the next of kin and in recompense for a crime I never committed when they are the ones that have killed and stolen and cheated."

He picked at a knot in the building's wood. He knew of the Roberts family. Maybe . . . just maybe, there was a seed of truth in her tale. "You are on a wanted poster, Corinna. What am I supposed to think? Should I believe a pretty face and silver tongue over a lawman's poster?"

Her hopeful expression crumpled into anger. "Some Angel of Justice you turned out to be. I thought bounty hunters were all about seeking truth before passing judgement, but all you want to believe is a lie because the lie is what will see your pockets filled with gold."

"I would never throw someone's life away for the reward." He kicked off the wall and slapped his hat against his thigh with a grunt.

"Then take a chance that I am telling the truth!"

He had never turned over a lady before, and perhaps that fact was making him weak and second guess his gut. *If* everything she was telling him was true, she would need protection while he tried to piece together what really happened. And to do that, she would need to be watched night and day—especially when she was likely a stone-cold liar who had everything to gain with running from him.

"Please, Tanner, you are my only hope of getting my life back. And if you do prove that I am innocent, I'll pay you triple the reward."

He frowned. Triple could buy the deed to their ranch and far more. He studied her face, his gut twinging. *Lord, is this why you introduced us? So I could prove her innocence and save the ranch, or perhaps turn her in to save my family's ranch?* He bowed his head, but only the wagon wheels churning in the street and the braying of mules met his ears. With no clear course, the only direction he could take was to wait on hearing from the

Lord, and to wait, he'd need to keep her safe from other hunters. "Fine."

"Fine? You'll let me disappear?" She straightened, eyes flicking toward the train station as the whistle blew for final boarding.

"No, everyone and their grandmother will be looking for you with that massive bounty on your head, and if I don't claim it, there are many less honorable men who will." He bent and collected her carpetbag and gently grasped her arm. "You are coming with me to my ranch deep in the Gallinas Mountains where I will hold you until I am certain one way or the other of your story."

"The mountains?" She paled and shook her head. "I can't go with you—especially a-alone."

"I know it is not ideal, but would you rather go to prison, even though you state that men are waiting there to put an end to you?" He frowned. "Seems like an obvious choice, but far be it from me to make a choice for any lady."

"Obviously, I would not like prison over

your ranch." She jerked her elbow out of his hand and brushed at the fabric there. "But I'm not marrying you either."

"Good. I didn't ask." Such a statement from the beauty only an hour ago would have crushed him, but that was before he knew she was a liar and an enemy of the law, and therefore, himself. *Potential enemy.* "I have no intention of marrying you to save your precious reputation before bringing you out onto the ranch. What does your reputation matter to me when you are supposedly a murderess? No. If people ask, you are going to be coming to the ranch to work as my cook and cleaning woman while I try to prove your innocence."

A wagon rumbled nearby, and Tanner slid into the shadow of the building beside Corinna as it passed with a pair of cream dogs racing along the back wheels, barking.

She crossed her arms. "And how will you be doing that, exactly, if we are out in the middle of nowhere, and you have to watch my every move?"

"I have just as many contacts as the

Roberts, I'd wager, and on the *right* side of the law with characters to match. Before we leave, I will get your story out to them with a drop spot for information while you hide out at my place."

"Your place?"

Her hands were shaking something fierce, and he checked his ire. She was a lady, a liar, and a murderess, but a petite lady, nonetheless. "Look, I don't know if you are an honorable woman, but I can guarantee that I'm an honorable man. I will never harm you or do anything that will dishonor my good name. And if I put you in jail, an innocent as you claim, it *will* dishonor my name, and you will be eaten alive. Do you trust me to guard you while I try to piece together your story?" He extended his hand.

She eyed his outstretched palm. "Do you promise to dig until you hit the truth? Because *I* can guarantee that they might as well have killed me already with the amount of false evidence they have piled up against me and that obscene reward."

He kept his hand extended. "Truth is justice. And I don't have enough of it yet. I have no choice but to keep digging."

She placed her impossibly small hand in his. "Do I have another choice?"

"Of course." He shrugged. "Prison."

CHAPTER 10

"**W**hat do you mean he is escorting you to your next home?" Dolly hissed.

"It means that I need help, and he is going to give me a chance." Corinna gathered the rest of her things into the trunk that she had forgotten to pack. It had been mortifying returning to the Rawlins building and knocking, awaiting someone to let her inside, but she was too practical to leave anything she might need now that she had another choice.

Dolly grabbed her arm, staying her flight about the room. "You have a rail pass! And a fortune to your name! Why would you go with Tanner Sterling? This does not add up, Corinna."

Corinna sighed and turned to the head waitress. Dolly was smart, and if Corinna did not assuage her suspicion, too many people would know of her whereabouts. "I am not at liberty to tell you much, but my fortune is not my own at present."

"What?" Dolly blinked. "Do you have an uncle who is laying claim to it, or something?"

"Or something very like it." Corinna shook her head and finished her packing. "I cannot say anything else, and I beg you not to mention the direction of my journey to anyone, especially not Lorna." She swallowed. It was dangerous enough that Dolly knew that Corinna was with Mr. Sterling, but if the Roberts came looking for her, they would have no qualms hurting those she considered friends for answers. "The point is that I do not have the means of seeing to myself for long. My assets are in the hands of others now, and Mr. Sterling has proved himself to be an honorable man. He won't take advantage of me."

Dolly gaped at her. "I-I know he claims to be a good man, but I cannot condone your disappearing into the night with him." She ran her hands over her face, moaning. "I feel like this is my fault. I can't send you off into the night with him just because you are in need of funds!"

"It's not even dark out yet." Corinna closed the trunk and relocked it, carting the medium trunk downstairs and trotted back up, finishing her thought, "And Pernilla didn't give you much of a choice."

"Mr. Harvey has standards, but even he would grant mercy in this situation— Pernilla, or no Pernilla." Dolly crossed her arms. "I can lend you money."

"And that is kind of you, but I currently do not have a means of repaying you your savings. I have a solution that is safe. And this isn't your fault, Dolly." Corinna rested her hand on the woman's arm. "My leaving is for the best. I never meant to deceive you, but circumstances stayed my tongue."

"Circumstances that I still do not understand," Dolly muttered as Corinna locked the last trunk and grabbed one handle of the large trunk and Dolly the other.

"I hardly do myself, but, if I *was* a spy for my father's empire, I'd offer you a job as a manager in one of my father's restaurants. You are the best head waitress I've ever met, and you deserve a promotion."

Dolly's cheeks pinked as they maneuvered the stairs. "And here, I thought you hated me after how I treated you."

"I didn't understand you at the time, but I have a feeling that, like me, there is much more behind your actions than you let on. Please, do not think you've brought on my leaving with Mr. Sterling." They dropped the trunk at the foot of the stairs, and Corinna flung open the front door and motioned Tanner, who was standing at the landing with his hat in hand, to come and fetch the trunks. He stacked the medium one atop the large, bent and grasping the sides, heaved it up. Her lips parted at the impressive feat. *No! He is basically your captor. You are worse than the heroines in the bounty hunter dime novels to admire his strength.*

She smiled to Dolly and extended her hand. "I hope to see you again one day, but if I don't, have a beautiful life, Dolly Matthews."

Dolly pressed her lips into a firm line and pulled Corinna into a fierce embrace. "You better write to me and tell me that you are well within the next month. If he so much as harms a hair on your head, I'll send Lorna's former Texas Ranger and now rancher husband, and he will take care of it. You hear? You are not without choices."

Corinna's cheeks bloomed at Dolly's declaration, but Corinna's core warmed that she could now count *two* true friends from her time as a Harvey Girl. "I can't promise to write straight away, but I will as soon as I am settled."

"You better, or I'll make good on my threat." Dolly narrowed her gaze at Tanner. "Keep her safe."

Tanner smirked. "She'll be safer than if she is in a padded jail cell."

"How comforting," Dolly muttered and bolted the door.

Tanner didn't waste much time in setting her trunks into the hired wagon that he hitched to his palomino. He unceremoniously hoisted Corinna into the wagon like a sack of feed and climbed up with ease after her, snapping the reins and guiding Silver out of town off the main road. He directed them to the range beyond the Montezuma and, she guessed, toward his ranch.

With the sun's setting, the air was growing colder by the minute, and she was thankful he had allowed her to return for her clothes and items—though she had forgotten to change out of her uniform again. A rut in the road sent her into his shoulder. She mumbled an apology and gripped the sides of the wagon. It was no spring buggy. Her derriere was going to be bruised and tender long before they reached the ranch.

The road crested, and they rolled over the wooden bridge. A grove of trees surrounded the road, marking the edge of the little town of Las Vegas and where Hot Springs began. She focused on the beauty of the Gallinas Mountain range as they crept closer and closer to the Montezuma. Silver easily pulled them up the steep mountainside toward the Montezuma Resort where she had spent the beginning of her Harvey Girl days with Lorna. Even now, the pointed roof of the Montezuma's tower was visible from the tree line.

Silver curved with the road as a castle-like building appeared. Its reddish-brown sandstone exterior on the first two stories complimented the mountainside with its gray slate roof. The architecture had made it feel homey during her time there, though, with its verandas, dormers, and bay windows, and exquisite with three towers, it boasted of the elegant time to be had for all guests.

Tanner snapped the reins and continued up the road beyond the Montezuma that eventually turned into a glorified trail, jostling her teeth. She kept her complaints to herself. Corinna *finally* had someone who had chosen to listen to her instead of tossing her in a cell for fear of the Roberts' retaliation. If she could only turn Tanner from only listening into a champion for her innocence, he might be able to give her back the life she had lost. *If my old life and restaurants are even there at all when I get back.*

She still shook in anger every time she stopped long enough to know that those rats were destroying her father's legacy and living in *her* father's house that he had built, surrounded by a lifetime of things gathered that were memories of their family. And those people were soiling her things with their presence if they had not sold them already. So, she put the Roberts out of her mind and chose not to think of them.

The wagon struck another rut, and she slammed into Tanner's shoulder. He glared down at her this time, and she scooted back into her corner, leaving an inch between them once more, but that inch allowed the sweeping wind to rush between them, leaving her chilled to the bone and her teeth chattering.

"Cold?"

She nodded, thankful he had finally chosen to break the silence. "I-it will be dark soon. Will we arrive anytime soon?"

"The ranch is further into the mountains, and traveling at night without torches is beyond foolish. We will set up camp and arrive late tomorrow morning."

Wait. What? She would spend the night alone . . . with him? Outside? "B-but the bears."

"Black bears rarely attack unless you provoke them. It's the wolves you need to worry about." Tanner snapped the reins, encouraging Silver to pick up his pace as the upward slope increased.

She gripped the siderail, weighing jail against the wolves. *There are different types of wolves there.* At least with the four-legged variety, she would stand a chance with Tanner guarding her back. "Wolves," she whispered.

"I've slept out of doors more than I have slept inside. You will be safe enough when I build a fire. They are smart enough not to approach it. And if they do, I have guns." He slapped the reins, coaxing the horse up the hill. "Come on, boy. Just a little longer."

"Guns? How many?" Her stomach churned. She never had the taste for weapons herself and hated it that her father kept a derringer in his nightstand when their area of Chicago had fallen prey to a string of thievery. But, when she had determined to flee, she had taken it. As much as she disliked weapons, they could prove useful. It was too bad she had packed it in the bottom of her carpetbag.

"I have four on me and my long rifle too."

"That seems excessive," she muttered, but was secretly glad that he possessed so many should a need arise, and she had no doubt he could wield them with ease.

"Not in my line of work. Sometimes, the men I take in would rather kill me than come with me. I need the weapons to be persuasive."

"Oh. Well, I'm glad I didn't wait for you to persuade *me* then." She snorted and slapped her hand over her mouth at the unladylike sound. She must be exhausted to have let that old habit slip through.

"I would *never* harm a woman." He scowled. "Even one who is thought to be a murderess. I am no animal."

She swallowed back the comment that he had grabbed her arm plenty hard earlier but decided that she needed to keep her potential defender on her side, so she nodded to her captor. "Good to know."

"But just because I won't harm you, doesn't mean that I'm a fool. I'll tie you up in an instant if you try to escape."

She gestured to the woods. "And why would I? This is just an elaborate jail."

"One person's jail is another's paradise, I suppose." He halted the wagon in a small clearing. "This is where I usually make camp."

It looked like someone had taken care to cut back nature and remove any debris from the packed earth surrounding the stones that formed a ring in the center of the clearing. At the edge of the packed earth was a stack of wood, as if ready for the next camper. The delicate trickle of water on stone caught her ear as a repetitive trill from a bird echoed nearby.

"Whip-poor-wills live here. There's a stream nigh, too, if you are thirsty."

"I've never had water from a stream. Do we need to boil it before drinking it?"

He flicked back his hat and stared at her.

"It comes right off the mountains. Can't get much cleaner than untouched, melted snow. It's the still water you got to look out for. Many a man lost his life to still waters." And then, as if remembering that she was the enemy in the camp, he clamped his mouth shut, hopped out of the wagon, grabbed a bedroll, and unfurled it. He reached his hands up to her. "Come on then."

Corinna eyed the distance to the ground. While she was attracted to the man, she didn't relish the idea of Tanner touching her for even a moment while they were alone in the woods. *It's not like you are going to suddenly become uncontrollable and kiss him again.* She glanced at his lips and gripped the side of the wagon, swishing her skirts out of the way. "I can do it."

"Sure, you can, if you want to break an ankle. You're too little to jump out on your own." He kept his arms up, waiting for her to accept his help.

"Fine, but for the record, I'm not that little." She rested her hands on his broad shoulders and allowed him to lift her out.

"If you want me to believe your story,

you best stop telling tales—or believing falsehoods. You barely reach my shoulder." He chortled and dropped his hands the instant her half boots hit the ground and smoothed his expression to stone once more.

She stood to the side and watched as he tossed Silver's saddle from the back of the wagon beside the bedroll. He gestured for her to sit on the bedding.

And we are back to being gruff as an old bear. She sank onto the bedroll, keeping an eye on the ground for any things that crawled as Tanner stacked the wood in a pyramid in the circle of stones. Using a flint and knife, he scraped a flare of embers into the dried pinyon pine straw he had tucked beneath the stacked wood. The flames licked the straw and slowly caught on the bark.

"Impressive."

He sat back on his heels. "Fire can be the difference between life and death out here. Wouldn't be much of a bounty hunter without knowing my way around a fire."

So much for complimenting the man. "Then it looks like I'd die without you."

"Just remember that and don't give me no trouble and try to run off on your own." He dug into a saddle bag and withdrew a leather pouch. "Bison jerky?"

"Not tonight, thank you. I'm not hungry."

He shrugged and sprawled on his back with his head propped on the saddle and bit into the dried meat. "Try to rest, Miss Corinna, but don't expect to make a break for it. I sleep light."

"Good." Corinna ran her hand over the bedroll. He had given her his blankets. Despite his anger, he was a true gentleman. She could trust him. Nestling under the blankets, she closed her eyes and smiled. For the first time in months, a spark of hope burst to life within her.

CHAPTER 11

The infernal woman was smiling in her sleep. He supposed all black widows slept soundly when they had captured yet another foolish prey in their web. Tanner knew what Corinna was, and yet, he still felt this pull to protect her, to find out the truth. *But it's not because I once found her pretty.* He folded his arms and flipped to his other side where he couldn't see her, the saddle hard against his cheek. No. It wasn't because of his former attraction at all. *For truth. That's why I'm risking bringing her out to the Sanctuary and for the reward.*

While she packed, he had jotted down a note that he had dropped with a list of recipients at the telegraph office. With any luck, he should have a new lead in a matter of a couple of weeks. He only hoped that the lead proved that what she was saying was true. He sighed. He had to keep that at the forefront of his actions. She may not be a liar, and he had to give her a chance.

Tanner remembered what it was like not to have a voice—to be helpless—to have no one believe him when he said he could take care of his family. No one listened to him as a boy of thirteen when his father died. No one thought a young boy capable of seeing after his six younger brothers. And so, they were carted off to the orphan train, and someone else took over their filthy flat in Chicago.

At first, Tanner had held on to the hope that someone would want a family of seven brothers, but by the fourth stop, one by one, his siblings were taken from him and given to strangers who only wanted free labor until the tracks ended with Tanner alone—unwanted. The memory of his innocent four-year-old brother, Noah, being taken from them first had tortured him every night. Noah's screams were the force that pushed him to track down each and every one of his siblings.

Tanner had grown a foot by the time he found the first one, Lawrence, who was so skinny from being underfed that Tanner had struck the man who had tried to keep Lawrence from returning with Tanner. By the time he found Noah, Tanner had turned fourteen and looked like a young man with his patchy beard. It took some doing, but at after two full years of searching, Tanner had gathered his family back under one tent. By then, Tanner discovered he was good at finding people, and he collected his first bounty—which allowed him to feed his six brothers for a week.

After the first year of his collecting bounties, they were able to get a loan from the Las Vegas bank to purchase a ramshackle cabin in the mountains, which they named Sanctuary Ranch. It wasn't much, but what started as a dream of being together and a hope for a new life, had blossomed into a home where his brothers were free to do as they pleased and make their own way in life.

He glanced at the sleeping woman across the fire. Between his brothers and his contacts, he would get down to the truth about Corinna Victoria Alistair Roberts. In his gut, Tanner hoped he misjudged her, as folks did his ability to provide for his brothers. But the fact that she had lied by omission did not sit well with him.

The unnatural snapping of a twig caught his ear. His fingertips grazed the Colt in his right hip holster. At the second snapping, he snatched the gun, rolled to a crouch, and reached to Corinna, gently shaking her. "Corinna, get in the wagon."

She mumbled and turned over in her sleep as if she were slumbering on a feather mattress instead of a bedroll on hard packed dirt. He shook her shoulder again. "Corinna."

"Huh?" She blinked in the firelight and looked up at the stars, dazed as she shrugged back under her blanket. "It's not even daylight yet."

"We are being watched."

She froze in her nestling under the blanket, whispering, "Is it a bear?"

"If it is who I think it might be lurking in the woods, we might wish that it was a mama bear."

She slowly rose to her knees and grasped his arm. "Who do you think it is?"

"Bounty hunters." He pulled back the hammer. "Take cover in the wagon *now*."

Corinna scrambled for the wagon, crawling into the bed of it, and in the corner of his eye, he caught her golden hair tumbling from her coiffure in her haste.

He removed a second gun from his left holster, staying crouched to make himself a smaller target. "I know you are out there. Come on out with your hands where I can see them, and you might just live to tell the tale of your encounter with the Angel of Justice! This is your first and last warning!"

"Hold your fire, Tanner! It's just us!" The second Sterling brother's voice rang out.

"Wade?" Tanner shouted, jamming his guns back into their holsters as he leapt to his feet and charged toward them. "What are you doing? Man alive, I could have shot you. You know better than to sneak up on me!"

"Not a chance." Wade Sterling stepped from the shadows, a long gun slung over his shoulders and whittled down toothpick in his mouth, with their two youngest brothers trailing behind, all of them hooting with laughter.

"Angel of Justice?" Jackson snorted, wiping tears from his eyes. "Is that seriously supposed to intimidate people?"

"I didn't come up with the name. Out-laws did, and it seems to do the trick in striking fear into their hearts." Tanner reached out, snagging Jackson in his arm and with his knuckles, rubbed the top of Jackson's brown hair. "What are y'all doing this far out from the ranch?"

"We were out frog hunting, and then we saw your fire from across the valley," Noah interjected, eyeing the wagon as if he spied something moving.

"You were frogging all the way out here when we have a perfectly good riverbank just beyond the cabin?" Tanner asked, disbe-lief coloring his voice.

Wade shrugged. "I was bored on the ranch and was looking for an excuse to get out. Figured we could hunt frogs, cook 'em up at our campsite, and the boys could head to the Harvey House tomorrow for some good eatin' and bring me back something."

"And what about you, Noah and Jackson? You bored too?"

"You always told us never to go out hunting alone," Jackson crossed his arms, smirking.

"I don't know how you three talked Lawrence, Gray, and Clint to take over your work loads," Tanner muttered.

"We drew straws—"

"Tanner?"

Her sweet voice wafted over to him and all the brothers stiffened, turning as one toward the wagon. The beauty peeked over the side of the bed, her eyes wide with her golden locks cascading over her shoulders and falling to her waist.

"Well, well, well." Wade worked the toothpick in his mouth and grinned at Tanner. "And good thing we did get bored because it seems that you have gotten yourself a little something in that wagon that either don't belong to you or is a secret that you should have told us about long ago. What do you got to say, big brother? You get yourself hitched?"

"I told you to stay down!" Tanner scolded as his brothers gaped. "What if they had been hunters?"

"I figured when you rubbed your knuckles on that man's head, they must be your brothers. It's nice to meet you all." She waved to the men with a little smile that brought out her single dimple and made her eyes sparkle in the moonlight.

His brothers were goners. He had better get word soon from his contacts. The last thing this family needed was another woman breaking up their family.

CORINNA TRIED to appear at ease before the massive group of men as the word *hitched* seemed to have frozen Tanner for a moment. William had been tall, but these men would've made *him* seem short. But, with them surrounding her in the wagon, she fought against the tendril of fear that licked at her heart. She knew Tanner would protect her . . . like a jailer his prisoner, but she didn't know these men, besides her brief interaction with Noah. *But you aren't necessarily the best judge of men's character with your previous choice in a husband.* She swallowed. *Be brave, but if you can't manage even that,* act *brave!*

"Well, is she your wife?" The one called Wade demanded.

"She could be. He sure was smitten with her at the carnival!" Noah interjected. "But the real question is *how* did he convince her to up and marry him?"

"She is not my wife. She's a *prisoner,*" Tanner spat the word as if it were the most horrible thing a woman could be in his eyes.

If she had been a vain woman, she would have been gravely offended, but even so, it stung to hear the disdain in his voice when she was innocent.

"She can't have done something too bad. You don't even have her tied up." Wade leaned on the sideboard, taking in her lack of ropes.

She adjusted her skirt to cover her half boot. "I haven't done anything wrong."

"Well, if she ain't no lawbreaker, and you aren't going to propose any time soon, can I ask her then?" The brown-haired male of the group interjected.

"Jackson, you had better watch your tongue. You are a sight too young for marrying." Tanner whopped him with his Stetson.

"Please. I'm nineteen and could've married three years ago if our closest neighbors hadn't moved into town." He shook his head. "Still think you should have let me court Darla."

"And how could you have provided for her?" Tanner broke through the circle and gave her his hand, gentleman jailer he was, and helped her down from the high wagon bed. "Boys, this is Corinna Victoria Alistair-Roberts, and she will be staying with us for a while on the ranch."

"How long is a while?" Wade crossed his arms.

"Long enough for me to prove she isn't a murderess." Tanner dropped her hand like she had burnt him and fixated on picking at a knot in the sideboard wood.

"Murderess?" The men muttered and gaped at her.

"Her?" Jackson chuckled. "Looks like the Angel of Justice can't recognize one of his own. She looks like she done dropped from heaven from the looks of her. She's the prettiest woman I've ever seen, and Darla was a beauty."

"And she's too little to be a killer. Look at her hands," Wade muttered, pointing at her hands with his toothpick. "Those are the hands of someone who isn't used to hard work. She's got a little red here and there, but she doesn't look strong enough to do the job you got her for."

"They do look mighty puny for a killer," Noah nodded in agreement.

"Excuse me, I'm right here. And for your information, my hands have seen plenty of work, but I make good use of hand cream." Corinna bit back a laugh at the men's assessment and ran her hands over her hair and twisted it to hang in front of her right shoulder.

"Because that is the most important accusation to address," Tanner muttered.

"I am not a killer. I am merely a woman who believed a so-called reformed man's intentions. I'm sure every single one in this group can claim they were deceived at one point in their lives. That you chose the hope of something promised instead of weighing every possibility before leaping?"

The brothers nodded, but Tanner scowled at her, unable or unwilling to admit fault.

But, if she could get his brothers on her side, then Tanner would surely follow! "Please, give me the benefit of the doubt while your brother sorts fact from the intricate web of lies my dead husband's family wove." She glanced at Tanner over her shoulder. "I do believe that our country attempts to presume innocence until proven guilty, yes?"

"Spoken like a guilty person." Tanner mumbled. "We need to get to sleep."

"But first, line up boys and give her your

names and ages to help her keep us straight," Wade motioned the two brothers and stepped forward and held out his large hand to her, waiting for her to grasp it.

She slipped her hand into his surprisingly gentle grasp. "Mr. W-Wade Sterling, wasn't it?"

"Yes, ma'am, but you can call me Wade." He gave her a kind grin, as if he was afraid she would start crying after Tanner's harsh words. "I'm second in line at twenty-six. Even though Tanner is two years older, I'm by far the wisest of the group."

"It is nice to meet you, Wade."

Jackson strode up and bumped Wade with his shoulder, grasped her hand, and bowed over it. "Jackson Sterling. I'm sixth in line and am nineteen, ma'am, and I can't tell you how happy I am to meet you and bring you back to the ranch, and just so you're aware of my intentions from the first, I intend on asking you to marry me."

She blinked at his rush of words. *And sixth in line? With Noah the youngest? Seven backwoods mountain men . . .* It seemed that

Tanner really did need a cook and a washerwoman.

"But don't answer now. You need to get to know me and fall in love with me over time," Jackson said with a wink.

Corinna cheeks burned, and she scrambled over how to respond without crushing the boy, but the next brother strode up and extended his hand.

"I believe you remember me from our almost-kiss," Noah said with such a wicked grin that it brought a bubble of laughter to her lips.

The men whirled to stare at the boy.

Wade glared at him. "You watch your mouth, boy. You may be eighteen, but I can still lick you good in a wrestling match and teach you some manners."

Her laughter burst out, breaking the tension. "It's not what you all think. There was a carnival hosted by the Harvey Girls, and I was taking an unanticipated shift at the kissing booth—"

"Which *Tanner* interrupted," Noah added, hooting with laughter.

The brothers shouted, clasping Tanner on the shoulder, but he shrugged them off.

"Not like *that!*"

"He did not kiss me on the lips," Corinna clarified quickly, shaking her head at Noah.

"Nice to see you again, Miss Corinna. I may be the youngest of the lot, but I am the smartest, which is different than wisest." Noah grinned. "And I'll be happy to help you sort through the web of lies to see that you are set free."

"Noah fancies himself a lawyer," Jackson supplied. "He found three law books on the trail about five years ago and took them home, dead set on reading them. He knows every obscure law by heart. He's hoping to help out Wade someday soon."

Wade elbowed Jackson in the ribs. "We are right proud of him."

Noah's chest expanded, and Corinna could tell all the brothers doted on the youngest, but Wade was clearly put out about Jackson revealing something.

"But you should remember his passion came out of a place of sheer *boredom*," Jackson snorted. "I could do all that learnin' too, but there is too much to do and too much exploring to do when I don't. Why, we just found those caves last year and they are so expansive, I've only been able to draw a map to part of it."

"So, we have an Angel of Justice, an explorer, and a man of the law." She looked up to Wade. Out of all the brothers, he had the darkest hair, nearest to Jackson's coloring. And while the other brothers may possess the willingness for a quick laugh, he seemed more serious, and his piercing blue eyes drew her to him. "What about you, Wade?"

He flicked away the toothpick and sank to one knee to untie the straps of his pack that held a rolled green blanket atop. "I breed horses and train them. Whenever I am done with a yearling, mare, gelding, or stallion, Tanner takes the horses to sell all across the territory and the states along the Atchison, Topeka, and Santa Fe railroads."

"Very impressive. But why don't you sell them yourself?"

Wade cleared his throat. "Well, raising horses takes up most of my time. I don't have a lot of broodmares ready to foal at any given time, but the training is what can take a stunning horse and make it a champion."

And yet, Tanner is concerned with funds . . . It must be a smaller venture.

"It is mighty late. If we are going to be up with the sun, we best get some shut eye." Tanner mumbled, as if put out by his brothers' friendliness, and grabbed her bedroll, tossing it in the back of the wagon. "Corinna, you'll be more comfortable in the wagon, away from the critters of the night. We will sleep around you to make sure nothing eats you while you sleep."

The rest of the brothers guffawed and slung their packs off their shoulders to make camp as Tanner helped her back in the wagon bed.

How did Tanner notice her squirming and staring every which way before she laid down by the fire? She swallowed back the sudden sting of tears at his thoughtfulness, even if he did think her a killer.

CHAPTER 12

Crossing through the narrow pass between the cliffs, Tanner kept his gaze fixed on the crest of the road. He slapped the reins, and Silver pulled them to the top of the hill where morning's light fell upon their cabin. Atop the hill, in a clearing that they had made larger, sat their log cabin. The original story and a half structure served as the center of the current cabin, with a stone chimney a good five feet above the roof. They had built two log wings off either side, effectively tripling it in size. Over the years, they had cut out a couple of rectangles in the walls for glass paned windows and even added a porch across the center, blending the old and the new so well that it looked like it had always been so large.

In front of the cabin stood the two mature apple trees that they had planted from seedlings when they arrived over a decade ago. The three falls of apples had proven a boon and a tasty addition to their usual fare. The trees never failed to bring back the memories of their journey to seeking sanctuary and finding this beautiful land fairly bursting with potential. The price had been right and Tanner felt confident he could pay down the loan each month. Now, they only had two years of payment left until it was the Sterling brothers' outright and no man could take it from them.

Sanctuary Ranch was more than just the first place they had called home after their parents died, and they had finally been reunited after nearly two years apart. It was a place where they could be themselves and not worry about townsfolk judging them for how little they had, or worse, sending the law after Wade if they ever discovered he had a warrant out for his arrest. But it had been many years since Wade's choice that had led to his hardly ever leaving the ranch, except for the occasional trip toward town. Even then, Wade never risked stepping foot into town. He only ever sent his brothers in as his proxy, which meant Wade never had the ability to meet a woman, much less court her. Tanner could only hope that one day Wade would truly be free from that awful chapter in their boyhoods.

Corinna sighed beside him. She lifted her hand to shield her eyes as she took in the sight. "It's beautiful, Tanner."

"Welcome to Sanctuary Ranch. She's a hundred and sixty acres of pure, wild beauty. The cabin was built in the previous owner's attempt to fulfill the Homestead Act, so she's not much, but she's home."

"What's the Homestead Act?"

"The Homestead Act was a significant part of our history," Noah piped up, leaning between them from his seat in the wagon bed. "In 1862, the government gave out parcels of land in order to have it settled—"

"Never ask him a history or law question, Miss Corinna!" Wade groaned. "He won't stop now that you've got him rolling!"

Noah continued to explain the details, which led to their loan from the bank to purchase Sanctuary cabin, but Tanner pushed Noah's words to the back of his mind until they were a dull hum. He flicked the reins, the wagon bobbling over the few stones in the road that they hadn't been able to remove because the deeper they dug, the more the rock turned into a boulder. Instead, they added more dirt to cover the rocks to make it as smooth as possible.

"And that was how we took over Sanctuary Ranch." Noah finished.

The brothers breathed a collective sigh of relief that Noah's oration was complete.

"I suppose it's rather fitting that someone accused of murder would find refuge here," Noah shrugged.

"*Accused* being the key word," Corinna returned as she closed her eyes and lifted her face to the sunlight filtering through the leaves. "It's so peaceful here."

"Won't be that way for long," Tanner chuckled and halted the wagon in front of the cabin, Wade's bluetick coonhound, Blue, already sounding the alarm with his deep whooping howl. Tanner hopped down in time for the front door to bang open.

"About time you came home!" Clint threw his arm around Tanner's neck, tugging him into a choke hold.

Tanner shifted into an evasive move and dodged his kid brother's playful punches as Gray sauntered out of the barn, followed by Lawrence with a long rifle slung over his shoulders, his arms draped over the barrel and butt, all grinning up at Corinna still in the wagon.

"Who do we have here?" Gray clapped Tanner on the shoulder. "Did you finally convince a Harvey Girl to marry you?"

"Why do you all always assume I have to trick a girl into marrying me? I'll have you know I'm in high demand in Las Vegas," Tanner retorted.

Corinna's cheeks flamed, but she pressed her lips together and looked to Tanner.

Ah yes, a proper introduction. He turned to lift a hand to Corinna, but Wade already hopped out and helped her down as Blue paced at Wade's feet. Wade scratched Blue behind the ears and Corinna gave the hound a tentative pat on the head that sent the dog's tail to whipping.

Tanner gritted his teeth against his rebuttal that *he* was to be the only brother who interacted with the prisoner. "Corinna, meet the rest of my brothers. Clint, age twenty-one and our resident cook, Gray, age twenty-two, who is the game hunter and supplies us with meat and sells furs in town to help make ends meet, and Lawrence, age twenty-four, who thinks he is cut out to be the next bounty hunter, but time will be the judge of that."

Corinna's eyes widened at the wall of men, but instead of shying away as he expected, she smiled up at them, dipping into a pretty curtsy. "It is a pleasure to make your acquaintances, Mr. Clint, Mr. Gray, and Mr. Lawrence Sterling."

"Who is she?" Clint whispered to Noah.

"An angel," Jackson answered, elbowing him in the ribs. "And I called dibs already."

Corinna smiled. "I'm afraid there is to be

no dibs. I'm to be the maid of the Sanctuary for a little while."

"Due to an accusation of murder," Tanner growled out. "You are always omitting the most important part of the story when speaking with my family."

"Yes, and your brother is holding me here until he can prove my innocence, or guilt, and therefore, collect the massive bounty on my head, or reward for clearing my name. Therefore, I hardly think that any of you should wish to seek my hand in marriage." Corinna tucked her hands behind her back. "I look forward to my time here with you all."

"You are to treat Corinna with respect, but don't you dare let her wander off this ranch." Tanner crossed his arms and tried not to focus on this all too bright version of the quiet Harvey Girl he knew. "There are bears and mountain lions out here, and you would make quite the delicacy, Corinna."

"Why, Mr. Sterling, it is never proper to call a lady such a thing," she chided, making his brothers guffaw and his cheeks burn.

"Now, show me to the kitchen so I can get to work."

The brothers looked to Clint.

"If the king of the kitchen will allow me to enter?" She nodded to Clint. "I never wish to step on a chef's toes, but I am rather handy."

Clint grinned. "I just did a heap of baking this morning and the dishes are piled nigh on a mountain. If you want to help scrub up, I'd call you heaven sent."

"Hold it, Clint. You know them ain't the rules," Jackson chortled.

"What do you mean? I don't mind." Corinna blinked. "Unless there are rules for the dishes?"

"Well, when you have seven men who all live under the same roof and pull the same amount of weight, dishes seem to be just another hurdle between you and your bed, so we let the dishes keep for a week in the sink," Wade supplied.

"Oh, and they get a real good stink on by then too, which makes the game even more fun," Noah added, grinning. "The more risk, the more reward if you win and don't have to do them. It's always a good time."

"I suppose one must create entertainment where one can," Corinna slowly nodded as if the very idea disgusted her but wanted to seem relaxed.

"Ain't that the truth." Wade grinned. "We do the dishes on Tuesdays, which just happens to be today, but only the unlucky loser has to do them."

"Do you draw straws?" Corinna frowned as if still confused by their whole system.

Tanner grinned. "Well, this is where we had to get a little creative."

"You mean *cheat*," Jackson snorted.

"We have a shooting contest with only one bullet, or arrow, each. Worst shot does the dishes," Tanner grinned. "And as I am the *Angel of Justice*, I never lose, and it helps the boys practice to avoid the dishes."

"And lucky for me, I can bet that I am not going to be the worst shot tonight," Noah hooted.

"What are you talking about?" Clint interjected. "You and I are *always* the worst, and I ain't losing today."

Noah rolled his eyes. "I meant that we have us a nice, lovely houseguest, and she is going to take her turn just like the rest of us."

"She is under arrest." Tanner crossed his arms. While he didn't put up with lying, he didn't think it was hardly fair for her to be subjected to Dish Mountain on her very first day when she didn't even put them there. But, as saying such a thing could be misconstrued as being soft, he reasoned, "We can't rightly hand her a weapon."

"I'm not arrested quite yet, Mr. Sterling," she reminded him. "You've merely taken me under custody."

"The rules state that *anyone* under this roof participates in a shooting match, and the worst shot does the dishes," the resident lawyer interjected. Noah crossed his arms. "Come on now, Tanner. You made the rules. You've got to follow them."

"And I'd say that someone clearly does not want to do the dishes," Tanner scoffed, but gestured to the barn. "Fine, but we are using arrows. Less chance of Corinna getting any ideas to murder us all."

At her wince that she quickly veiled, he felt a twinge of remorse for his jab. He felt the urge to apologize, but remembering her lies, he pushed down that urge. The only way to protect his heart was not to have one where Corinna Victoria was concerned.

CORINNA DECIDED NOT to let that comment stick in her heart. Tanner Sterling obviously had some issues with trust. While he had suspended his disbelief enough to keep her safely away from other hunters, she couldn't blame his hesitation to be friendly with her again. She well recognized the signs of building a wall around one's heart. *Well, I don't have to be Tanner's friend. All that matters is that he is having his contacts search on his behalf for the truth.*

She followed the men to the barn where Wade disappeared inside for a moment and reappeared with a sheath of arrows and a bow, the men cheering.

"So, you really do have a contest with a

bow and arrow?" Corinna shook her head in disbelief as they strode around the barn to where a barrel with two white circles painted on the top was set in the field an impossible distance away.

"Cheaper than gunpowder, easier to make than a bullet, and it's how we hunt," Wade explained as Tanner rolled up his sleeves, exposing his bronzed forearms.

The brothers lined up from youngest to oldest, starting with Noah who struck the target three inches from the center, followed by Jackson and Clint, who all had similar strikes. Gray and Lawrence outshot them all. Then, Wade stepped up and struck dead center, and with a chuckle, handed the bow to Tanner.

Finally, something he is not the best in. She crossed her arms and watched Tanner take aim. He drew in a steady breath and released it, along with the string. A *whiz* sounded and the point split Wade's arrow down the middle. Her lips parted. She knew Tanner was a wonder with the gun, given his legendary status, but she had assumed that if he was proficient with a gun, why would he venture out to a bow and arrow?

"Your turn." He held them out to her.

She bit back a groan, grasped the weapon, and stepped up. She was going to make a fool of herself, but she needed the brothers to see that, while she was a terrible shot, she was a good sport and didn't mind playing their game. She attempted to nock the arrow like the men had done. She drew back the string, but in doing so, her grip on the arrow slipped and the arrow tumbled to the ground.

Tanner scooped it up and stepped behind her.

"What are you doing?" She reached for the arrow.

He didn't release it. "If I don't show you how to hold it, you may just shoot us after all. I am usually the doctor of the group, and I assure you that me giving stitches is the last thing they want to experience."

"I'm not sure—"

"It's for safety." Tanner lifted the arrow and situated himself directly behind her, guiding her arms into the correct position and cradling the bow into a manner that felt less awkward.

He gently grasped her shoulder and tugged her against his chest. "You've got to relax, Corinna. Lift your elbow to be level with your eye while keeping your fingers on the arrow and string. Take a breath and pull on the drawstring."

She was *trying* to, but it was impossible with him at her back. She had never been held like this, much less by a man of his physique. His massive chest brushed against her shoulders and his arms created a barrier between her and the rest of the world. What would it be like to have these arms want to protect her? She would never need to look over her shoulder again with him on her side . . . if he ever decided she was worth trusting.

"Breathe," he commanded softly in her ear.

Good gracious. She kept herself from shivering and drew in a ragged breath. His hand slowly inched away from hers.

"And release the string," he whispered into her ear.

She shuddered and let go.

Clint and Noah yelped, diving for the ground as the arrow struck the ground at their feet.

"ell, it looks like the dishes will be done by Miss Corinna, after all," Tanner smirked as he removed the bow from her grasp, seemingly not in the least affected by the whole instruction affair. "At least I tried to make it a challenge by helping you."

"I could have killed your brothers." She tossed up hands. "Let's just assume I'm the worst shot next time and save you all from the danger of having me shoot."

"No, no, no. That is not how the game is played." Noah rolled to his feet and dusted off his clothes. "Besides, when you live this far away from anyone, it is a good idea to know how to defend yourself. You never know if you'll be facing off an angry mama bear or have a venomous snake slither in the outhouse, but I vote we try the Colts next time to make it a fairer fight."

"Agreed. Take me to Dish Mountain, please." Corinna held out her hands as if they were cuffed, bringing chortles from the brothers.

Tanner rolled his eyes and led her into the cabin. It appeared more spacious than it had from the outside with its lofted ceilings. In the center of the ceiling, there hung an old wagon wheel with antlers intricately woven around the wheel with large tallow candles lining the border. It would be quite cozy when lit. Beneath the rustic chandelier was a braided rug that appeared to have been made from plaid shirts that were more faded in the center than at the edges, as if they had added braided fabric over the years until they possessed a large rug.

At the back of the room was a fireplace that appeared to service the kitchen as well as the main room. Before the hearth, there were five wooden chairs and two rockers, and from the lines in the floor between the threshold of the main room and what she supposed was the kitchen, she guessed the chairs were dragged to and from each room after meals in the evening.

Tanner pointed to the steep stairs at the right of the room. "That leads to the loft room where we all used to bunk, but we use it for extra dry goods and storage now. Wade and I sleep in the left room. The rest of the men sleep in the right and left wings of the house."

Meaning, never go in the left room, or the wings, but why would the two of them share the one room upstairs when there is a storage room? She nodded and followed Tanner through the door by the fireplace that did indeed lead to the kitchen.

The fireplace was shared, but on this side, the fireplace arched with space for a pot to hang. Thankfully, there was a small stove for preparing meals. It would be difficult to make anything in large quantities with it, but she supposed she would have to learn, given it was her one talent with which she could unfreeze the heart of any man.

"Soap is at the right of the sink. The pot in the fireplace has hot water for scrubbing. Can you manage it?" Tanner eyed her arms. "It is mighty heavy. Do you need us to move it for you?"

"I am stronger than I look, and I lost fair and square. No one should help me clean."

"We will be just outside. Yell if you need anything." With a wary eye, Tanner left her alone.

Corinna sighed and pressed her hands to her lower back and took in the room. She had never been so relieved to see a stack of dishes before. She needed to make herself useful and, hopefully, prove that she was not the type to go murdering her husband, no matter how terrible William might have been to her. She hummed her favorite hymn and set to work, scrubbing away the filth of a week's food on the plates. It was a wonder they did not have rats treating this place like their own personal Harvey House.

Clint ambled into the kitchen, reaching for an apple in a barrel. "Looks like you set a record for fastest dish washer. Takes us well into the night to finish them all." He picked up a dish and flipped it over. "Even cleaned the underside. Impressive."

She blinked at him. "And . . . you don't usually?"

He shrugged. "It's fifty-to-fifty odds that we remember to flip it over."

She swallowed back a gag. "Would you mind if I prepared the meal?" She looked up at Clint, not wanting to step on his toes, but if they were as unclean cooks as they were dish washers, it was a wonder they did not get food poisoning.

"Please. I hate cooking. Come on." He waved her after him outside. In a dugout in the shade of the barn, he opened a small door, bent, and led her down the steps to the icehouse. There were a few blocks of ice and the air held a chill. From the light splaying in through the open door, she found four rows of wide shelves mounted in the dirt wall, all bearing wrapped bundles. "Everything in here is fresh from two days ago. We slaughtered one of our longhorns, so the rest of the meat is in the smokehouse. Tanner brought a handful of females and a bull back from Texas about five years ago, and they've been feeding us since."

She grabbed a bundle and unwrapped it to find a stack of T-bone cuts that would have made her father proud to serve in his restaurants. They would prove tender without any pounding before cooking. "Why did you take over the kitchen if you hate cooking? I thought each brother did what they loved."

"Nope. I got stuck with it because I am the only one who doesn't burn everything to a crisp. When they found out I was the only one that could manage my ma's biscuit recipe to the point of them only being partial bricks, I was forced into the role." He sighed and gathered a crock, which she assumed held the butter. "I should have burned them. I'm fairly certain Tanner failed on purpose."

Corinna giggled as she followed him up the steps and ducked out of the small door. "Why would you guess that?"

"You've probably noticed already, but

Tanner's good at everything he sets his hand to."

Oh, I have, believe me. To Clint, she merely shrugged.

He pressed his lips into a line, pausing, as if unsure if he should continue. He held the door to the kitchen open for her. "Tanner may seem all gruff, Miss Corinna, but he has a heart of gold underneath that stone demeanor of his."

"I caught a glimpse of it before he thought I was guilty."

Clint nodded. "Just give him a day or two to sort through that storm in his head, and he'll come around. He can never stay mad for long."

Corinna set the steaks on a plate. "Can you show me around the rest of the kitchen, and I'll get started?"

Thankfully, the kitchen was fully stocked with nearly all Corinna needed and for the spices she was missing, well, she could improvise. Her most popular dishes at Victor's Steakhouse had been the result of an experiment when their dry goods order was late. She sprinkled salt and pepper over the meat and reached for the crock of beautifully churned golden butter. Scooping a generous amount into a bowl, she minced a red pepper, garlic cloves, and an onion, mixing it in the butter she had set aside and added a hint more salt and pepper, stirring the seasoning. She plucked two sprigs of rosemary from the bush just outside the backdoor that she had spotted on the way back from the icebox. Stripping the rosemary from the sprigs into the butter, she stirred it one more time before scooping the butter mixture and rubbing it over the meat.

Letting the steaks rest, she chopped potatoes, along with an onion and more garlic, and tossed them into the skillet with another scoop of butter. She set a cast-iron pan atop the stove and worked on the steaks, expertly searing the sides in the rich golden butter. For another side, she sliced Clint's loaf of bread, that seemed better than edible, and toasted the slices, scraping butter atop each, and sprinkled them with salt and rosemary. By the time she rang the dinner bell, she was coated in sweat and was certain she would match the smell of the cowboys who came to the Harvey House, but she knew her meal was perfection.

The brothers lined the table, each commenting on the smell. She hoped it was a good murmur. Tanner was so difficult to read, but the others' excitement was clear. She refrained from twisting her hands. She was confident in her skills as a cook, but anytime one used a new stove, it did involve a bit of a risk that usually led to a humbling moment.

Tanner held out a chair and motioned her to it.

"Thank you, Tanner." He was proving himself most thoughtful, even when suspicious. She slid into her seat as the men did the same. Tanner took a seat on an overturned barrel.

"Let's bow our heads," Tanner called over the group.

All swiped off their hats and held them over their hearts as Tanner prayed over the meal and petitioned the Lord that truth would be revealed. "And thank you, Father

God, for the hands that prepared the meal. Amen."

Her heart twinged at the sweet addition before she realized he must always say such things and might even have thought that Clint had made the meal, given she had no idea where Tanner had been during the cooking—just somewhere near in case she tried to run.

"Clint," Tanner said around his first mouthful. "Noah said you were getting better, but this—this is exceptional."

"This is heaven." Clint stabbed another forkful and shoved it in his mouth. "But it wasn't me. It was all our Miss Corinna. Once Tanner clears your name, promise you'll marry me, Miss Corinna?"

"Oh, no, she is going to marry me," Noah interjected.

"Too late. She's bound to marry me," Wade teased, sending her a wink, "if she'd have me."

"You'd have to get through me to ask her," Gray laughed. "What about you, Tanner? You going to throw your hat into the ring too? I'll warn you, I'm prepared to woo this lady."

"The meal isn't *that* good." Tanner mumbled around his mouthful. "When I say those words, I'll mean them."

"Sheesh, someone needs to take a nap." Lawrence stabbed another forkful. "And just for that, you are not invited to our wedding."

Corinna couldn't keep her laughter at bay. The brothers were impossible not to feel a kinship with even after such a short time. With these men, she felt like she could have a few more friends soon. *If Tanner doesn't haul me off to prison first.*

"Do you have any family who would object to our union, Miss Corinna?" Jackson finished off his steak and patted his belly.

"No, but I'm afraid I might be a little too old for you, Jackson," she teased, desperately hoping to squelch that twinge that came from admitting there was no one but her now.

"If she is this amazing with cooking a T-bone, just imagine what a filet mignon will taste like," Gray shook his head over his mouthful of steak. "Have you ever cooked with deer before, Miss Corinna?"

"I haven't yet, but I would love to try."

Gray lifted his forkful of potatoes in a salute. "I'll be on the lookout for one this week and see what you can do."

The meal was devoured nearly as soon as they sat down, and as she didn't want to be the only slow eater in the group and keep them all from their duties, she left her steak only half eaten and rose with the men.

"I'll help you clean up," Noah interjected and took her plate, but she spotted him swipe the remainder of the steak into a handkerchief and stuff it into his coat pocket. "But, remember, no more washing dishes until next Tuesday."

She grimaced over the thought of the dishes piling up, but she would not buck the system when she was trying to win them over. She wiped down the table and en-suring all food was gone, she stacked the dishes as neatly as she could in the sink. She dabbed at her forehead with the corner of her Harvey Girl apron and spotted the dust coating the hem. She needed to clean herself up, but where should she go? She doubted the cabin had running water.

She peeked into the den, but only found Wade, Clint, and Jackson. At the sound of wood being chopped, she withdrew to the kitchen and out the back door to find Tanner with his shirtless back to her. Her lips parted as he swung an axe into a block of wood that splintered on contact. He yanked the axe head out, his back muscles tightening with the effort before he turned to stack the wood into a pile, revealing a very perfect torso with several scars on his shoulders where it looked like he had taken a bullet and more. The scars spoke of the fearlessness of the man and his pursuit for justice. What would it be like to be protected by such a man? To be trusted by him? To have him as her defender?

"Did you have a question? Or did you come out for the view?" Tanner chuckled and gripping the throat of the axe, flung it into the stump he had been using to prop up the blocks of wood, and reached for a red flannel shirt draped on a nearby boulder.

She gasped and whirled around, her

cheeks flaming at being found out and for not realizing she had been staring, mesmerized. "S-sorry. I, um—could you help me haul the tub inside? I'd do it myself, but I don't think I could manage."

"You can turn around now," he called as he buttoned the top of his shirt. "A galvanized tub? I don't think we have one of those."

"How do you all—" She stopped herself and flushed, realizing what she almost asked.

"We bathe in the river over yonder." He pointed toward the woods behind the cabin. "It ain't very comfortable in the winter months, but it gets the job done.

"The river . . . the river that we drank out of earlier?" Her lips parted.

"Yes? Is that a problem?"

She covered her face and shuddered. "Where did you draw the water?"

He grinned, seeming to understand her aversion. "That river is fast moving. What you had was clean. But the river is a fair walk from the cabin."

Good.

"And I'd have to go with you and watch out for snakes, bears, and the like."

You what? She attempted to keep her panic in check and merely nodded as if it were the most natural thing in the world. Normally, she would go without, but between sleeping in the wagon and cooking over the hot stove, she knew she was not smelling her best. And her apron needed to be laundered, along with her uniform that she had worn for a few days now.

He narrowed his eyes. "You still want to bathe? It will be freezing, even for an unseasonably warm day like today."

"I will make do. If you give me just a moment, I'll collect my things." She hurried upstairs to the room Tanner had pointed out as hers and had the men deliver her things to. She flung open the lid, retrieved her bar of soap and soft towel with a clean dress and underthings, which she had folded inside the blue gown with the pretty sprigs of flowers embroidered all over. It was lovely but had a practical cut that would hold up well while she worked. She peered out the dusty window to her escort to the river below. *Hold your head up and don't act like you've never bathed in anywhere but a heated tub.* She trotted down the stairs, nodded to the men in the den, and headed out the back door again. "Ready."

He cradled a long rifle in his left arm. "Need help carrying anything?"

With a corset tucked away in my clean gown? Her cheeks heated. "Thank you, but I have it." It was kind of him to offer though and it gave her hope that maybe Tanner would forgive her.

"Suit yourself." He charged down a worn path and motioned for her to keep up. "I poked my head into the den and told the boys not to come down to the river. You'll be safe enough."

"Thank you," she managed to pant out. He was an impressively fast walker, which left no moments for her to attempt to fill with conversation, what with concentrating on not tripping over a rock and falling flat on her face.

Trees arched over the path, creating a canopy where the sun filtered through the leaves. She lifted her gaze to the beauty surrounding her, peace filling her as birds called to one another in the branches. At a high-pitch *chuck-chuck* coming from her right, she spied a darling little chipmunk clawing its way up the bark of a blue spruce. She had seen only a few during her position at the Montezuma Resort and hadn't seen a single chipmunk in town. She waved at the little creature and hurried after Tanner.

He paused along the bank, and she nearly rammed into his back. He looked down at her, his brow lifting like she was an annoying puppy that he had somehow taken charge of when he didn't even want one in the first place. She withdrew a pace, mumbling an apology and glanced at the riverbank where the waters moved at a steady pace, save for a little bend in the river that created a pool and was protected by four large rocks.

"This is a calm part of the river. It's deep enough to bathe, but not swift enough to carry you out. Again, no one will disturb you here, so don't worry." Tanner pointed to a boulder up the path. "And I will be sitting up there with my back to you."

"Y-you're staying?" She gasped. "You cannot think I will bathe while you are there, barely a stone's throw away!"

"I can throw a lot farther than that rock." He crossed his arms. "Look, if you want to bathe, this is your only option. And even if I could leave you, I really shouldn't. All sorts of animals come here to catch fish and drink their fill. I need to watch the area from this way. I will trust that you watch the other way, which I *promise* I will not guard. However, if you scream, I'll come, so if the freezing temperature of the water surprises you, swallow it if you don't want nobody to come a runnin' to rescue you."

Corinna swallowed her protest and nodded, watching as he climbed the massive gray boulder and faced away. She kept her eye on him for a few more moments and stepped behind a large brush and reached for her top button, stripping down to her chemise and corset. She removed her corset but decided to leave on her underthings. She considered leaving on her stockings too, but she didn't wish to ruin them on the jagged rocks. After she washed and changed into fresh clothing, she could hang up her wet underclothes to dry.

She grabbed her discarded gown, glanced over her shoulder once more, and seeing him still sitting and facing the direction he promised, she darted out from the brush and edged onto the pebbles of the shallows, fresh water stinging her toes and making her gasp from the cold. She forced herself to her calves and then her drawers. Shivering, she draped her dress in the water watching as the water soaked the edges of the gown and it gradually sank.

Who knows when I'll be able to wash again if there is a cold snap. She plunged to her waist sucking in a breath. The icy waters brought new life to her weary spirit and made her want to squeal, but remembering Tanner's warning, she suffocated her cries by submerging herself, scrubbing her fingers as quickly as possible through her long locks before reaching for her shampoo on the bank. A wind swept through the trees that had her diving back into the water to shield her soaked torso. She washed and rinsed her hair and grabbed her bar of soap, rubbing it over her skin until suds formed. She rinsed and grabbed her gown that had floated to the shore, scrubbing it with soap and rinsing it too.

"Almost done?" He shouted.

She started and crossed her arms over her soaked chemise and glanced over her shoulder. He was still facing away.

"A few more minutes!" She dove under the water once more, relishing the ripple of water through her locks, and scrambled out of the river, tossing her wet dress on the brush. The wind kicked up again, making her teeth chatter and her nails turn blue as she dried. She dressed quickly and tucked her wet underthings in her wet gown to hang inside her room before the fire.

She ran her brush through her hair and fluffed and scrubbed the roots of her hair with her towel to encourage it to dry faster. She draped her towel over her shoulders and spread her hair atop it. Her cheeks burned at the thought of him seeing her in such a state of undress, but it couldn't be helped. "I'm ready, Tanner. You can turn around now."

He slowly turned, his gaze resting on her bare toes, and as he must have seen her blue skirt with its flounced hem, he lifted his eyes. His striking blue eyes rested on her damp locks that cascaded to her waist. He looked away, his jaw working. "Come on, then. It's about time to start preparing supper."

"I'm sorry for taking so long."

"Sure." He strode ahead, one hand wrapped about his long rifle, the other clenched into a fist.

Sure? What did that even mean? She hated this silence between them. He and Lorna had been the two people she had come to trust enough to show them her true self, not the tongue-tied Harvey Girl she had become.

He was going too fast, but her pride guarded her tongue, so she raced forward to catch up. Her foot jammed on a root and her other caught in her skirts as she tumbled forward. She slammed into the ground, wincing at the rocks biting her hands. She swallowed back a whimper.

Tanner knelt beside her, his strong

hands grabbing her shoulders and helping her to sitting. He gently grasped her hands and turned them over, tracing her palm with his fingertips. "Ah, Corinna, you are bleeding again. Cut isn't too bad, though."

"I thought you waited until truth to judge someone, Tanner," she whispered, daring to voice the bitterness springing in her heart.

His gaze met hers under furrowed brows. She had never noticed how thick his lashes were. "I-I am sorry. It's hard not to think of you as the enemy."

"I know." She rolled her lips in as his fingers inspected the cut. "I had thought we were friends . . . that's why I trusted you about the bracelet."

"I did too." He reached into his back pocket, withdrawing a scarlet bandana. He narrowed his eyes on her wrist. He tugged up her right cuff and her left. He stiffened, eyes flashing up to hers. "You have scars on your wrists."

She tugged her hands back, pulling down the lace trimmed cuffs to hide what William had done to her. "Yes."

"They look like they were rope burns." He gritted his teeth and fairly growled, "Who did this to you?"

She shook her head, drew a piercing, bracing breath, and pushed away from him, rising to her feet. "Does it matter? You only wish to have me tied up and throw in prison anyway."

"I wish for justice." He rose with her, his fists curling. "And what happened to you matters to me."

She plucked a colorful leaf from an aspen and rolled the fiery leaf between her fingers. "William."

He flicked the brim of his hat up, his gaze resting on her cuffs. "Why? I thought you said he treated you well . . ."

"Treated . . . before he discovered my lack of funds." She crushed the leaf and flung it aside, walking back toward the house.

"And so, he tortured you?" His voice rose as he closed the gap between them and walked alongside her.

"No. He didn't intend for me to get hurt."

"Don't defend him, Corinna."

"I'm not—if he were alive today, I'd, of course, press charges for how he treated me. But I really do believe that he didn't want to hurt me." *Not at least after he tied the ropes so tightly at first that they bled.* Remorse had flickered in William's eyes then, and he had loosened the bonds slightly, but he did not apologize. He was too far gone for that. "He had to find a way of keeping me from following him and creating a scene in the lobby, begging him to understand, so he tied me up and left me alone in the hotel room."

He scratched his brow, his voice low, "And you couldn't get free."

"Not until my wrists were bleeding from trying to work out the knots." She crossed her arms, tucking her hands where he couldn't look at them. "We best get back. Dinner will take some time to prepare. Care to lead the way, *warden?*"

TANNER FROWNED as he led the way up the path to the cabin, his gut burning that William Roberts had left her tied up in a hotel room alone. *If he wasn't dead already, I would hunt him down myself and see him rot in jail.*

Corinna's comment of *warden* stung. But Tanner *had* been treating her like the enemy, but he didn't know how else to guard his heart against the beautiful woman. Beautiful women were always trouble. It was what tempted Pa to fall into the arms of a mistress and destroy their family. Only by the Lord's redeeming grace, Tanner, Lawrence, Gray, and Noah had a deep kinship with their Franklin half-brothers Alexander Wade, Jackson, and Clint.

But because of Pa's adultery, Tanner's mother died of a broken heart. And then Pa took that other woman, Bertha Franklin, to their flat, who Pa never even bothered to marry. They lived in sin and didn't even care to hide it from their neighbors, which saw all their friends falling away. No one wanted to associate with them, lest they be tainted by the friendship. The brothers bonded in their loneliness despite their initial distrust of the others. Three years later, Pa died from the influenza, quickly followed by Bertha, who had stayed by his side through the illness. The brothers were left friendless, broken, and alone.

Tanner glanced away from the trail and focused on the trees, breathing deep. Whenever those memories arose, it was best to put them back in the box before he sank into a mood for days. There was only so much darkness one person could handle, or it could consume a body. And he was letting that darkness taint his judgement. He had watched Corinna over many a Harvey House meal—he only saw kindness and a willingness to work. *And those scars.* He couldn't dismiss them. If she did kill her husband, it might have been in self-defense. *And if she didn't, you've been treating her like a parasite for sins that another committed.*

"Oh!" Corinna cried out and shoved him into the bushes.

"What in blue blazes!" Tanner rolled to his back, already spying what he had nearly stepped on and what was now focused on Corinna and curling up for a strike. He drew his gun as the rattler lunged for her, fangs wide.

"Tanner!" She screamed as the blast erupted at her feet and she sank to the ground in a faint.

He charged for Corinna and snatched her away from nearly grazing a stone in her fall. "Corinna?" He ran his palm down her cheek and gave it a gentle pat. "Corinna?"

She moaned and clutched his shirt front.

He gripped her to him, the scent of her soap reminding him of that day at the booth . . . before he knew that she was on a wanted poster. "Corinna? Wake up!" He gave her a little shake. "Corinna?"

She didn't stir.

His blood pounding in his ears, he swept her into his arms and raced down the path where his brothers charged to meet him, each carrying weapons.

"What happened?" Wade demanded, eyes already searching the forest over Tanner's shoulder.

"Rattler. She pushed me out of the way and nearly took a bite herself."

"Brave girl." Jackson muttered.

"Foolish, given you could've shot it," Wade added. "But brave."

"He would have gotten me. I wasn't looking where I was going." He looked down at her pale cheeks. She was going to take a bite for him—even after all he had done in treating her like a criminal, threatening to tie her up like she was a danger to him. The memory of the red scars around her wrists nearly choked him with grief. She must have been so frightened. She had been alone. And when she finally met the one man she thought would help her, he judged her—as if he had a right. *Lord, forgive me.*

"What's wrong with her?" Noah frowned.

"She fainted from fright. I tried waking her, but—"

She stirred in his arms, moaning as she gripped his shirt even harder.

"You are safe, Corinna," he whispered, but as she did not release her hold on his shirt, he gave her a little jiggle in his arms. "Wake up, little lady."

She moaned again.

"What should we do? We don't got any smelling salts." Noah asked.

"Dunk her in the river?" Jackson suggested. "That always does the trick when I'm too sleepy to start chores."

"Couldn't hurt," Noah nodded. "River is a good bet. Let's get her back down the path, and you can show me the snake remains on the way. Rattlers make some fine boots—unless you shot him to bits."

"D-don't you dare throw me in the r-river," Corinna muttered, pushing against Tanner's chest. "Tanner? Tanner, did the snake bite you?" she whispered.

"I'm fine, thanks to you." Tanner set her on her feet but kept a grip on her arm. "You steady yet?"

She shoved her hair from her cheeks and nodded. "Sorry. I haven't fainted in years."

"Clint fainted once when face to face with a mountain lion," Gray reassured her, patting her on the shoulder.

"Tarnation, Gray! That was supposed to be our secret!" Clint lunged at Gray, who ducked the blow with a laugh.

Wade ignored him and grasped her elbow, gently taking her from Tanner. "Let's get you something to eat. Eating nearly always helps."

She looked over her shoulder at Tanner. "Are you coming?"

Lord, let me separate my fears. Let me see Corinna with eyes that are not tainted with the past. He offered her a smile. "I won't ever turn down food, especially when you are the cook."

As he hoped, her face transformed at his compliment. "I don't think any of you Sterling brothers ever turn down food."

"You have yet to taste Clint's meatloaf," Tanner chuckled. "Not even a starving bear would touch that."

Corinna giggled. "Well, if the level I am being measured against is Clint's meatloaf, I think anything I make will pass the Sterling brothers' taste test."

CHAPTER 14

$\mathcal{O}$ver the next two weeks, Corinna fell into a rhythm of cooking and cleaning the cabin. Thanksgiving had been a fun affair as she cooked up so much food that the seven brothers couldn't even eat it all. While Tanner had been gentle in his actions toward her, the ease between them had yet to return completely, but she supposed it would take time to build trust. His brothers, however, already seemed to trust her completely as they always asked her to marry them after every meal in their ridiculous way of saying thank you for the tasty fare. Tanner only smiled his thanks and set off to write more letters to his contacts.

He had been sending messages to town through a different brother each time. Yesterday, Tanner had a reply from a man in Chicago, a detective named Jude Thorpe, saying he knew of the case against Corinna and he too believe she was being set up, given he had been trying to arrest members of William's family for years. It was a relief to finally have a detective believe her who didn't demand Tanner bring her in to be thrown in prison before searching for truth. Maybe there was hope for reclaiming her old life after all.

Corinna reached into the wicker basket to lift out one of Tanner's freshly washed shirts to hang on the line. She held it out before her. He possessed the broadest shoulders she had ever seen on a man. His brothers were a close second in size. She ran her fingers over the red shirt, remembering the first time he had fished her out of that raging river. It would be difficult to leave the man and her friendships.

"Corinna, you think you can fetch the eggs today?" Noah called as the men trailed out the back door. "Don't think we can gather them today."

"Eggs?" She blinked. The boys had specifically kept her out of the henhouse, claiming the rooster was too wild.

"We've got to see to the horses in the far pasture. It will take all of us to wrangle them, and we won't have time," Jackson said, shoveling in his pork sausage and biscuit as they walked toward the barn.

She swallowed her chiding the men that the dishes need to stay in the house.

"Just make sure you watch out for the rooster. He's been mighty aggressive of late and nearly took out my eye," Noah warned, downing the dregs of his black coffee.

Gray rolled his eyes as he shrugged on a coat. "Don't let them scare you."

Corinna released a short laugh.

"You just have to be fast in getting those eggs because if you are too slow, like Noah, *then* they will attack," Gray finished.

"I see." Corinna forced a smile even as the thought of confronting the birds made her heart race. "I've seen you all do it often enough. I am sure I can manage."

Tanner exited the cabin last, a biscuit in hand. "Will you be okay to be left alone, Corinna?"

He's leaving me by myself? Progress indeed! "Quite. Go wrangle some horses, and don't worry about me." She smiled at him.

"Take care." He returned her smile. "Enjoy the quiet."

"I will!" She called after Tanner. He was certainly not at ease with her, but this little bit of trust in her filled her with more hope than even that telegram from Detective Thorpe had. Corinna watched them from the laundry line as the last rider disappeared behind the grove of aspens and into the pinyon pines beyond. She sighed and grabbed the wicker basket by the back door. She dragged her feet to the henhouse, eyeing the door to the wire coop. At the back of the coop, there stood the wood nesting boxes where the chickens could lay their eggs in comfort.

The clucking hens drew their sharp claws along the hardpacked earth, stabbing unsuspecting bugs with their beaks while another hen pecked at the smallest hen in the group, who sported a bald spot between her shoulder blades. The rooster flung himself between the hens and with a great flapping of wings and a show of his talons at the bully hen, the little hen tucked herself behind the rooster as the larger hen raced to the corner of the henhouse.

"So many talons," Corinna muttered, tugging at her cuffs to ensure the least amount of skin was exposed. She shifted from foot to foot, attempting to rally herself to push open the door. "Certainly, you can run into the unknown, but facing down a rooster in a henhouse terrifies you. Don't be silly. You can do this!" She charged inside, sending the birds to squawking and flapping their wings, creating such a wind storm the dust picked up and swirled into Corinna's nose. She held her breath and picked her way through the stinky coop around hens that came running up to her skirts, clucking and pecking at them. Her heart sped and she hurried past them to the nesting boxes.

She spied a lovely olive-green egg. With shaking fingers, she grasped the egg and gingerly placed it in her hay-lined basket and reached for the second egg. She wrinkled her nose at the brown clumps clinging to the egg that left little doubt what it was. She continued reaching into the nesting boxes until she glanced over her shoulder to find the rooster staring at her, feathers rising as he spread his wings in warning. She took a step away from the boxes and at the squawk underfoot, she shifted her weight to free the hen's leg.

"Sorry!"

The rooster gave a mighty flapping of his wings and screeched, lunging for her. She dropped the basket and covered her eyes with her upraised hands. His sharp talons snagged the black sleeves of gown. She shrieked as she flung her arms down in an attempt to free herself from the rooster as the henhouse erupted into chaos. She raced for the door, but the rooster was already coming at her, blocking her escape and nipping at her with his sharp beak. She ran from corner to corner of the coop, but the rooster was relentless and two of the largest hens joined the fray, flapping their wings and pecking at her.

She snatched up the fallen basket and leapt atop the wood roof of the nesting boxes, cringing at the squish beneath her fingers. "Back you odious bird! Why are you all attacking me? I know I took your eggs. Do you want them back?" She lifted an egg, intent on returning it to a nesting box, but it slipped from her finger and smashed on the earth.

The cacophony of cries of treason filled the air. There would be no escape for her until the Sterling brothers returned.

TANNER HAD LEFT the trail a little early to check on Corinna, but he couldn't find her anywhere in the house. He knocked on her bedroom door. "Miss Corinna? Corinna, are you in there?" He didn't want to bust inside, but she was nowhere to be found. "I'm coming inside." He turned the knob and stepped into the small room. She had moved the storage to behind two old blankets that she hung on a line, making the room smaller, but neater in appearance. The bed was made and her clothes were still hanging in the closet. Didn't look like anything was amiss. Beside the rocking chair in the corner by the lone window was a pile of his brothers' shirts. He lifted the one folded in the seat—his blue plaid shirt that he thought had been ruined and tossed in the rag bin. He turned it over to examine where the rip had been. It was completely mended, and if he didn't know where to look, he would have missed the small perfect stitches. Heiress or not, the lady was a hard worker.

If she wasn't in the house and her things were still here, could she have been hurt while try to lug fresh water from the path? He charged down the stairs and ran toward the path just beyond the clearing, but the chickens squawking and screaming halted him. He spun on his boot toward the coop. The door was closed, but the chickens were acting like a predator was inside with their flapping and hop-flying about. He trotted closer and stopped short, squinting at something curled atop the chicken's wooden nesting boxes.

Corinna was curled into a ball atop it. Her head was cradled in her arms as if trying to ward off an attack. "Corinna?"

She jerked up, her golden hair spilling to her waist and frizzy about her face that was smudged with dirt. "Tanner! Oh, thank the Lord. Are you armed?"

His hand immediately grasped the handle of his Colt as he scanned the packed earth of the coop and the nearest trees for danger, though he didn't know why on earth she would choose such an exposed position. No snakes could be seen. "Is someone out there?"

"No," she muttered and narrowed her gaze at the rooster. "But someone in here is going to make a mighty fine fried chicken dinner tonight."

Tanner blinked. "What?"

"Please help me out of here. I can't get down. Why else would I choose to fall asleep atop a filthy chicken coop?"

"I hadn't figured that one out yet myself." He holstered his gun.

"I wouldn't put that away so fast." She pointed to the rooster. "He is far too aggressive."

"I don't think shooting him is the answer." Tanner chuckled.

"It is if you want to be able to come in the coop any time soon. They've staged an uprising." She bit her lip. "Can you come get me without violence?"

"I've captured far more dangerous criminals without bloodshed. I think I can handle Mortimer the rooster."

"Well, I dare say that Mortimer has a bounty of his own out for me."

He laughed and pushed open the door. The chickens barely acknowledged him. But the moment she reached out for him, and he scooped her in his arms, the hens and rooster swarmed them, pecking and squawking, and tearing at his pants and boots with their talons and reaching for Corinna. He charged out as Corinna squealed into his chest.

He slammed the door on the rooster's beak and set her down. She lifted the basket in her hands and gave a victorious shout at the birds.

He scratched his head. "I've never seen them act so aggressive in all my days."

"Well, they put on a good act." She set down the basket and counted the eggs. Four out of ten were all that remained intact. She sighed.

"Did you feed them any differently? You did spread it in a circle, right? If you give it to them scattered, or in a straight line, the weakest hen tends to suffer."

"Well, that explains a few things." She groaned and reached into her apron pocket, seed spilling from her fingers. "I forgot to give them the feed while I collected the eggs." She reached to run her fingers through her hair and stopped at the sight of the brown staining her hands. She wrinkled her nose. "I was only so afraid after what the boys said that feeding them flew right from my head."

"Did they feed you another whopping tale while I was inside? You do know that my brothers have been teasing you about the chickens, right?"

"How? They've been telling me that the flock was possessed for days." She stared up at him.

"And you believed them?" A half smile escaped at the normally so put together lady, who now sported hay in her hair. He slowly plucked a piece of hay from her golden hair and another. "That's because they knew you were already wary of them, and they were planning on teasing you. I don't think they thought you were in any real danger."

"They got me good." She dropped her head, shaking it and laughing. "Well, I suppose I'll just have to get even with them. Do you have any suggestions?"

He grinned. "I can think of a few."

"Howdy, Corinna!" Wade called from the back of his horse as the brothers guided the herd into the corral. "Come and see."

She smiled up at Tanner. "Thank you for saving me. And I want to hear your ideas for revenge soon."

CHAPTER 15

The next morning and afternoon, Corinna scrubbed the floors, still mulling over the options for a return jest. Tanner had a surprising number of ideas—as if he had been thinking on them for years.

"Corinna! Time for a break. You need to learn how to ride before your hands blister from all that unnecessary scrubbing with boiling water." Wade motioned her to follow outside.

She wiped her hands on her sturdy Harvey Girl apron and, grabbing a carrot from the bin in the kitchen, followed him under the canopy of trees where a few birds chirped and called to one another and toward the corral. It was so peaceful here, unlike any place she had ever lived. In Chicago, there was always someone shouting on the streets and at the Harvey Houses, there were always far too many girls about to have any real quiet moments. "Are you certain we should be doing this? I have so many chores left to do before dinner."

"They kept before you arrived at the ranch. And this is important. I can't believe that you never learned to ride! How else do you get around?"

She shrugged and leaned against the fence as he slipped under the rails. "It's never been a need before, given we always had a carriage and driver."

"And you never rode for fun? We grew up in Chicago too, and I saw fine ladies ride side saddle in the parks." He held his hand out for her.

"You did?" She grasped his hand and bent to scoot under the fence rail. "What neighborhood did you live in?"

"One you, no doubt, never heard of." He

gave her a soft smile and whistled for a nearby black beauty and gathered a bridle from the fence rail.

"You might be surprised. While my father had a fortune, we were parvenus. We didn't always live on East Erie Street."

Wade released a low whistle. "You have a home there?"

She nodded. "Yes, but our money is considered new. I wasn't raised as a fine lady, but as a woman poised to take over her father's empire. I was either always studying the ledgers, ordering food for the restaurant, or cooking to have any time for leisure." She lifted her hand to rub the mare's nose. "She's beautiful."

"That she is. She was the last foal of my prized Friesian stallion, Falcon. Her mother is young, though, and should be having a foal in the spring. But, as this mare is too spirited for a beginner, you will be riding Lone Star, the one that started it all. He is nearing seventeen and is very gentle." He whistled again and lifted a hand toward a massive red roan with a white star on its head.

"Have you always had an interest in breeding?" She pulled the carrot from her apron pocket and held the offering out to the animal.

Wade drew in a sharp breath from clenched teeth, and taking her hand in his, flattened her fingers, resting the carrot in the center of her palm. "You want to keep your fingers, yes?"

"Oh, thank you." Heat crept up her cheeks. "So, as you can tell, I know little to nothing about horses."

"I didn't always either. But I spend more time with them than I do with humans."

"You've never ridden into town since I've been here. And I've never seen you in town before either." She lifted the carrot toward Lone Star, hoping to coax him over.

"Would you have remembered me?" His brows lifted as he guided her hand to Lone Star's mouth.

She giggled as the horse's lips grasped for the food from her palm.

"Of course. There aren't men as tall the Sterlings that come the Harvey House. I would remember you." But, realizing how it might sound, she wiped her hand on her apron and added, "We have our regulars, so a new face would be remembered."

Wade frowned and reached for the bridle, guiding the bit into Lone Star's mouth. "I don't go into town."

"What? Ever?"

He shook his head, fastening the buckles and drawing the bridle over the horse's head. "I haven't since the day I arrived."

He didn't seem excessively shy. He was a little quiet and that was probably because the brothers were always shouting, but he always had a kind word for her and conversed easily. "May I ask why?"

He slowly nodded. "It's a secret. Tanner would be upset if he knew I told you, but," he smiled down at her with a sadness in his eyes, "the reason I can't leave the ranch is because there is a warrant out for my arrest. The punishment for what I've done is hanging."

She gasped. "You didn't kill someone, did you?"

He gave a mirthless laugh as he slung the saddle blanket into place and ran his hands over it to smooth it down and reached for the saddle. "We'd make quite the pair in that case."

"We would . . . but I didn't actually murder anyone."

"I didn't either, but a judge won't likely grant me mercy." He glanced up from tightening the girth. "I'm not sure what Tanner has told you of our past?"

She snorted. "Pretty much nothing."

"That's what I thought. Well, to start, we have different mothers."

"But," she frowned. "Your ages are intermingled?"

He nodded. "My mother, Bertha Franklin, was our pa's mistress. We didn't merge families until after Mrs. Sterling died a year after birthing Noah. Tanner was ten, and I was eight at the time. When we were orphaned three years later, the seven of us were put on an orphan train, despite Tanner's best efforts to keep us together. It was heart wrenching as we were spread across the West—some to kind families. Tanner was not claimed."

"No one wanted him?" Her heart

clenched. *So much pain for a boy of thirteen and then, to face such rejection.*

He shrugged. "Too old. I was the last to go myself. When I was adopted on the orphan train, it was by a cruel rancher. He bred horses, and my job was to muck stalls, care for the herd, and he even let me watch him train the horses, and eventually, join him in the training." Wade rubbed his jaw. "I didn't think I'd ever see my family again until Tanner found me a year later. The rancher refused to give me up. Said I was a natural with the horses, and it would cost him a fortune to find a trainer with my raw talent."

"How awful. But how old were you?"

"About twelve, so I didn't have much of a choice legally. I really was gifted with horses, even though I hadn't been around them long. I could stand on their backs while they trotted about the arena and was real good at trick riding. The horses loved me—trusted me. And I loved and trusted them, which was something I had never been able to give before. They didn't want anything from me but love and respect, and they gave the same." He rubbed Lone Star's nose, resting his forehead against his horse.

"But, when Tanner arrived, surely your brother wouldn't have given up on you simply because the rancher didn't wish to release you?" Corinna knew Tanner to be relentless, passionate, and a man bound by honor. While she ached in hearing the tale, she needed to know what had happened to Tanner that made him the man he was today.

"No. Mr. Joe fought Tanner and about near killed him. I couldn't stand to let Mr. Joe beat Tanner to death, so I grabbed Mr. Joe's prized stallion, this roan, to distract him enough for Tanner to escape. Mr. Joe chased after me with a long rifle, but Lone Star was too fast. He ran like the devil himself was on our heels. Tanner followed by a different route but kept us in sight."

"Did you try to return the horse after you escaped?"

Wade pressed his lips into a thin line and shook his head. "Not at first. The man had worked me harder than I ever had worked in my life and didn't pay me a penny. Didn't even give me new clothes and hardly any food. I was skin and bones when Tanner found me. No. I took that horse because there was no way I was ever getting back on a train and around adults that would force me to do what they thought was best." He cleared his throat. "I rode him all the way to New Mexico."

She rested her hand on his arm, lending him her comfort.

"Once we were all together at last, reality set in and I knew that if I didn't fix things, I'd be hung if caught. But there was no way of giving back the stallion without facing Mr. Joe again and possibly being taken again. He legally *adopted* me . . . said I was his, but there was no kindness in that man's heart—only greed." He shook his head. "I saw what he did to break horses' spirits and knew he'd do much worse by me. So, with Tanner's next bounty, he bought me a mare for next to nothing, since no one could train her, and after a long time of gentling her, I bred her with Lone Star and had eight foals by the pair. I trained and sold my herd through my brothers. I made more than enough to pay for the stallion I stole, and I wrote a proposal to Mr. Joe to drop the charges and I'd pay him double what the horse was worth."

She gasped. "That must have been a massive sum."

He nodded. "It took me years to save it."

"And I'm guessing Mr. Joe didn't drop the charges?"

Wade shook his head. "His son wrote back and said I hadn't accounted for all the stud fees and prized foals that would have come from his line that *I* possessed. He was out for my blood. He refused the sum. I offered him triple the worth of the stallion and he refused it again." Wade cleared his throat. "My juvenile face is on a horse thieving poster across America. That's why I had to change my name from Alexander Wade Franklin to Wade Sterling when I was twelve, and I can never leave Sanctuary Ranch."

A wanted criminal by twelve? "That is horrible, Wade." She rested her hand on his. "If I am ever cleared from my false charges, I will hire the best lawyer in all of Chicago to attempt to clear your name. No judge would convict you of a crime from so long ago when you were but a boy—an abused one at that. Especially with the offer of triple in payment, no judge would sentence you."

"One could hope, but I don't want to test that hope." Wade dipped his head and motioned for Corinna to join him on the left side of the horse. "I made my choice, and I'm at peace with living my days up on this mountain away from the people who would wish me dead."

"Not everyone is like that rancher. There are those who would show you compassion."

"Like they did for you?" He rested his hand on the saddle horn, his piercing gaze meeting hers.

Fair point. "Well, I married into a crime family. But, if you take that away, Dolly Matthews treated me kindly and would have let me stay on at the Harvey House if it hadn't been for Pernilla."

"Quite the burden for a name." Wade led the horse out of the corral.

She laughed, following with her hand on

the horse's mane. "I think it's rather pretty, but the way Pernilla conducts herself is another matter entirely."

"You ready for your first lesson?" Wade wove his fingers together. "Let's get you up in the saddle. Step in my hand, Miss Corinna."

She put her little boot in his large hands, and he lifted her easily.

"He's sixteen and a half hands tall, but kind. He will sense you are a novice and be gentle." He swung himself up into the saddle behind her and tugged the horse's reins, setting them to walking down the trail to the river, the horse's hoofbeats muted on the worn path.

Corinna wrapped her hands around the saddle horn. "When is the actual lesson going to start? I thought I'd be riding a saddle over a barrel for at least a day before I started to ride. Don't I need some instruction on the proper form?"

He laughed. "Use your legs and don't fall off."

The horse picked up his pace, sending Corinna to sliding from the saddle. Wade chuckled and grabbed her waist, steading her.

"Use your legs, Corinna!" Wade reached in front of her and took the reins. He pulled back on Lone Star. "Slow down, boy."

"What are you two doing?" Tanner glared at them from down the path with a bucket of fresh water in each hand.

Corinna nodded to the horse. "Wade was just teaching me how to shoot better, obviously."

"Please get down, Corinna." Tanner set the buckets at the side of the path, his face reddening.

Wade frowned. "She's not in any danger, Tanner."

She felt the laughter from moments before slip away. Judging from Tanner's scowl, he believed *she* was the danger to Wade. Tears pricked at her lashes. She thought they had gotten beyond this. She thought Tanner was beginning to trust her. She should have known better than to believe in a man again. Before the tears could spill over, Corinna patted Wade's hand. "Will you set me down please?"

Wade glared at Tanner and swung his leg over the saddle, his boots thumping on the dirt. He reached up for her. She rested her hands on Wade's shoulders and dismounted.

"Thank you, Wade. I'll see to my chores. It seems Tanner wishes to speak with you about all the ways I've disappointed him and how evil I am." She turned on her heel and raced back to the house. If Tanner wanted to believe her guilty, she might as well run now before Tanner threw her in jail.

CHAPTER 16

anner's gut twitched at the fury in Corinna's eyes as she stomped back toward the house, but what else was he to do when Wade seemed smitten with her? The man had hardly been around women and heaven forbid he fall for a woman who very well may be imprisoned in a matter of weeks. He hoisted up the full buckets and headed for the house.

Wade stormed after Tanner, leading Lone Star. "You were always stubborn, but I didn't think you were plain dumb, Tanner."

Tanner jerked his head up. He set down the buckets at the corral fence line and clenched his fists. "I'd think very carefully over what you call me, Wade. I'm not in a charitable mood, to say the least."

"Do you honestly think I'm in love with Corinna?" Wade crossed his arms, Lone Star tossing his head in seeming agreement. "Is that why you've been so quiet the past few days? Well, let me make one thing real clear —I'm *not.*"

"Why wouldn't you be? She is beautiful." Tanner narrowed his gaze at the man. Out of all the brothers, Wade was no doubt the loneliest.

"That isn't reason enough to fall in *love* with a woman. Looks don't equal love." Wade reached for the girth to unsaddle Lone Star.

"It was reason enough for our pa."

Wade's hand froze in unbridling the roan. "Well, I never claimed to be him, and he's not the one I looked up to." He slipped off the bridle and turned to Tanner. "You are."

Tanner hadn't expected that. His fingers uncurled. "Why?"

"When my ma brought us to live at your flat in Chicago, you were kind to me and mine. You called us brothers." Wade ran his fingers through Lone Star's mane and gave him an affectionate pat and sent him out to graze.

"It wasn't you and our brothers' faults that Pa did what he did," Tanner mumbled and picked up the buckets, crossing the yard toward the house.

"No, but I had always been looked down on wherever we lived—my mother being what she was." Wade's jaw worked. "You never treated me any different than Lawrence, Gray, and Noah. You even made sure we went to church because your ma would have wanted you to keep going. Do you really think I'd let myself fall in love with Corinna after all you did for us?"

"What's that got to do with Corinna?" Tanner climbed the back steps and set the buckets under the porch.

Wade slapped off Tanner's Stetson. "Blazes, Tanner! You are going to make me spell it out, aren't you? Do you think I would ever set my sights on a woman you were clearly in love with?"

"Me? In *love* with her?" Tanner snorted.

"She is wanted by the law, Wade. I'd be a fool to get tangled up with a woman with a past like that."

"It wouldn't be the first time you did something outside of the law." Wade leaned against the porch column, crossing his arms and reaching for the whittled toothpick in his pocket.

"Just because I didn't turn my own kid brother into the town sheriff does not mean I work outside the law. It means I am a human with compassion. You were a child and made a choice out of fear and a need for justice. You weren't a horse thief—you were an innocent boy who was in harm's way." Tanner sank onto the porch, his legs dangling over the edge.

Wade plucked a pocketknife out and reached for a stick, handing them to Tanner to whittle. "And doesn't that purity apply to Corinna? She chose to marry a man she believed was of good character. She was deceived. . . just like your ma. But Corinna lied out of fear because she had no hope of justice. Why can't you show Corinna grace, the way you showed us when your father's mistress arrived on your doorstep the minute after Mrs. Sterling was buried?"

"I can't—not when I have Pa's blood in me." Tanner drove the blade into the stick, scraping away the bark, wishing he could scrape away every bit of Pa left in him.

"What's that got to do with it? Blood ties don't make a man who he is—God makes the man and allows him to choose who he will become. Who will you be, Tanner? Will you be held back by fear of following our pa's footsteps, or will you accept that God has redeemed our past and given us a future as bright as the noon day sun?"

Tanner snatched off his hat and slapped it against his knee, angry that Wade saw through his annoyance with Corinna to the heart of the matter. "And you think that promised future holds Corinna for me?"

Wade sank down next to him and rested his hand on Tanner's shoulder. "I see you watching her with a smile on your lips as she interacts with our brothers. I see how she pays extra special attention to you. She cares for you, Tanner. She sees your honor, and it calls to her."

"Calls to her?" Tanner nearly nicked off his thumb at that turn of phrase. "Spoken like a man in love."

"Spoken like a man who is a prisoner on his own land that's not even his yet. Don't you think I want a wife and children? I may never be able to court a girl and marry, but *you* don't have to be alone. Why won't you let yourself be happy?"

Tanner sighed and handed over the knife and whittled wood to Wade. "Because the last time I was happy, it was torn away from me in an instant, and while I can face bullets and knives, that kind of pain scares me to my core. I don't ever want to feel that helpless again."

"You are far from helpless, Tanner Sterling. What's the fear keeping you back from pursuing her?"

Tanner picked at the flecks of bark on his hat, flicking them into the dirt at his boots. "My fear is that despite my gut telling me that Corinna is innocent and a sweet, caring woman, that I am blind to the truth —that she is a liar, and that beautiful lying women are always trouble. I would never feel anything for a woman like that except a need to run far away."

Wade nodded. "I have the same fear, but just because our pa did everything wrong doesn't mean we will too. There's a big difference between us and him."

Tanner glanced over to his brother.

"We fear the Lord and seek Him first because He is our rock. Pa's rock was a bottle and a woman that was not his own. When we offer our hand to a woman, it will be for her alone, because unlike Pa, we choose honor. Don't let your fear of being like him hold you back from a good woman like Corinna. And if you don't feel like you want to offer for her hand, remember that the Lord brought you into her life for a reason . . . even if it isn't for marrying— there is a reason."

The thought of Corinna leaving him forever did not sit well with Tanner, but he couldn't keep her here forever. "And you think that reason is?"

"To put on your gun belt again and be her angel of justice."

SHE'S A LIAR, and beautiful lying women are always trouble. I would never feel anything for a woman like that except a need to run far away. Corinna pressed her hand to her mouth as Tanner's words drifted through from the kitchen's open window. She raced upstairs and away from his wrath, but Tanner's words were tattooed on her heart. She hadn't meant to eavesdrop. She had taken a few moments to freshen up in her room before returning to the kitchen to finish her scrubbing when she heard him.

She dashed a fist under her eyes. She had foolishly allowed herself to be drawn to him —to seek his approval, to attempt to bring a smile to his lips. *Fool.* Corinna pressed the heel of her hand on her heart, kneading at the deep ache within. How could she have thought that Tanner was softening to her? He was never going to see her as anything but a criminal—even if she was acquitted, he'd think of her as a liar, and therefore, no better than his pa's mistress whose lies and lust had killed Mrs. Sterling. She swiped at the tears cascading down her cheeks and drew a bracing breath.

If Tanner won't help me, no one will. These brothers were devoted to one another, and if she didn't leave soon, she would likely be following Tanner back down the mountain in handcuffs. She glanced through her bedroom window out onto the forest with its secrets hidden in the shadows. *I am as good as dead anyway, might as well try to run despite the dangers.* She grabbed her brown cloak. She didn't dare pack a bag. If anyone saw her, they would think she was merely cold. She grabbed the henhouse basket as a decoy and strode through the barn and snatched Tanner's leather canteen from the wall. It was filled. *Trust Tanner to always be prepared.*

She strapped it on under her cloak. Keeping the basket in hand, she moved to the chicken coop at the edge of the clearing. She cast a glance up and down the path and toward the house. They must be busy with their tasks.

"Corinna!"

She clutched her cloak closed to keep Tanner from seeing the canteen strap. She tried to force a smile as he jogged up to her, but at the concern on his expression, it faltered, especially at the sight of the brothers racing to the paddock. "Tanner? What's wrong?"

"Noah just got back from the far pasture. Said the horses got loose. We all need to track them down before that rogue herd tries to claim them and—"

"And you need my help?"

"No. Frankly, you would slow me down significantly," he grinned as if to soften his words.

The same pang stabbed her heart. *Of course, he only sees me as a nuisance.* "Ah, then it is the other thing. You don't want me to run off," she shrugged. "How far could I get on foot?"

"If a wild animal comes onto the property, there's a gun above the kitchen door that's loaded." He paused, lifting a hand. "On second thought, if you don't know enough about a gun, it's more dangerous than good. Just bar the door and I'm sure you'll be fine but hold the gun just in case. Can you reach it?"

"That's what chairs are for!" She shooed him with her hands. "Stop worrying and go. I'll be fine."

He ran his hand over the back of his neck, seeming like he wanted to add something.

Maybe an apology? That you didn't mean what you said? That you do believe me?

"Corinna, I think we need to talk—"

"Hurry, Tanner! I'll lose the whole herd if that wild mustang gets hold of them," Wade shouted from the back of Lone Star.

"Maybe later?"

She couldn't lie—not when that's what he really thought of her. "Good luck."

Tanner gave her an apologetic smile, turned and ran to the paddock, whistling to Silver as Wade raced off with Noah in the lead and the dog following. Tanner bridled Silver, and gathering a handful Silver's blond mane, swung himself up behind the horse to ride away bareback.

It's now or never. She stowed the empty basket on the porch and hurried into the kitchen to grab any food about to fill her apron pockets. She eyed the gun. She knew the basics thanks to the men's dishes competition every week. She scooted a stool under the kitchen door so she could catch the end of the shotgun. She grasped it and lifted it from the rack. It was far heavier than she had thought, but she would be safer with it—at least she would feel safer.

Clutching it in her hands and keeping the barrel pointed heavenward, she raced into the woods, not minding the burning in her lungs. Carrying the shotgun was awkward, but determination nipped at her heels. Soon, the river's babbling called to her. She crested the hill and spied the river. She released a sigh. It was low enough to wade across. If she had oriented herself correctly and crossed the river and continued West into the heart of the mountain range, she could get to the other side to Santa Fe. There, she could board a train with her rail pass and disappear. She would change her name, dye her hair, and live a life without friends and companionship if she had to. She wanted to live. She needed to be free.

She didn't pause to take off her shoes. She lifted her skirts in one hand and waded across, panting at the cold, a whimper escaping. She eyed the bank. She couldn't simply cross here. Tanner would spy her footprints like a flag from a fort. She waded down the river and around the bend until she reached a place where a moss covered log draped from one side of the river to the other, blocking her path, but as luck would have it, she spied a series of rocks that would prove excellent stairs.

She disappeared into the woods beyond, praying she was angling herself in the correct direction. She peered at the position of the sun. *No help whatsoever. For all my reading of bounty hunter stories, I should have remembered how to figure out true North.* But, as she was *in* the mountains, she couldn't rightly use them as a guide. She had to keep going.

After a few moments, she slowed her pace from a run to a determined stride. If she went too fast too soon, she might as well collapse under a tree now. No, slow and steady was the best bet.

Sweat trickled down her spine and at the snap of a branch behind her, she drew up short, pointing the shotgun in the direction of the sound. The Sterling Brothers never mentioned neighbors. She spun, desperate for a place to hide. *Where's a cave when you need one?* She darted behind a tree and sank to its base.

She shivered as she clutched the gun, praying for deliverance as the crunch of boots sounded nearer and nearer. They stopped, and then, with a crunch of leaves, disappeared again. She released her breath in a *whoosh*. After what seemed like an hour, but it could have only been a quarter of an hour since she heard the footfalls, she dared to rise. Corinna looked up and down the path, and seeing no one, stepped out. A form dropped from the branches of the fir overhead.

She screamed as boots hit the earth.

CHAPTER 17

"Now, Miss Corinna, is that any way to greet me?" Buck Bridger grinned at her. "Aren't you a sight for sore eyes?"

"B-Buck?" She slowly lowered the shotgun, uncertain of his intent. He had watched her often at the Harvey House, but time had proven him to be harmless enough. And from all their conversations, she knew he often went hunting in the mountains. *But he doesn't have a long rifle in hand.* "W-what are you doing—"

Buck lifted his hands palms out to her. "Looking for you. You left town without a word and no one would tell me a thing. Miss Pernilla finally said that you were fired. I checked with the station master, and he said that you never boarded the train as far as he knew. I figured you needed my help."

"I thank you, but I am well." She doubted her words rang true with a shotgun in her hands. She shifted the double barrel to rest against her shoulder. She couldn't afford to set it down—not isolated as she was, but neither did she want to accidentally harm a man.

He nodded to her canteen and shotgun. "Looks like you are going somewhere. Maybe escaping from someone? I think you need a friend."

Panic seized her. She couldn't go with him, even if he didn't mean her harm. Her plan left no room for another to know anything about her escape. "I-I'm fine."

"Doesn't look like you are fine, Miss Corinna." His brows furrowed. "Why don't you let me help you? Hiking into the Gallinas Mountains is no Harvey House picnic. You could get hurt, or worse."

She couldn't win in a fight against this mountain of a man, but perhaps she could outwit him. He had never been improper—only too obsessed with her. "Very well. Will you help me get to Santa Fe?"

His brows rose. "There is a trail south of here that will bring us round nearer to the base of the range to Glorieta. It will take us an hour to get there atop my mount and another three after that." He hitched his thumb toward the woods. "I left him tied up a few yards back. I wasn't certain I was on the right trail and wanted to make sure you weren't some ornery trapper."

She blinked. Did she dare trust this man? "You would do that for me?"

Buck smiled down at her. "Well, I would have done it for you only weeks ago, but now that I know how much you are worth, bringing you into Santa Fe will be a pleasure."

She paled. He knew about the reward? "W-what do you mean?"

He pulled a folded piece of thick paper from his pocket and handed it to her. "I didn't believe it at first, but why else would you be so against my advances? You must have been trying to protect me from your past that is clearly catching up with you."

Is he delusional? But in every novel she had read with an obsessed stalker, the heroine played to his self-esteem, maybe she could do the same? "You must understand, I couldn't allow any man to court me while this false claim was unresolved." She bowed her head. "As much as I may have wanted to be courted by—" *By Tanner.* The thought made her stomach clench. She hadn't wished for any man to love her before or after William.

His eyes brightened. "You mean, the warrant is a mistake? And that's why you didn't go out with me?"

"I am no murderess and am being framed by evil people. I've never so much as hurt a mouse."

"Then, you love me?" He reached out for her hands.

Lie! Lie! She tried to push out the words to finish her flirtation, but the lies of her past that had gotten between her and Tanner stayed her lips. She never wanted to lie again—even if it meant putting herself into jeopardy . . . as foolish as it seemed, she wanted Tanner to know she had changed. He had accused her of being a woman who used her looks to get her way. She wouldn't do that now. She swallowed back the lie that could save her. "Buck, I am honored that you would seek to win my hand, but I don't love you."

"Because you are in love with that Tanner Sterling, aren't you?" His demeanor darkened as he dropped his hands.

Despite Tanner's words to Wade, she had let herself lean on the man. She had come to know his character and longed for his affection and a place to belong. She could hardly admit it to herself, but her answer overflowed from her heart. "Yes."

"I see. I suppose you are only good for the bounty then." He lunged for her.

"No!" Corinna screamed as Buck grasped her wrist. She swung the barrel of the gun toward his head, intent on startling him. He dodged and loosened his hold enough for her to turn the shotgun on him.

He bent in a crouch, readying to leap at

her again. "You going to shoot me, Corinna? Seems that poster was more truthful than you let on . . ." Buck chuckled as if he didn't fear the bite of a bullet. "If you pull the trigger that is."

"I am *not* a killer!" She yelled and lifted the barrel to the sky and pulled the trigger, praying Tanner would hear the blast echoing off the mountains. Birds sprang from the treetops, cawing in fear. She dropped the gun, forgetting the second shell as the gun released the bullet with a crack, sending Buck diving to the right. She grabbed up an armful of her skirts and ran toward the direction of the river. "Tanner!" She screamed, begging God for a miracle— to save her.

Buck's boots pounded the earth be-hind her.

"Tanner!" She screamed again, despera-tion tinting her voice as Buck's hands en-closed about her skirts, and he yanked her against him. "Tanner!"

"I can see why he didn't turn you in right away. I'm tempted to keep you for myself, but seeing as I owe a gambling debt to one of the most dangerous men in New Mexico, I need the funds sooner rather than later." He pulled a length of rope from his back pocket and wound it about her wrists. "Your Angel of Justice and I have been hunting bounties for so long and gettin' the other's prize that I'd say he owes me one."

"Tanner!" She screamed again as he tightened the rope, dragging her memories to the surface of William and his tying her up after their wedding as he ransacked her belongings. When she had screamed then, he had not taken pity. She didn't think Buck would strike her, but what was a blow now if she were to hang? She screamed with all her might. "Help me, Tanner!"

"Come now, I won't hurt you." Buck Bridger scolded as he clamped a massive hand over her mouth, but not roughly. "We all got jobs to do, and I'd be a fool to let a pretty face stop me from a bounty of two thousand dollars." He drew a bandana from his back pocket and wrapped it about her mouth, gagging her tight. "I don't like treating a woman like this, but you give me no choice with all your caterwauling. While I may be willing to risk the Angel of Justice's ire, I don't want to risk *his* bullets raining down on me. The man never misses." He tugged on her bound hands. "Now, let's get down the mountain before Tanner figures out them horses were let out."

WADE AND NOAH were down in the valley, trying to encircle the herd. Tanner held Silver's position, wondering what Corinna was doing. He had left her alone. He would have never done that with any other criminal, but Corinna was innocent—of that he was certain.

Wade's words had seeped into his heart and in his gut and he felt an urgent need to speak with Corinna and apologize and confess his feelings to her. While he tried to keep his distance from her, it had been impossible on the ranch and at every mealtime. His heart was no longer his and it frightened him. *Lord, what if she can't forgive me for doubting her and for the harsh words I spoke? What if she doesn't return my affection?* Even admitting such a fear in prayer, his gut twisted, and he feared he already loved her too fiercely to ever feel right again if she left him.

Tanner gritted his teeth, recalling his reaction to the warrant and guilt pricked his insides. *After how I treated her, I doubt she would hold any sort of affection for me. God forgive me in my judgement of her. You are the only judge.* A gunshot sounded. His heart seized. "Corinna!"

He looked to his brothers, but they were in the valley and likely hadn't heard it over the din of chasing horses. He wheeled Silver around and raced toward the shot. It wasn't in the direction of the cabin but on this side of the river. No one should be on their land, and there was no reason for Corinna to be firing a gun so far away from the cabin, which meant it had to be another bounty hunter. "Lord! Help her!"

A second shot sounded and the faint

sound of Corinna screaming his name had him kicking Silver into a dead run, ducking low under the branches and gripping with his knees as Silver leapt over fallen logs. She screamed again, nearer this time, desperation making her voice crack. He seized his long rifle, vision blurring in anger at whoever was hurting her—calling himself all kinds of a fool for leaving a helpless woman alone in the mountains where any animal, two, or four-legged, could harm her.

Tanner burst through the grove of aspens to see Buck Bridger with his arm around Corinna's waist, pinning her back against him. She fought against Buck, and when her strike to Buck's nose made him loosen his grip for a moment, she darted away, only to have her tugged back by a length of rope. His blood boiled, knowing how William had tied her up and seeing the panic in her eyes now, he knew she was back in that dark place.

"Buck!" Tanner roared. "She is *my* bounty. Release her at once and I'll let you walk away with your dignity."

"What you talkin' about? She was wandering around of her own free will *with* a gun, Sterling. You cannot keep the little angel as a pet!" He stroked his well-trimmed beard and studied her. "That might fall under aiding and abetting the law. Maybe I should arrest you as well."

"I was keeping her until I received word, that I am expecting any day, in regard to her absolute innocence." Tanner kept the rifle ready, even as Silver pranced under foot, clearly reading his anger at Corinna being held against her will. "I'd appreciate if you would release my bounty in the meantime."

"Your bounty?" Buck hooted. "Nah, I think you left her unguarded, and unbound, and armed in the woods."

In the woods with a gun? He glanced at Corinna who was still struggling against the ropes. Was she running from them?

Buck snorted, reading his confusion. "Looks like she got away from you after all."

"I don't care why she was in the woods. These are my woods." He aimed the rifle. "You know my reputation. Let the lady go."

"No." Buck jerked Corinna in front of him like a coward. "I'm doing nothing wrong in taking this murderess into the sheriff's office."

"She is not a murderess."

"Then she will go free, but I'll get my bounty." Buck grinned.

"And how long do you think she will last there?" Tanner retorted.

"I've arrested women before! Don't be fooled by her looks, Sterling." He tugged the rope, bringing her to her knees.

"Watch it, man!" Tanner shouted, pulling back the hammer of his rifle.

"I was taken in by her looks, but that was before the poster, and it all made sense when I saw it. She's guilty as sin."

"You've only arrested women who were clearly breaking the law. Corinna has *yet* to be proven guilty. It's all circumstantial evidence that I believe was completely fabricated so the guilty party could go free. Now release her, or I won't hesitate to shoot you where you stand." Tanner aimed and fired a warning, sending the dirt by Buck's feet spraying.

Corinna used her captor's momentary distraction to knee Buck.

He groaned and fell to his knees, dropping the rope.

Corinna bolted for Tanner.

Tanner gripped Silver hard with his thighs, leaned, and seized her forearm and swung her up behind him. He threaded his right arm through her tied arms and kicked Silver into a full gallop as she clung to his shoulder. He prayed she wasn't hurt further and that she could manage to keep her seat.

Tanner wove through the woods as Buck's shouts filled the air. Tanner headed for the secret cave that he and his brothers used as a secondary storehouse. They would be well hidden there until his brothers returned to the cabin and could help fend off Buck and any help he might have hidden in the woods. While Buck might try to rile Tanner for entertainment, the man was a dead shot and never left without a fight.

Confident that he had lost Buck for now, Tanner bent under the branches, tugging Corinna down with him to avoid the low limbs. With her pressed against his back, she felt small and helpless. In that moment, he knew he would do whatever it took to keep her safe—no matter what the law dictated.

He halted Silver and leapt off the horse and drew Corinna down. He reached for his hunting knife in the sheath on his belt and in a single slice, freed her. He gently massaged the raw skin at her wrists. She let him, tears streaming down her cheeks as she sank into him.

"Tanner. You came back for me." She sobbed. "I thought it was all for nothing—that you decided I was guilty. I thought I was going to be taken to jail, so I ran. Then, B-Buck found me. I thought he—"

Bullets he could handle, but a sweet woman crying? With a grunt, Tanner pulled her into his arms and patted her back in the fashion he saw Reid comfort Lorna. It worked for her, maybe it would stop Corinna's tears. He patted a little firmer on her back and her sobs abated.

She pushed herself back to look up at him, but her little hands stayed on his chest. "Will I never be safe again, Tanner? Will that one rash decision of a desperate spinster cause me to lose my life?"

"It seems one choice can shift our whole lives. It did for me." *Like pulling a pretty woman from a raging river that hasn't ceased being in my thoughts since.* He stroked her hair from her cheek and cradled her face in his hands, everything in him wanting to press a kiss to her rosy lips, to tell her that he would protect her and that no one would ever hurt her again. But there was too much left to do to promise such a thing—too much left unsaid.

"I married William for love . . . and despite everything, I was saddened when I discovered he had been murdered." She tugged a necklace out from her high collar with two pendants on it. She held one pendant in her hand—a coin with her husband's name engraved in it. "William had this coin engraved instead of an engagement ring—one for me and another for him." She lifted the second coin bearing her name. "I thought it romantic to hold such a secret between us .. . until we eloped. He left this coin on the floor, along with a string of words that brought me to my knees."

"Did he strike you?"

"He may as well have. I tried to follow him, and his true colors were brought to light." She stroked the coin with the look of a much older woman. "He called me a worthless spinster, a burden, a deceiver, and a disappointment."

Lies. All lies. "And yet, you wear those pendants?" He gaped at her. "Why would you want to remember him after what he said to you?"

"I did not know the man who spoke those words. William had been tender, kind, and adoring during our secret courtship and engagement, but the legacy he left behind him proves him to be that of a rat—a rat who left me in that hotel room, broken and alone. I wear these pendants to remind me never to fall in love again. To remind me of all that I have lost, while still holding on to that one fleeting moment when I thought I was loved. And yet, never was loved." She sighed. "The memory of first love is an odd thing that holds on even when one's perception of the other is destroyed. The memory is fraught with a hope of finding it again in earnest while fearing that if it does come again, it will only prove to be a lie once more."

"I am so sorry he treated you that way and for the pain he has caused you and the fear he still causes you."

"Thank you," she whispered. "By God's grace, I have forgiven him, but I will never *forget* what he did to me and my family—" she released a short laugh. "How can I when I am haunted yet? I did not kill him, but when they have branded me a murderess, I am doomed unless an angel appears, and a miracle of justice occurs. Thus, I vanished from the face of the earth, lest I be hunted down for the sins of William."

He wanted to be the one the Lord used to bring about that miracle. *I'm here, Lord. If You want to use me to take this woman's hand and lead her through the fire to safety, I will. Use me.*

"I've lost my home, my fortune, and the dearest father a girl could have. I shouldn't be surprised that they require my life as payment for William's crimes as well."

He lifted his hand to her curls, his fingers wandering over the silkiness of them.

He placed his forehead on hers, hoping the contact would calm her.

She stiffened, but did not pull away, closing her eyes as if relishing in his comfort as much as he enjoyed hers.

"I believe you, Corinna."

"What?" Her eyes flashed to meet his. "You do? Did you get a telegram that confirms it?"

"I believe you because I know you and what you are capable of. You care deeply about people and are selfless. There is no way you could have killed William. Nothing has been confirmed yet about your involvement."

"But you believe me because you trust me?" Her wide eyes brimmed with hope.

"Wholeheartedly. And—" Shame churned his belly. "And I am so very sorry, Corinna. Everything you called me was true —I tout that I seek justice, but the moment a shadow of doubt fell over you, I abandoned the belief of you being innocent until proven guilty." He hung his head. "I don't know how you will ever forgive me for treating you like—like a black widow spider. That is not you. It's never been you and you did not deserve my harsh words and treatment. My mother would be ashamed of how I have treated you. Even though she was the victim of adultery, she never spoke over the woman who wronged her like I have you. I am so sorry."

"The evidence against me didn't make it easy for you to believe me, Tanner."

"But I shouldn't have treated you like I did—I drove you to run. Judgement is the Lord's job, not mine. Can you forgive me? Is it possible for us to begin again? As friends?"

"A friend? Is that what you really want? I-I heard what you said to Wade."

His stomach churned. "W-what?" Did she know already that he was in love with her? Was she trying to let him down even now?

"I heard you tell Wade that I am a liar, and that beautiful lying women are always trouble and that you could never feel anything for a woman like me that except a need to run far away." Tears spilled over her rosy cheeks. "And so, I ran."

"You heard that?" Tanner grasped her little hands in his, longing to kiss away what she thought she heard. "That's not the full story."

"How can we be friends when I know that's what you thought of me only a few hours ago."

He lifted his fingers to her chin and slowly, gently raised her gaze to his. "That was not the whole story. Wade asked what my greatest fear that was holding me back from pursuing you."

She blinked. "You want to pursue me? B-but I thought you were only guarding me out of a sense of duty?"

"Corinna, I am a fool for doubting you, and I have let fears rule my choices for too long, and I want to change that." He lifted her hand to his lips. "Starting with us. Will you forgive me for letting my fears rule and the harsh words I spoke in ignorance?"

"I forgive you, Tanner. Will you forgive me for lying about my name?"

The weight on his shoulders lifted, allowing a full breath into his lungs. "Thank you, and of course. Let's begin again, shall we?"

"So, what do we do now, *friend*?"

Maybe he shouldn't have used the word friend, but at least it was a far sight better than enemy or acquaintance. "I'm afraid that we can't just keep you in the Sanctuary any longer while we wait for evidence to arrive on our doorstep."

Her cheeks paled. "You think the danger is so great?"

He ached to take her in his arms and quiet her fears. "Yes, and I can't rightly go looking for evidence to clear your name when every bounty hunter within a thousand miles has your poster and is out for the reward. Since Buck didn't follow us, I'm guessing he is fetching help."

She crossed her arms, putting some much-needed distance between them before he did something he had no right to do —not without a kissing booth in sight.

"What do you suggest we do, then? Where do we go?"

Tanner reached out both his hands to

her, willing her to take them. "Do you trust me?"

With her hair spilling to her waist and eyes wide, she seemed much younger than the six and twenty years the poster proclaimed. She slowly reached out, fitting her hands perfectly in his. "I trust you with my life, Tanner Sterling."

CHAPTER 18

"Well, it's about time."

Tanner spun to face the cave entrance. How had he become so careless? *What if it had been Buck?* "Lawrence! When did you get back from town?"

"Just returned to find all the boys were gone, and the house was empty. Thought I'd check the storehouse in case you were making a supply run." He grinned. "Seemed like I was interrupting something mighty interesting, though."

"The horses were let out," Tanner supplied as she pulled her hands from his.

"Ahh, well, I have news." Lawrence flapped a telegram in the air.

"What?" Corinna and Tanner cried at the same time.

"Looks like there's hope for Corinna Victoria Roberts after all," Lawrence said with a triumphant grin.

"Jude Thorpe responded?" Tanner's heart surged with hope. If anyone could help them, it was the renowned detective from Chicago who captured the serial killer haunting the world's fair.

Lawrence nodded. "He was thrilled for the chance to get some new evidence to help put away the Roberts crime family. And he has a plan on how to clear your lady's name, but he needs two weeks to see it through."

Two weeks? Tanner gritted his teeth against the timeline. He had already taken off as much time as a new foreman should, and Reid would be forced to give away the spot to another, less distracted, man. Tanner knew exactly how much funds remained in his leather wallet. They had enough to make a final trip to town for supplies, but with a trip to Chicago in the mix, as well as travelling and keeping hidden, the funds would be gone quickly. And there was no way now he would allow Corinna to pay him for clearing her name, not after everything. *The Lord will provide.* "All right then."

"In the meantime, I found out an interesting piece of news that you will want to hear. While I was studying the new wanted posters on the sheriff's wall, a telegram arrived for the sheriff, listing a bounty of twelve hundred dollars—for a criminal who was spotted by none other than former Texas Ranger Gaston Reid, boarding a train in Colorado Springs."

"So much?" Tanner's guard raised. "Who is the criminal?"

Lawrence flicked back the brim of his hat and crossed his arms. "Reid claimed it was Billy the Butcher. Reid apparently alerted the Colorado Springs sheriff and had the bounty approved fairly quickly."

"Billy?" Tanner rested his hand against the cavern's stone wall. Billy the Butcher had been hard enough to find, and he nearly ended Tanner during his capturing. "Billy is supposed to be dead. I was bringing him back to Chicago to collect his bounty when he got shot on the train over the Mississippi River. He fell. There's no way he could have survived the fall."

"Well, he's alive. It's rumored that he faked his own death and had the whole thing planned out." Lawrence frowned. "And given it was you that captured him the last time, I'm surprised you didn't consider this a possibility. Maybe retirement was a good idea, Mr. Angel of Justice."

"I've been retired for all of a month." Tanner knew where this was headed. Lawrence had been out to prove himself for months. Capturing Billy the Butcher would easily mark Lawrence as an elite bounty hunter. "You are *not* ready. Billy is as ruthless as they come. Do you know his weapon of choice? A hunting knife that he is far too familiar with and carves his victims to the point that the police can hardly identify them. If you are not careful, you'll become another on his long list of kills."

Lawrence's teasing glint faded, and he stabbed his finger at Tanner. "I followed you in capturing the Death Rider gang. I can do this." Lawrence challenged. "You are the only one who doesn't think I am ready. The town sheriff practically *begged* me to go after him."

"Because he's a coward. Colorado Springs isn't that far away from Las Vegas, especially by train, and the sheriff is scared. Billy knows I live in the Gallinas Mountains. He swore he'd take me down before he died when I captured him last time." Tanner closed the gap between them and jabbed Lawrence's chest. "You are not to go to Colorado Springs and follow Billy's trail. Do you hear me? The man is not named *the butcher* for nothing. Billy's brain does not work like everyone else's. He is probably just gathering intel at the moment and is planning on returning to Chicago where he can commit crimes in the city he knows best. All the while, he is waiting for the perfect moment to attack any man who dares to track him. He comes up with plans that are so layered it is almost impossible to see through them. I worked for two years to catch Billy. The only reason I quit being a bounty hunter is because the most dangerous man I had come across was supposed to be dead from trying to escape while in custody, and he couldn't hurt my family when I retired."

"We need the money." Lawrence narrowed his gaze. "I'm going, and you can't stop me."

Tanner rolled his shoulders back. "Watch me."

"We aren't helpless kids anymore, Tanner," Noah interjected, joining them. He gripped the reins to his lathered mount.

"This isn't about you." Tanner gritted out through his teeth. "And why are you here? You need to get the herd."

"I saw you charge up the hill. Wade's got the herd under control. I overheard the last bit of news. And, with all due respect, this does pertain to me as well. You've done a great job keeping us on this ranch for over a decade. You got us clothed, fed, and even educated to some extent. It's time you release your control, and let us take care of you for a change." Noah rubbed his horse's nose but kept his gaze steady on Tanner.

"Over my dead body will I allow Lawrence to face Billy alone." Tanner clenched his hands. "And if I have to fight my own brother, I will."

"Even if it means sacrificing the safety of Corinna by leaving her to catch Billy again?" Noah looked to Corinna. "Because I can tell you right now that the others won't stand for it. She's as good as a Sterling now and we stick together and what she needs is you to stay by her side and for Lawrence to hunt this bounty."

Lawrence nodded. "We are men. We are born protectors. Let us protect."

Tanner kicked a rock that ricocheted off the wall. "I want you to be your own men. I want you to succeed in whatever you choose to do, but I cannot let you fight *my* battles for me. I need to face Billy, once and for all." *I will not allow anyone to hurt my family again.* "This is not a choice I am making out of fear, but wisdom. I know Billy better than anyone."

"And how will you do that with Corinna? None of us have the pull that you do. If she is left alone, other bounty hunters will come and will see us as hiding a fugitive." Lawrence retorted. "They won't respect our so-called claim to her."

"We may even be put in jail ourselves for keeping her here, knowing full well that she is wanted." Noah gave Corinna an apologetic smile.

Corinna cleared her throat. "If you gentlemen ask me, which you clearly have not, the answer is simple enough."

"We are not turning you in for the bounty," Tanner ground out. "I'd sooner pack up this ranch and vanish again."

Her sweet laughter rang out, breaking the tension between the brothers. "Good. Because that is not what I was suggesting. I will go with Tanner to put away this Billy man."

"Setting aside the fact that Billy is a serial killer and therefore, extremely dangerous, you cannot simply waltz into a train station with a herd of bounty hunters on your trail. News has no doubt spread that you are on the ranch under my care." Tanner crossed his arms.

"Which is why Tanner will not be seen boarding with a woman. I can find something in the storage in my room to change my appearance. I can board as a young man and then, I can change in one of the stations along the way."

"Everyone knows you in Las Vegas," Tanner argued, even though the idea had merit. He could keep her safe and then hide her while he searched for Billy.

"But no one will think anything of two males boarding a train in Watrons." She smiled, as if knowing she already had him beat.

Lawrence studied her. "If she stays in disguise until you pass the Harvey Houses, she should be just fine and not be recognized."

"Did Reid mention where the train was headed?" Tanner asked.

Lawrence nodded. "Chicago."

"As I suspected, he is already planning something," Tanner groaned.

"Hopefully, he is not already back to his old ways, but the location is a perfect place for me to hide. No one will ever suspect I've returned to the city I have fled," Corinna interjected.

That's a fair point.

Lawrence nodded. "I'm guessing his enemies put two and two together and realized that their long-lost Billy was still alive and came for him in Colorado Springs. He had to get out quickly, and to a place he knows, even if it meant blowing his cover with the law. Honestly, Billy might be glad to see you." Lawrence chuckled and slapped his hand on Noah's shoulder. "Come on, let's get their packs ready and tell the others what is going on."

Corinna rested her hand on Tanner's arm, waiting until the two brothers were out of the cave before asking, "Do you think this will work?"

Tanner shrugged. "I can't allow myself to think of anything but victory. Confidence is half the battle."

"And the other half?" She whispered.

"Skill, which comes from endless training and years of dedication. And I am the best." He grasped her hand. "Do you trust me to take care of you?"

"Always."

CHAPTER 19

Corinna peered behind the blankets she had hung between her room and the pile of storage items, searching for the trunk Tanner had said contained their old clothes. Even though the idea of dressing in disguise frightened her when she suggested it, Corinna knew without a doubt that Tanner could protect her. The thought of returning to Chicago made Corinna's stomach churn with dread, and yet, a thread of excitement was bursting forth. Soon, all of this would be over—one way or the other, but she knew the Lord had worked out every detail leading up to this moment, and that He already knew the ending. *Lord, please let it not come tumbling down upon me.*

Corinna only needed to keep hidden until Detective Jude Thorpe finished his investigation. And to hide, she would need to change her appearance for a couple of days. Her plan was, after all, the safest way for her to keep hidden from the hunters while ensuring that the Sanctuary stayed out of the hands of the ravenous banker who would not show them mercy, even though the property had been hardly worth anything when the boys had acquired it.

If I had my funds, I could pay off their loan in a heartbeat and hire the best lawyer in Chicago to secure Wade's freedom. If Tanner managed to clear her name, she would force Tanner to take the funds as a reward, even if she had to pay off his debt to the bank without his knowledge. It would be a small step to repaying her debt to him and his kind brothers. It did her heart wonders to finally have someone know the truth and believe *her.*

Spying the trunk, she crawled over a broken cane back chair and knelt to carefully lift the lid of an ancient trunk that appeared to be on its final moments, given the hinges were so rusted. She lifted out a small faded blue plaid shirt and smiled at the thought of it once fitting someone downstairs. She located a pair of pants that were more patches than original material and tears pricked her eyes. This trunk held proof of Tanner's love for his family. Every item was carefully folded and stowed as if it meant far more than heirlooms. Something in the corner of the trunk caught her eye. She grasped a small leather book and flipped it open.

Denver, Colorado 1884
Someone adopted Noah today.
He cried out for me, and I vowed I would return for him. He's only four, but I know Noah would remember my promise. They wouldn't tell me the couple's name who took

him, but the couple can't live far from here because they had a wagon, and their team was not sweaty.

She swiped tears from her eyes at Tanner's orphan train journal. She gently closed the book and held it to her chest, aching for the boy who had written these words, whose family had been torn apart when he felt like he could provide for them. Even at that young age, he had proven himself a tracker.

Her gut twinged in guilt as she flipped to one of the last pages, but Tanner had known this journal was in the trunk when he sent her looking for it, didn't he?

Boerne, Texas 1886

I found Wade. My shoulder aches something fierce from the bullet. I knew I would be getting hit one of these days in my line of work, but I didn't think I would take it from a rancher who wouldn't see reason. Sure, they lived in a shack of a ranch, but he said Alexander Wade was taken care of, but I saw each rib in Alexander Wade's chest. His cheekbones are sharp. I don't feel bad about fighting the man, but I do feel bad about Alexander Wade stealing that stallion, even though it was to keep the rancher from killing me. I heard of an old cabin for sale in the Gallinas Mountains from a fur trapper. No one stays there, so we could squat out there a while before someone buys it. It's time we get ourselves away from everyone for a

while. Adults have never done us
any good anyway.

Her heart ached from fourteen-year-old Tanner's lot, but she couldn't help but admire his determination. When she had been fourteen, she was in finishing school all year and training with her father in the summers. She had been a hard worker, but she couldn't imagine traveling alone across the country searching for loved ones and earning her keep as well without any help from anyone.

Fearing Tanner might come searching for her, Corinna returned the book to the corner and dressed quickly. The plaid shirt smelled musty from age, but the pants were sturdy enough despite the patches. The first pair of boots she pulled on were far too big, so she tried two other well-worn pairs until the smallest of the lot fit. She found a rope in the trunk and threaded it through the belt loops, confident they wouldn't fall. With her corseted waist, she knew she looked too girlish, but hoped the baggy shirt would hide her curves. A woman could not rightly give up her binders when traveling, especially when alone with a man.

Her cheeks heated at the thought of her coming journey, but she was past propriety now. She trusted Tanner, or else she wouldn't have suggested it. But, if her few society acquaintances could see her now, they would never associate with her again. *But who cares about those who didn't even bother to come visit after Father's funeral?* It had been a dark year with all the threats following her elopement. She was no longer that innocent girl with hopes and dreams for a future.

Now, she only wished to live. And to do so, she had to put aside society's carefully laid rules and focus on finding this criminal so that Tanner's family was safe and provided for in the coming years.

She closed the trunk and moved back behind the blanket wall. Rolling up a fresh yellow gown and underthings, she packed them in her carpetbag. She glanced at the box of her dearest possessions under her bed.

Kneeling, she retrieved the box and set it inside her trunk. The box would be safe until she asked for it to be returned. She ran her fingers over the quilt atop the four-poster bed. She would miss it. Before she could allow her tears to rise, she closed the lid, gripped her carpetbag, and descended the stairs to say her farewells, landing with a *clomp* on the bottom step. The brothers stared at her, mouths agape.

He didn't know it was possible for Corinna to be even more attractive to him, but with those old pants hugging her at the waist and hinting at her shapely limbs—He jerked his gaze away and cleared his throat, his brothers all coughing back their laughter at his reaction.

"What? Do I look ridiculous?" Her cheeks bloomed.

"That's not the word I'd use," Tanner muttered.

"You two had better be going." Lawrence crossed his arms and sighed. "I could have already been on the train following him by now if I hadn't felt honor bound to bring you that information from Jude Thorpe, Tanner."

"And I am grateful you did." Tanner clapped him on the shoulder and turned to Corinna. "We need to board the last train out of the Watrons station, and we might just catch him before he disappears down his rat hole in Chicago."

"Here you go, Tanner," Wade held up the heavy bulletproof vest composed of metal plates that he had created for Tanner years ago. "Wear this at all times, you hear?"

"It's saved me too many times in the past to take it off while working." Tanner shrugged on the vest, secured his gun harnesses, and loaded his weapons into place before shrugging on his great coat that hid the bulk.

Corinna's lips parted. "So many weapons . . . while on a train?"

He smirked. So, she finally saw him as dangerous? *Good.* But Tanner figured it wouldn't do much for the woman's nerves if he told her just how many train robberies he had foiled, nor how many times criminals panicked and attempted to take him out. "It is better to be prepared than in want in a pinch."

Clint handed her the carpetbag. "And speaking of being prepared, I've taken the liberty of adding a few things to your pack. I stocked it with some things from the kitchen. When you are settled and ready, we will send the rest of your things after you."

"Thank you, Clint. You are always so thoughtful." She turned to Noah. "Keep studying. You'll make a fine lawyer one day."

"That's the dream." Noah lifted his Stetson and plopped it on her head, tying the string beneath her chin. "Keep a hat on, Corinna. No boy has hair that lovely."

"Thank you, Noah. I'll send it back with Tanner." She shook his hand and then Lawrence's, Jackson's, and Gray's. "Gentlemen, it's been an honor to meet you all. Thank you for your hospitality."

"You come back real soon," Clint pressed a kiss atop her hand. "I'm finally getting away from that stove with you here showing these boys what a real home cooked meal tastes like."

"There are nearly thirty Harvey Girls between the Montezuma and Castañeda. You should all find yourselves wives." Corinna turned to Wade. "You all would make wonderful husbands."

"For now, we'd rather keep you as our sister." Wade grasped her hand and kissed the top.

"Speak for yourself," Gray interjected. "I might go find me a wife, now that I know what kind of food I've been missing, and it would be nice to have a conversation with someone about my interests."

"Which are what exactly?" Noah jabbed him in the ribs. "Hunting? Oh, and hunting?"

Wade rolled his eyes at his brothers. "You keep yourself safe, Corinna."

"Thank you, Wade. I will do my best to have your name cleared," she whispered.

Wade pressed his fist over his heart. "You have given me hope." He pulled Tanner into a hug, muttering into his ear, "And you had better tell her how you feel before it's too late, Tanner."

She lifted a hand to the men, emotion clouding her voice, "I don't know if I'll ever see you all again, but I must thank you all for your kindness and for believing in me when no one else would. Farewell, Sterlings."

The brothers followed them outside, and Wade helped her mount a buckskin as Tanner swung up onto Silver. With another wave and fond farewells, they left the clearing that was truly his sanctuary. Now, he entered the battlefield and Corinna was the prize. He needed to keep her safe, and to do that, she needed to vanish in plain sight while he was chasing down Billy the Butcher in Chicago. And he had just the idea on how to accomplish it, if Jude Thorpe agreed to his plan.

The trail to the Watrons station was much easier of a trip than it had been in the wagon from town to the Sanctuary, as Tanner rode his palomino and Corinna a rather sedated buckskin. The silence stretched between them, and he didn't know how quite to break this awkwardness that had bloomed since that fateful day of the kissing booth and all its revelations. She had forgiven him, but he needed to rebuild trust, friendship, and then, maybe she would be open to his pursuit.

At the edge of the woods, Tanner halted his horse and turned to her, keeping his voice low. "Corinna, while we are on the train, please try not to speak unless necessary, and keep your head down. You're far too pretty for anyone to believe you to be a boy."

A smile curved at her lips. "If you say so."

"I do." Tanner winked and nudged Silver through the trees.

When they reached the station, he halted his horse and climbed down. She eyed the ground from atop her mount. Wade only bred horses that were sixteen hands at least and had always been there to assist her in dismounting, but Tanner couldn't rightly help her down without betraying her weakness. He watched her from the corner of his eye as she clutched the saddle horn and swung her leg over the mare, sliding down.

He held himself back from assisting her as her feet dangled, and she dropped to the ground. Miraculously, she didn't fall and give herself away.

Satisfied that she was safe, Tanner left her to hold the horses as he approached the station and leaned against the ticket master's sill. "Two third-class tickets for Chicago and two for the livestock hold."

"Chicago? That's a far piece from here." The man counted out Tanner's money, locked it in the till, and handed the tickets to Tanner along with two dimes in change. "You are the second fellow in the past week to buy that fare from me. I remembered because I've never sold that one before."

Tanner's senses flared. *I was right.* He flicked back the brim of his hat and leaned closer to the ticket master. "Do you remember what he looked like?"

The man narrowed his eyes to Tanner. "Who's asking?"

"Tanner Sterling, bounty hunter."

"Oh no. No. No." The ticket master lifted his hands and withdrew a step back inside his little booth as the incoming train's shrill whistle sounded in the distance. "I don't want no trouble. If that passenger has a bounty on his head, it means he wouldn't think twice about coming back for the man who ratted him out the moment he is out of prison." He closed the window, locked it, and turned his back to Tanner.

Tanner tapped on the glass until the man finally propped it open an inch.

"What?"

"I need you to send a telegram for me to Grand Central Station in Chicago."

"Fine." He slid a paper pad toward him with a stubby pencil.

> Thorpe, Coming to Chicago. C. to be maid in household! Reply to Topeka station.

Tanner handed the note and coin to the man, and trotted back to Corinna, who was holding the reins to both horses. "You ready?" Tanner smiled at Corinna, resting his hand on her shoulder like he would a brother.

She nodded, fear flickering in her eyes.

"Let's do this." Tanner handed the reins off to the porter to be taken to the livestock car.

The black train screeched to a halt at the station, steam billowing out from between the wheels. No one disembarked, and they were the only ones to board. He hoped that was a fact no one cared to recall if pressed by Billy the Butcher's followers. Tanner motioned her to board behind him.

Disguised as she was in her baggy men's clothing with her hair stuffed up in the oversized Stetson, no one paid her much mind, especially when Tanner scowled and used his massive build to carve a path through any passengers who took the chance to stand and stretch while stopped at the station.

He sank on a vacant bench at the rear of the car. She perched beside him. He took up most of it with his wide shoulders, but since she was so tiny, it worked. She was sitting too primly to pass for a boy though. "Slouch," he whispered.

Her shoulders instantly slumped.

As the train pulled out the station and swayed, her head bobbed and she rested it on his shoulder when a car jarred at a turn. She jerked up, eyes wide. "Sorry."

He looked down at her and his heart ached to kiss away the concern lining her features. He bent his head to hers, longing to comfort her. "You lean on me as much as you need."

CHAPTER 20

ean on me. Even a day later, his words warmed her heart. She gazed out the window at the Topeka train station while Tanner trotted out to the telegraph office to check for a reply from Jude Thorpe. Oh, how she wanted to lean on him. Did he know how much his words affected her, especially with her nerves all in a bundle to be traveling again?

The last time she had been on a train, it had been as a Harvey Girl freshly delivered from training in Topeka to the Montezuma Resort with Lorna Elliot. Her time had not been long under the Harvey House, but the sisterhood she had formed with Lorna, and the unexpected friendship with Dolly, had given Corinna a strength and comfort while she had to guard her tongue to keep her secrets from spilling out. And then Tanner had discovered all her secrets and still stood by her. Perhaps Lorna and Dolly would as well if she ever got a chance to see them again.

She fought against wringing her hands at being back in Topeka and all the fond memories it held. The thought of Lorna returning to the ranch to discover that Corinna had vanished brought tears to her eyes. Lorna had become a very treasured friend, no matter how brief their time together had been. *Lord, if it is Your will, bring us back together one day, please.*

The warning whistle blew, and she spied Tanner through the glass, racing up the train steps as the passengers, who had been dining at the Harvey House, flooded the platform behind him. Tanner slipped through the aisle and sank down beside her, his cheeks aglow beneath his stubble.

"Good news?" She whispered.

He nodded. "I have my answer."

Curiosity drove her to ask for details, but, with people milling about the train car, it wasn't the time to dig for answers, or what question he had sent to Detective Thorpe. Everyone soon found their seats as the wheels churned, and the train whistle blew again. The station in Topeka faded behind them, and Corinna itched to change now that anyone who might recognize her as a Harvey Girl was behind them. Her pretty yellow gown was clean and waiting. It wasn't well suited for travel, but anything was better than the pants she had been wearing for two days. She grabbed the carpetbag from under their bench seat.

"What are you doing?" Tanner grasped her wrist.

"Changing." She lifted the carpetbag. "Shall we meet in another car?"

"You can't dress as a stylish lady now. It would gather too much attention. To blend in, you need to become a servant."

She sank back down beside him to avoid eyes being drawn to their conversation. "A servant without a place to serve? Wouldn't that draw even more attention?"

"That was the answer to my telegram. I secured you a position working for the Thorpe's as a maid. You will be well protected there."

And you are just mentioning this now? She frowned. "And they know my history?"

"Oh, yes. Jude's wife, Winnifred Thorpe, was the one who sent the answer."

"Why would she do that? And why would a detective allow his wife to be a part of the case?"

"Their marriage is unique. Mr. and Mrs. Thorpe met on a case that she was working. She is skilled herself in the art of disguise, which is why I thought this idea might work, but I'll let you find out more from her when we arrive." He propped open his carpetbag and shoved a large package in her hand. "I snagged your black Harvey Girl gown before we left. Figured it could work for a maid's uniform if you found a different apron with more frills and one of those little hat things at one of the bigger cities."

"You mean a cap?"

He snapped his fingers. "Yes. Take your carpetbag with you as I, uh, didn't grab anything else but the gown. Change and I'll meet you in the lunch car. We can't have people seeing your sudden change. It's too memorable."

"Lunch car," she agreed and slipped into the car's lavatory. It was a tight space to change ensembles, but she could manage with much wriggling. She slipped into her soft underthings and petticoat, sighing at the luxury. It was wonderful to look and feel beautiful again. Certainly, the gown was black, but she had always loved that color against her skin while she worked in the Harvey House. And it reminded her of her father, who had always dressed in black while working in his restaurants.

"Father, I miss you something fierce," she whispered and bowed her head. *Lord, could You give my father a hug from me? And tell him that no matter what happens, I will be well.*

THE SMELL of the city was the same as it had been in his childhood, the sharp wind unforgiving. Only four months ago, Tanner had been traveling toward Chicago with Billy the Butcher, the highest bounty of his career, until Billy had pulled his escape over the Mississippi River in St. Louis. Tanner had continued on to Chicago to give his testimony in the criminal's city and left with nothing in his pockets. The police department wanted Billy dead or alive, but without a body, there had been no bounty to collect.

But this time, his mission was even more important than paying off his family's land . . . if he did not clear this woman's name and put the culprits responsible for her persecution behind bars, her life still might be forfeit. And, if he did not find Billy, his family would die. Too much rested on this trip to his childhood city.

Corinna kept her head bowed under the plain straw bonnet they had purchased in some little town in Missouri, declaring her to be the meek hardworking woman she had become over the past year, and not the heiress she was in her own right.

Tanner kept a firm hand at her back, guiding her through the crowd, watching for any threat in the crowded train yard. He pointed to a man under the clock. "That's him."

The towering detective, Jude Thorpe, leaned against the column, his expression grim until he spied them. Detective Thorpe lifted his hat in greeting to Corinna, revealing his thick, wavy brown hair for a half a second before he smashed his bowler back into place. "My father-in-law and I have uncovered some rather disconcerting news. Is Mrs. Roberts up to hearing it?"

Corinna cringed. "Please do not call me by that name. I am Corinna Victoria Alistair now and forever. William will not mar my identity anymore. Please address me as Miss Corinna."

"Yes, ma'am." Detective Thorpe motioned them outside the massive train station to a waiting carriage, pausing for them to enter first before sliding inside and closing the door behind him. Detective Thorpe rapped his knuckles on the roof and the carriage pulled away from the station. "The driver knows where to go." He leaned his elbow on the open window. "My wife, Winnie, has taken an interest in your case as your restaurant is a favorite of her family's. We still attend every Thursday evening with her father."

"Your wife is Winnie Wylde, the daughter of the inspector?"

"Now Winnifred Thorpe." Detective Thorpe grinned. "And believe me that when I received Tanner's letter asking for assistance with your case, she *strongly* encouraged me to take it, saying that she believed you were innocent the moment she heard the rumors that you fled, which I thought strange given—"

"Given that most people flee when guilty," Corinna supplied. "But why did she think me innocent?"

"Because of the fact that she remembers you in the restaurant, and she is well educated on the Roberts crime family." Detective Thorpe shook his head. "Anything involving them usually stinks to high heaven."

The carriage rolled to a stop under an arched porte-cochere of a substantial mansion on Lakeshore Drive. Placing her hand in Tanner's and stepping out of the carriage, she glanced up to the four-stories tall home with a turret on the east corner, the pretty stone covered in vines that would look lovely in Spring when they bloomed.

"This is quite the home, Detective Thorpe!" Tanner released a slow whistle. "Quite the step up from when I met you."

"Too true." He laughed. "My flat could have fit in the east wing of the carriage house, and Winnie, angel that she is, treated the flat as if it was just as much of a castle as this place when we married. Winnie's aunt gifted it to us earlier this year."

"That's right!" Corinna snapped her fingers. "I read about a society matron wedding a viscount before I left. I just never knew it was the inspector's sister-in-law."

"But to *gift* you this place?" Tanner shook his head. "That must have been quite the marriage to give up a mansion like this without a second thought."

"It was a good match," Detective Thorpe agreed. "Aunt Lillian loves to travel and met her true love on this last trip to Paris and was married in a whirlwind, quite unlike her, if you ask me. I thought the viscount had ill intentions, but when I investigated the lord's background, I found him to be a widower of good character and great means. And then, Aunt Lillian gifted us this place, leaving us no doubt that she was far happier abroad than home."

Detective Thorpe pushed open the door, nodding to the butler, who scowled as if affronted that Jude had opened the door by himself.

Tanner's jaw dropped at the marble foyer with its massive chandelier hanging on a long chain between the second and upper floors. He was clearly uncomfortable. Corinna fought the urge to slip her hand into his, recalling that it was neither her place to do so, nor in the character she was adopting . . . which meant she should have entered through the back entrance.

A petite blonde woman, great with child, appeared in one of the doorways, and Corinna vaguely recalled her as the lady Winnie. Puffing as she waved them inside, Mrs. Thorpe's hand rested on her stomach. The moment they were all inside, she shut the door and turned a broad smile to them. "Welcome!" She bobbed her head to Tanner and Corinna. "I'm Winnifred Thorpe, and my husband and I are so happy to have you both. This is all so exciting!"

At her husband's lifted brow and hint of smile, she pressed her hand to her lips.

"Excuse my enthusiasm! What I meant is that my Jude has been oh so insistent that I no longer help with any kind of detection work *outside* of the home, what with the babies coming, which I agreed to, but it has been so hard being confined to the house and resting all the time. But it will be worth it in the end to have our twins. Forgive me, I'm rambling again!" She looked to Jude. "Did you explain everything yet?"

Jude shook his head. "I'm not as well versed with the running of the household staff and expectations."

Winnie laughed. "If I hadn't been in my confinement period for the past two months, I wouldn't either, but lucky for us, I do not handle boredom well and know this mansion inside and out now. Come, Miss Corinna, I'll show you to your quarters and explain everything. Gentlemen, help your-selves to the tea cart. Miss Corinna, I've got a tray being sent to your room." She gri-maced. "If anyone saw you taking refresh-ments in the parlor, I'm afraid the façade would be up in moments. Mrs. Flynn, the housekeeper, is sharp. And we already broke one rule with having you enter through the front door with a guest and my husband."

"Thank you so much for looking past everything to trust me under your roof," Corinna replied with a smile, hoping to still any misplaced guilt that Mrs. Thorpe might be experiencing. She caught Tanner eyeing the refreshments and set a few sandwiches on a plate and handed it to him. "And just because I can't eat now, doesn't mean you can't." Corinna moved to stand by the win-dow, her hands folded before her skirts, already assuming the role in case the butler surprised them.

"Thank you." Tanner's eyes met hers, a warmth flooding her heart at his smile before he turned to Detective Thorpe. "Have you heard anything new, detective?"

"There has been movement in the underground crime families, including the Roberts family." Detective Thorpe reached for a tea cake and poured himself a cup of tea. "Everything is pointing to Billy the Butcher's return. My men are on the brink of discovering his location."

"So quickly?" Tanner said around his mouthful.

Detective Thorpe shrugged. "My theory is that Billy's return has caused such a stir that his usual methods of staying out of sight are being challenged."

"Unless that is what he wants us to believe to lull us into thinking that we've got him when he actually has us right where he wants us," Tanner muttered.

"Yes, but we will prepare for every possibility. He will not win this time," Detective

Thorpe answered with confidence and sank beside his wife on the settee.

Tanner joined Corinna by the windowsill. She allowed herself to relax in his presence as she looked out upon the pristine lawn—all was too idyllic for the turmoil surrounding her life. "I suppose this is goodbye for now, Tanner," Corinna whispered. "I don't suppose I can talk with you being I'm the maid now and you the houseguest."

"I'm sure Mrs. Thorpe will tell you where I'm sleeping. If you are ever frightened, just come find me. But you are safe here, Corinna. Jude has the house surrounded with his undercover detectives and Inspector Wylde lives on the property too in a cottage."

But I'm not being guarded by you. The thought of Tanner being near and yet having to keep herself distant from him, tore at her heart. She didn't want to be separated from him, but what was she to do? She couldn't declare her fondness of him. She couldn't even ask him to stay after it was all over. He did not love her. It seemed she was to remain an old maid for all her days.

"Corinna?"

She had stayed silent too long. She smiled up at him. "That is a comfort. Thank you, Tanner. I know how much you and your brothers have given up for my safety, and I want you to know that I will see to it that you all are rewarded."

"Justice is reward enough."

"Yes, if you are a detective, but you are a bounty hunter. Consider this me hiring you to clear my name."

He shoved his hands into his pockets and leaned against the window frame. "It's nothing."

"It's everything to me." She squeezed his arm, wishing she was free to tell him all that was in her heart.

"Are you ready?" Winnifred smiled and rose from the settee.

With a final look to Tanner, who seemed like he wanted to say more but couldn't, Corinna followed her new employer up the winding servant's stairs, wondering how

Winnifred was completing the task with such grace while carrying twins as Corinna was winded by the time they reached the fourth floor.

Winnifred led her down the hall of the servant's quarters. "This is the women's side. The door in the middle of the hall leads to the men's side, which is strictly forbidden—not even I have ever dared to see the rooms on that side, and I have a *ridiculous* sense of curiosity." She counted off the doors. "Ah, yes, the fourth door on the left. This one is yours." Winnifred pushed it open to reveal a plain room with a small fireplace, an iron bed with a fresh uniform draped over it, a dresser with a pitcher and vase for washing up, and a single chair in the corner with the promised tea tray atop it.

Corinna crossed inside and peeked out of the single window. It had a view of the front lawn and Lakeshore Drive.

"I hope you'll be comfortable. Now, I know you are only pretending to be a maid on my staff, but we'll of course need you to perform your duties to keep suspicion at bay. I hope you don't mind?" Winnifred twisted her hands. "I've always tried to stay as true to a character as possible."

Corinna smiled. "Of course, and this is quite a comfortable room. I was a Harvey Girl for months. I'm not only used to hard work, but I enjoy it." *It keeps me too busy to think, and heaven forbid I start thinking about Tanner again.*

"Good! And how exciting!" Winnifred sank atop the mattress, gripping the foot of the bed. "If I had known about Harvey Girls, I most likely would have tried to join them when I was a girl. I love adventure."

A girl? She can scarcely be older than myself. "And you are on one of the greatest adventures now." She gestured to Winnifred's stomach.

Winnifred fondly ran her hands over her growing babies. "Oh yes, Jude and I have wanted a baby for years. It was quite disheartening at first. All my friends had babies, and just when I was about to give up hope, the Lord blessed us with twins!"

Corinna swallowed back the sudden lump in her throat. "It would be a gift indeed to have babies to hold and love."

Winnifred rested her hand on Corinna's arm. "I saw the way that Mr. Sterling was looking at you. Maybe marriage and babies are not too far off in your future with those wedding bells ringing over his head. Why, he reminds me of how Jude would look at me—ours was a forbidden romance too."

"Oh, no. He's not interested in me like that." While he apologized and she forgave him, he had not spoken of pursuing her again, and it would do more harm than good to dream of love with such a man as he.

"Well, I will not pry. My husband tells me I pry too much, and as I am aware of that fact now, I try to hold myself back as much as possible." She clapped her hands. "Now, shall we talk about your position and back story?"

"Tanner said you were gifted in the art of disguise."

"How kind of him! I went undercover a

few times. The first time was quite the learning curve, but in the end, I helped put away one of the most dangerous serial killers to date. I feel it is my duty to aid you and Tanner in doing the same. So, let's talk about your story. I was thinking that since I hired you without the housekeeper's knowledge, you could be a friend of Jude's sister Mary with a name that matches your initials. What names works for you?"

"Coral Vale?"

"Perfect. Now, for the rest of the conversation, I will address you as Coral so I do not call you by an incorrect name in front of anyone, but if I do, I'll play it off as only an entitled, rich lady would." She reached into a hidden pocket of her gown and produced wire-rimmed spectacles. "I use these when I'm undercover. They have glass lenses, so it will not affect your vision."

Corinna accepted the glasses with a giggle at Winnifred's clear excitement. For the next hour, Winnifred helped Corinna craft the perfect story so that if anyone asked, they both had the correct answers that were nondescript enough as not to invite more questions.

At last, Winnifred rubbed her belly and swung herself to her feet. "I best take my rest before I get in trouble. Jude is such a dear, but he worries." She shrugs. "But his worrying usually sees a new novel for me to read while I rest, along with a box of my favorite chocolates, so I can't complain. Rest well, dear. I shall see you in the parlor when you serve afternoon tea."

Corinna sank into the bed as the door shut. Winnifred had a fairytale life. She sighed. It was too bad that Corinna had wed the evil prince instead of the knight in a shining Stetson. Maybe her life would have turned out perfect too if she had waited. *Stop. Stop wishing away your mistakes. It only makes it harder.*

She changed into her uniform, pinned on her cap, tied a fluffy bow at the back of her trimmed apron, and donned the wire spectacles with clear lenses, completing the disguise. She blinked behind them and peered into the tiny looking glass atop the mantle in the tiny servant's quarters. Something so simple did indeed alter her appearance. *Less than two weeks to go. Then, you'll either be locked up, murdered by the Roberts, or have your fortune, restaurants, and life returned.* And she would never see Tanner Sterling and his brooding expression again.

CHAPTER 21

The next afternoon, Corinna readied the parlor for Winnifred's afternoon tea. She had seen her maids do the task often enough in their mansion on East Erie Street.

"There you are," Tanner whispered from the doorway.

She glanced over her shoulder and self-consciously touched the rim of her spectacles. "You best not linger, or you'll get me in trouble. The housekeeper, Mrs. Flynn, was quite firm in the fact that she wished for me never to speak with any of the family or houseguests."

He closed the door behind him with a

chuckle. "I know. She was quite stern when she found me in the library just now. . . as if she thought I was trying to steal one of the books there when I was really looking for you. You would think that she would treat houseguests a little better than alleged criminals."

"Perhaps she is related to you?" Corinna couldn't help but giggle.

Tanner smirked. "Very funny. I was seeking you out because I may be gone for a few hours while I track down Billy."

"*Hours?* I thought you said he was a mastermind. Do you have a significant lead then?"

"Yes." He scratched his chin. "Hiding out must have taken away some of his edge, because Billy practically left a trail for me to follow."

"A trail?" She scowled. "But isn't that suspicious?"

"I'm a bounty hunter—I'm always suspicious." He crossed the room to her, taking her hand. "I won't be gone long, but please, don't leave the house while I'm away. This is the safest place in Chicago for you."

"Mrs. Flynn and the staff are heading out for the rest of the afternoon for their monthly day off, and she has given a list of chores for me to do that is longer than my arm before they return." Corinna smiled up at him. "I'll be far too busy to even take a stroll on the grounds. You worry about yourself and keeping yourself *alive*."

"I didn't become the best by being careless, Corinna. Visit Silver for me? It's not practical to use him in the city, and he's not used to being stabled." He winked at her as he slipped away. "Have fun dusting the castle!"

After setting the parlor to rights and having the tea ready with a fire blazing in the hearth, Corinna completed her next tasks in the withdrawing room, and then the drawing room. By then, it was nearing evening, and she found she hadn't had much time to worry, much less think over what Tanner was about. But, as his room was next on the list, all thoughts of Tanner flooded her as she pushed open the door to his room.

Unlike his brothers, who let their presence be known with their things laying atop chairs and underfoot, Tanner's room was neat and tidy. She supposed though, he didn't have time to mess it up much, nor did he have much in the way of possessions on this trip. But, still, the bed was made up and she could hardly see anything that needed tidying, but Mrs. Flynn would fire her if she didn't remake the bed in the household manner. She tugged the corner of the quilt out from under the bed where Tanner had tucked it.

"Corinna!" Winnie pressed her hand to her side, breathless, as she flapped a note at Corinna. "You must get this to Tanner. Someone sent a tip that the meetup is a trap! I can't go anywhere, and the lines are busy because Mrs. Hopkins next door will not hang up, and the servants are out!"

Corinna dropped the corner of the bed sheet. "Where's the meetup? I can warn him."

Winnie thrust the paper into her hands.

"This meet-up location can't be right," Corinna murmured.

"Why would you say that?"

"Because this is the address to Victor's Steakhouse." Corinna shook her head, not having time to comprehend what this could mean, as she ripped off her apron and bolted down the stairs and for the back door, ignoring all in her path. Racing to the stables, she slowed only enough to keep from spooking Silver, threw on the saddle blanket and saddle and cinched the girth, thankful for Wade's insistence that she learn.

"We've got to save Tanner," she whispered to the horse, hoping Silver would understand her.

At his owner's name, the stallion tossed his mane and whinnied. She flipped over a wooden bucket for a step, climbed into the saddle, and clung to the saddle horn and reins, kicking Silver into a gallop. "Yah!"

The wind ripped through her hair, her cap falling to the ground as she wove about the streets to reach her father's flagship restaurant. Her pulse quickened with *why* Billy the Butcher had chosen that spot to meet with Tanner, including it potentially being a trap for her set by the Roberts, given the anonymous tip. But how could she ever live with herself if she chose to save herself when she might be able to save the man who meant everything to her?

If this was her final evening on earth, at least Tanner would be spared from the brutality of the Roberts family. She had chosen herself once before, and she would not do so again. She pressed her heels into the horse, and the palomino galloped down the streets, earning her shouts from carriages and pedestrians. She halted him behind the restaurant in the alley and located the potted fern where her father stowed a secondary key. The bottom of the pot had slime on it from years of sitting on the back step, making it the perfect hiding place. In the light of the setting sun, she could barely see it, but catching the corner of the key, she slid it out and fit it to the back door's lock, letting herself inside.

She ducked into the coat rack that served to hold all the used, but mostly clean, aprons from the kitchen staff. She steadied her haggard breathing and listened for voices. No one was near the kitchen. She slipped away from her safe space and darted to the swinging door that led to the main dining room.

In a sea of linen covered tables, a candle flickered on the center table where a man sat, his face concealed in the dancing shadow of the candle. In his hand, he swirled a glass of amber liquid. He leaned back in his chair and spun a long, wide knife with jagged teeth on the table—Billy the Butcher's signature weapon.

She pressed her hand to her mouth at the thought of what the knife had been used for and what the man, whom she believed had to be Billy, intended to do with it this night. Tanner wasn't in her line of sight, but that didn't mean he wasn't present. She had to find him without being caught herself.

She dropped to her knees and crawled under one of the tables. Hidden by the long linen cloth, she drew in a steady breath. She needed to control her panic if she was to have any chance at warning Tanner.

"I was wondering when you would show up," Billy's hardened accent filled the room.

Her heart still. Was he speaking to her?

She squeezed her eyes shut. *Lord! Let me save Tanner, please!* She dared to peek out again.

"Tanner Sterling, I am your judge tonight. And I have found you wanting," shouted Billy the Butcher toward the corner of the restaurant where a potted palm stood.

"And how can you be so sure that you possess the upper hand, Billy?" Tanner stepped from the shadows, guns drawn. If Corinna didn't know him so well, the sight of his fierce expression and dangerous glint in his eyes would have made her tremble. But Tanner was not frightening to her. He never could be.

She watched from under the table, aching to shout her warning, but something held her back. This Billy must have a plan, and now that Tanner knew Billy was aware of him, surely, Tanner would be on his guard. But neither knew she was there as well. She could help!

"You are under arrest, Billy."

"I thank you for your attempt to reignite our friendship, Sterling, I really do. Especially with this being our final evening together." Billy jerked his arm, and something fell from the chandelier. "It's time for the Angel of Justice to meet his maker."

"Tanner!" she screamed her warning, but the heavy pot slammed into Tanner's head, bringing him to his knees, his weapons tumbling from his hand.

Billy turned at her scream, the candlelight flickering on his jaw. Her heart leapt to her throat at the familiar cut of his jaw, his handsome eyes, and disarming smile.

No! No. It can't be. "William?" She crawled from her hiding place, clutching the table. "William. It can't be you, is it?"

His mouth parted, wonder in his voice. "Corinna? My darling, I thought I would never see you again."

She fought against the voice in her head shouting at her to run away. She silenced her fears. *Tanner is in danger.* She slowly strode forward, palms out toward him. "William, what are you doing to that poor man?" Her gaze flicked to the blade in his hand that was aimed at Tanner's exposed neck. One flick of William's wrist would end her beloved's life.

"Doing? Why, I'm working, my dear."

"Working?" She shook her head and took another step toward him. "This isn't you, William."

"And how would you know?" William snorted. "We haven't seen one another in a year, Corinna, but I must admit, you look even more lovely now than you did on our wedding night. You have a glow to your cheeks."

"You are too kind." She gestured to his blade. "But I know that this is not you, given I knew the man who wooed me well. Is someone forcing you do this, my darling William?"

His eyes warmed. "My dear Corinna, you always brought out the best in me. I will find you later, I promise, but you need to leave. I don't want you to be a part of this." He gestured to Tanner's limp form. "I am proud of my work, but it is not a sight for a lady such as yourself."

"I'm already a part of it, William," she whispered. "You are in my restaurant, holding a knife on a helpless man."

"You've turned a blind eye to things in

the past. Let this one depart from your memory too."

She had to keep him thinking that she found him above reproach while still slightly bitter. It wasn't lying when she was undercover. Winnifred had regaled her tales of flirting with a serial killer to save her neck. Corinna would have to do the same, even though the thought of lying again burned her insides. The truth could be just as useful. "I may have put out the memory of you kissing another while you were courting me, but I was so desperate for your affection that I believed your explanation. This is another story. I am not that same heart sick spinster that you abandoned—alone and tied up in a hotel room."

He sighed, rubbing his forehead with the hand that gripped the knife. "I never wanted to leave you like that, Corinna, but I made promises to my family, and if I did not fulfill them, I was going to be next. I wanted to marry you in earnest."

"Earnest? What do you mean?" She pressed her hand to her heart at the hope springing inside, despite the danger. "B-but you married me."

He lifted his brows. "For someone so high and mighty as your father, one would have thought that he would have explored every avenue for forgery in a legally binding document."

"Forgery? You mean to say that our marriage certificate is not valid?" She gripped the back of the nearest wooden chair.

"Remember that girl I kissed? Madge was my fiancée and the one who forbade our actual union. Her brother was a master at forgery. He made the certificate you signed, dressed in one of those fancy collars, and married us."

She pressed her hand to her stomach, this morning's contents threatening a reappearance. "You mean that we were never actually wed?"

He gave her a saddened smile. "I am a confidence man, Corinna, but I never wanted to con you."

"Another lie, no doubt." She crossed her arms, not having to pretend. "Is that line crafted so I will fly to your arms before you fulfill your name?"

"No matter how I treated you after our ceremony, I would *never* murder a woman I loved." He smiled at her, the action sending shivers down her spine.

Out of the corner of her eye, she saw Tanner shift. He had a plan. She knew it. If she could only keep William talking, surely Tanner could get them free.

"Loved, William?" She pressed her hand to her chest, as if deeply touched. "Me?"

"Yes, you, my little Corinna. I always wondered why you did not marry before I found you, and it was my deepest regret that we were not truly married. Otherwise, I would have taken you with me, and we could have spent this time together in wedded bliss. If it hadn't been for my fiancée, who became my bride for a few weeks before she met an untimely end, I would have done so." He glanced down at Tanner, who had stilled once more. "But I am wondering why is it that you are here in this restaurant when you have all but vanished from civilization? You seemed surprised to see me, so I am thinking you came here for Sterling." His gaze darkened at her. "Does he hold your heart now?"

The flicker of jealousy in his crazed expression was enough to alert her to his intentions. "You know that I have never looked at a man before you." She hoped he would not think of the *after*—after was another story. Tanner had filled her heart and thoughts almost since the moment she had met him.

"Which is why I loved you all the more." He turned the blade and sighed. "I really wish you would leave, Corinna. I do not wish for you to see me as what this nincompoop named me as—the *butcher*."

"You don't have to hurt him, William." She held out her hand to him. "Why don't you come to me? It's been too long since we have seen each other and—" She swallowed, dipping her head. *You are undercover. Tanner knows this. You must act the part to save his life.*

"And?"

"I miss you. I miss you so much it hurts," she whispered, the tears in her voice for Tanner.

William's eyes softened and he crossed the room, taking her hands in his. "You always did see the best in me, Corinna. Even when my family was determined to kill me if I failed in conning you out of your fortune, you made me feel like I was a changed man for those few months of the last con."

She lifted her gaze to his dark eyes, recalling how his smile and glance would make her knees weak. She had to do this for Tanner. *Winnifred said to act as if my life depends on it—how much more convincing can I be when Tanner's life depends on it?* She rested her hand on his cheek. "William, don't leave me again. If you do this, there is no coming back, for even I cannot excuse an outright murder from the man I hold most dear. Please, remember your love for me, and stay with me." She lifted the pendants from the chain about her neck. "I still wear them for us, William."

"You really want us to marry?" His knife hand dropped to his side.

"It's what I've always wanted. What do I care about money and wealth if I do not have you?" She tugged him with her. "Let's leave now and take the life that was denied us before. With you by my side, the charges against me will be thrown out, and then I can have access to my money, which could be yours if you marry me in earnest now that your wife is no longer with us. Please, William. If you love me yet, let's run away together."

"You would forgive me for leaving you the first time?" His brows furrowed.

Lord, help me act my way through this. Let William not see the fear and disgust. She sighed. "I had forgiven you long ago, William." And it was true. Despite the anger that fueled her to make better decisions, she knew that if unforgiveness festered, it would only make her bitter. But love? She never truly loved him.

He must have seen the truth of forgiveness in her mien. He slid the knife on a nearby table and pulled her to him and kissed the top of her head. "Very well, let's go. Revenge can await another day when I can justify this man's end as self-defense."

"And I shall gather a bouquet from the tables," she smiled up at William, releasing an inane giggle. "After all, a girl only gets married once, except in our case."

TANNER FINALLY RUBBED AWAY his gag using the sharp edge of the cabinets. Using his teeth to worked away at the knots binding his hands, his mind spun at the fact that Corinna had been married to Billy the Butcher and her choice to leave with the murderer as his willing captive. She had sacrificed herself for Tanner. After the way he treated her when he thought she was the enemy, she gave up her life for his.

He bit a loop of rope and yanked, his hands freeing. He unfettered the ropes binding his feet and leapt up, grabbing the back of a chair when the room spun. He lifted his hand to the lump at the back of his head. He drew a steadying breath and glanced about for weapons, catching a glimpse of his Colt's barrel on one of the chairs.

While Billy had taken all of Tanner's weapons from his person, he had only bothered to stow them out of reach as Billy meant to slay him. He threw on his weapons as quickly as possible when pounding footsteps sounded at the front of the restaurant. He whipped out a gun in each hand and threw himself behind a column.

Detective Jude Thorpe and his men rounded into view of the broad front window.

"Jude!" Tanner shouted. "It's Tanner! I'm coming out." Keeping his guns in hand, he lifted his arms.

Jude eyed the cast iron pan on a rope that still hung from the chandelier and back to Tanner. "What happened? Where's Billy?"

"Billy got to me first. He would have ended me if Corinna hadn't stepped in." Tanner quickly filled Jude in on Corinna's plan to save him.

"Brave, foolish girl," Jude muttered. "But I can't say I'm surprised. The woman must love you."

"She would have done the same thing for any of my brothers, but if it hadn't been for her, I would be dead now," Tanner swallowed, uncomfortable with talk of love when he hadn't even allowed himself to tell Corinna what was in his heart and had been since he met her. "What took so long? I sent a note to the station where I was and when to meet me if I didn't return within the hour."

"Sorry for the delay. There was an overturned cart at every intersection surrounding this place. We eventually gave up the carriages and ran here. It was, no doubt, the Roberts doing as they awaited your finale."

"Enough talking." Tanner gritted his teeth. "We need to go after her."

Jude nodded. "Any ideas where he took her?"

"To see the nearest parson."

Jude's jaw dropped. "She wouldn't . . . would she?"

"For me, I think she might."

CHAPTER 22

*C*orinna was careful to remove a red rose petal here and there to leave a path for Tanner. It was a weak attempt to mark their trail, but what else did she have that wouldn't attract William's attention than the bouquet she had swiped from the dining room?

"I must say, I am quite surprised that you wish to legally marry me." William slapped the reins of the worn mare pulling the ancient hack.

"William, when you have waited as long as I have for a true love . . ." She let the words drift off, her mind on Tanner. "One would do anything to ensure that true love's happiness." *And safety.* Tanner would come for her, she had little doubt, but would he be able to stop the wedding in time? William would be caught, yes, but she would be signing away her future *again*. She would be branded a criminal's wife, and her restaurants would likely fail due to the association, and any dreams of a future husband would vanish.

But Tanner would be safe. Perhaps I can give the restaurants over to my godfather before William's family seizes the deeds? But one glance at the greed lighting William's face, she knew it was only a castle on a cloud of a hope unless Tanner was able to find her before William stole her away into the night and into the shadows of Chicago forever.

William directed the hack into a dark street between two large buildings, slowing the horse.

Her senses prickled. She *knew* this street. It was the one that her father strictly forbade her from ever taking, even though it was a short cut to their home. Was he taking her to Victoria House?

William turned down another block, and

another, until he pulled the horse to a halt on East Erie Street in front of her family's four storied stone home. "It's a good thing that my uncle joined the clergy in his youth. He was ordained and everything before the family took him back into the fold. I heard that he and the rest of the family heads are living in your house. Shall we wed and then throw them out before we sell it?" He grinned. "It would give me great satisfaction. With your money, I will be voted the head of the family for the best confidence scheme, and with that power, we can disappear, and the law can never touch us."

She gave him a tentative smile. "As they should name you as the head. Positions like that should be earned and not merely given out because of a place of birth."

He lifted her hand to his lips. "You are too good for me, Corinna." He hopped out and reached for her.

She placed her hands on his shoulders and fought back a cry of fright as he lifted her out with such ease that she knew he could toss her out of the upstairs window without much effort. Her mansion provided the height needed. He could manage her demise and make it look like she had leapt for her death after wedding such a vile man. *Don't think like that. The Lord will protect you. He placed you in the path to save Tanner's life. Trust Him to have a plan to save yours as well.*

She lifted her eyes to the starry sky above, wondering if this was the end when Psalm 37 flickered to life in her heart, the verses blooming to life. *Commit thy way unto the Lord; trust also in Him; and He shall bring it to pass. And He shall bring forth thy righteousness as the light, and thy judgment as the noonday. Rest in the Lord, and wait patiently for Him: fret not thyself because of him who prospereth in his way, because of the man who bringeth wicked devices to pass. . . For the arms of the wicked shall be broken: but the Lord upholdeth the righteous. The Lord knoweth the days of the upright: and their inheritance shall be for ever. They shall not be ashamed in the evil time: and in the days of famine, they shall be satisfied.*

She straightened her shoulders as she climbed the steps. *I rest in You, Lord. Break the wicked who would see me dead this night, Lord.*

William withdrew a gold key from his pocket and fit it into the lock, grinning at her. "It's a good thing I never returned the key I took from you. Maybe I, too, was hoping that one day we would be together again."

He pushed open the massive door to reveal the breath-taking marble foyer that opened to the rooms of the first floor. In the center stood the impressive marble staircase that if you stood at the bottom step and looked up, you could see the fourth-floor ceiling. She rested her hand on the column of little sphinx statues at the first step that had so impressed her as a child. She closed her eyes as home washed over her, memories flooding her mind and heart. It had been too long.

A crash sounded from upstairs, and William drew her behind him in a surprising gesture of protectiveness. A pinhead of hope burst in her heart. In his own twisted way, William did seem to care for her. And she could use that to her advantage. The pounding of feet on the second floor sounded above, and four heads peered over the railing.

"Billy?" A woman shrieked. "Bud! Billy is back, and he brought the girl."

William's shoulders visibly relaxed. "You have nothing to fear now, Corinna."

"No?" She gaped up at him. "She seemed fairly upset."

"That's my mother and the sister to our head of the family. She won't let them kill me, or you, the woman who can make me the head of the family." William wrapped his arm about her waist. "She will adore you simply because you will dethrone her brother and increase her stature as well. Your presence will bring all good things, my love."

She folded her hands in front of her skirt, gripping the few remaining flowers and hoping that he didn't notice the size of her rose bouquet had shrunk so dramatically. She kept her eyes on the marble stairs and gasped as the man, she was guessing was Bud, appeared in her father's favorite burgundy silk robe and William's mother in

Corinna's own pretty wrap. She gripped the flowers. How dare he? How dare they make light of her father's robe and her things? After all his threats and the grief they had caused her family, it took everything in her not to rail at him.

"Ma! Glad you were here. Wasn't sure what I'd be walking in to," William said, wrapping her in his other arm.

"Good thing, or else you wouldn't be breathing now." Bud narrowed his eyes on Corinna. "You either."

"Well, I hope you are prepared for some good news. Corinna has now come into her fortune and we can drop those nasty charges, because as I stand here, I am not dead and therefore, she did not murder me. We are to marry in earnest. Is Bobby upstairs? We need him to marry us."

His mother clapped her hands and smiled at Corinna, revealing several missing teeth, and the few she still possessed were yellowed with little white clumps at the top, as if she had been snacking on crackers in bed. "Well, well. The rich girl has fallen for my handsome boy. I'm not surprised. They all do. How many girls did you get to fall in love with you, Billy?"

Corinna stared up at William. She didn't know why she was surprised, given how little she apparently had known about him before their first marriage ceremony. She had to escape before the wedding! She had thought he would refrain from killing her, but mad men rarely did what one thought they would.

"Ma, I don't want my bride's head filled with all that only minutes before our wedding." He winked at Corinna. "All that matters is that *she* is the girl I want to go through with marrying, and I will do anything to make up for when I abandoned her."

An idea bubbled inside. "William?" Corinna smiled up at him, hoping that she looked like a girl in love. "In the attic is my mother's wedding dress. Would you mind if I changed before the ceremony? It would make me feel close to my mother." *And buy me time as well as a potential escape route.*

"Anything for you, my darling." William kissed Corinna's cheek. "Ma, I need you to bring Corinna up to the attic to change. Can I trust you to help her and *not* harm her?"

Mrs. Roberts shook her head. "She is the key to my boy's future. Of course, I'll keep her safe."

He opened his palm and wiggled his fingers. "But, just in case, may I have your ankle knife, Ma."

She sighed and hefted up the dressing robe to her knobby knees and withdrew a blade. "Fine. I was only going to scare her a little—nothing like a little fear to keep a daughter-in-law in line."

"I know, but Corinna would never hurt me. Would you, honey?" William chucked her under the chin.

"You know that you are my first love, William," she whispered, lowering her lashes.

Mrs. Roberts waved Corinna up the stairs. "Lead the way. We've explored much of this house, but the attic seemed haunted, so we let it be to let the ghosts settle."

"I'd be happy to." Corinna's smile was the closest to genuine for the first time that evening. If she could get into that attic, she might be able to save herself after all. She led the way, and at the landing for the attic, she turned to William's mother just as thunder rumbled and rattled the walls, making the older woman shrink into Corinna's dressing robe. "Thank you for assisting me. I know it is not the best part of the house, but after we are wed, I'll have lights brought up here and have the place cleaned out, even if William and I can't stay here, for obvious reasons. I would hate for there to be a place in our home that gives you discomfort, Mother. May I call you 'Mother?'"

The woman smirked. "*Ma is what Billy* calls me. Mother is for the hoity-toity set."

"I quite agree. Is it well with you that I call you Ma too?" *If she thinks me doting, surely, she will let her guard down.*

Ma narrowed her eyes at her, a gleam coming to life. "What's my clothing allotment to be?"

"As much as you wish. What is mine is yours, *Ma*." She dipped her head, hoping she wasn't laying it on too much as she pushed open the door and climbed the last flight of stairs into the attic. She moved to the corner of the floor where the window of the house would meet her neighbors.

She swallowed as she spied the old board beneath the window—the very board that used to join her house to Florence's old home. She had almost forgotten about it until it was the only way she could think of to escape. As children, they tried crossing to each other's houses. They had thought nothing of the height until Corinna had almost fallen when the governess had discovered her and screamed, startling Corinna.

She turned her back to the board and knelt to flip open the lid of the trunk that bore her mother's gown. She wished she did not have to go through with this part of the ruse. To even allow William's mother to see it felt like a violation of something pure, but what other choice did she have? Tanner would need time to find her. Mrs. Roberts' footsteps set the floorboards to creaking, and a tiny flapping of wings sent the woman squeaking and running for the door.

"You'll be fine to dress alone. I dare say

you've been managing just fine for a while," Mrs. Roberts called out and slammed the door.

She surged to action. They would be coming for her within minutes. She flung open the old window, gripped the plank, and slid it from her windowsill to the ledge of Florence's old attic. The plank had been small as a child, and now, it was far too tiny to even think what she was about to do. Her father had completely lost his temper when he discovered what she had been doing and awoke her to the dangers of walking across a plank four stories high, even with the slope in Florence's roof on the third floor below that would block a fall somewhat. She had never done it again. Lightning cracked overhead as wind whipped back her locks.

She had never attempted the crossing while it was raining, but she either had to possess the courage to cross or marry that rat in earnest this time and die a slow painful death. *Lord, protect me.* She gripped the plank with both hands, tested her weight on it, and rose to standing, her knees knocking as she slid her right foot forward. She spread her arms for balance and took her first step away from the windowsill as lightning crackled in the dark dome. It wobbled a half inch but held true.

A sharp knock sounded on the attic door.

"Corinna?" William's deep voice sent a jolt of fear through her. "Corinna, are you dressed?"

"Almost!" She threw over her shoulder, hoping her voice carried.

The pounding on the door increased. She pushed herself to take another step, and another, as shouts erupted on the landing outside the attic door. Something slammed into the door, the horrible crunch warning her that little time remained. She glanced over her shoulder as the door splintered.

"Corinna! What are you doing?" William appeared in the doorway, gaping after her.

She scrambled forward and fell to her knees as rain pelted her back. She gripped the board and crawled.

"Corinna! Stop. You will hurt yourself." He pleaded, running to the window, and stretching out his hand to her. "It's just wedding nerves. Please, come back!"

While she knew most of his drive to marry her came from claiming her fortune, his tone held concern. *Maybe he won't send me to my death, even if I ignore him.* She crawled forward, the slick wood making her dig her fingernails into the board to keep from losing her grip.

"Corinna!" His tone sharper. "This has gone on far enough. Come back."

The board wiggled violently beneath her grasp. She glanced back at him. His fingers were around the board, steadying it.

"If you do not come back, I'll see to it that you do not escape." He trilled his right hand against the board. "Do not test me."

Against her better judgement, she released a short laugh. "How can I trust you not to kill me the moment our wedding certificate is signed, William? You have proved yourself again and again to be a liar, a thief, and a *murderer*."

"If you think those things about me, why should I deny them?" He sighed and slammed his fist into the board.

Her fingers faltered and slipped. Her scream cut off as she landed on her stomach. The board jolted again. She twisted her face to him, the rain plastering her hair across her cheek. "No! William, please! Have mercy."

"You had your chance to come back." He shook his head. "But I do rather like your plan better. Yes, come back little bird and I shall marry you and mayhap I will extend your life until after the birth of our firstborn."

"Corinna!"

Tanner. His voice filled her with hope. Tanner was safe—alive. And she was not alone. "Tanner! Tanner, help me!"

"Ah, it seems I have found the root of your reluctance."

Terror seized her as she looked back at William once more.

He knelt at the windowsill, his once handsome face contorted with evil. "I loved you, but it appears you love another, and that will not do. I will be second to none."

"William," she whispered. "Don't do this. Please, let me go."

"You know I cannot do that. Goodbye, my little bird. Fly away one last time." He grabbed the board with both hands.

Corinna screamed.

BILLY WAS GOING to send her to her death. *No! Lord, please.* As Billy gripped the board, his intentions were all too clear.

Tanner leapt on top of a barrel beside a coal shed and onto the roof of the shed as he drew his weapon. Taking aim for Billy's wrist to keep the impact on the board between Billy's hands at a minimum, Tanner released a prayer and pulled the trigger. Billy shouted as the bullet struck true and in a single motion, Tanner holstered his weapon and reached out his arms for Corinna as Billy released the board to cradle his wrist. The board wobbled free of the ledge and Tanner's angel fell. *Lord! Save her!* "Corinna!"

She angled her body to fall on the sloping roof of the neighbor's third story, sliding down the clay tiles. He stretched his hands up as she gripped the gutter of the third story, crying out as her fingers lost their hold and she plummeted, falling directly into his arms. She slammed into him, smashing him down into the tin roof of the coal shed and stealing his breath. Shots fired from the police toward Billy. He twisted on the roof, covering her body with his own, unable to move further until his lungs filled again.

"Tanner!" Her breathless cry stirred him.

"Corinna?" He caved his shoulders so that he could shield her and see her at the same time. "Corinna, my darling, are you hurt?"

"No." She reached up and caressed his cheek with her hand. "You saved me again."

"You saved me," he returned, kissing her atop the hair. "We have to stop meeting like this."

"Agreed." She moaned.

"Are you hurt? Please don't try to hide it from me."

She twitched her limbs and shook her head. "Miraculously, I don't think so. You?"

"Likely a few bone bruises, but nothing

that time won't heal." He bent his forehead to hers, breathing a prayer of thanks.

A bullet pinged on the tin beside them, bringing Tanner back to the present. He needed to get her to safety, but he couldn't remove them from the roof without exposing her to Billy's gunfire. The angle protected them for the moment, but if Billy leaned out the window, he could easily kill her.

A bullet slammed into his back, smashing him into Corinna as he desperately tried to draw air into his lungs.

"Tanner!"

He grunted. The jacket deflected the lead. Another bruise, but better than Corinna being hurt. "I'm fine. I've got the vest, remember? Stay down!"

Hands reached up for them. He scooted with Corinna under him to the edge. "Let the policemen catch you and hit the ground at once. I'll follow." He released her, waiting for her to drop before slipping off the roof himself. Grasping her little hand in his, he tugged her away from the detectives and, shielding her with his chest on her back, raced away from the gunfire.

In an alley across the street, he towed her into a doorway and guiding her into the corner, he pulled her against his chest in a fierce embrace, emotion clogging his throat. He had almost lost her—the love of his life who had no idea what she meant to him. He was ten kinds of a fool. He pressed a kiss to her hair again and then lifted her hands, kissing the inside of her wrists. "I thought I lost you, Corinna."

"And I had given up on ever being happy again, and yet, here we are," she released a laugh, tears spilling over.

He pressed his forehead to hers. "I think I love you more than any man has ever loved a woman."

She gasped, looking up at him. "You mean it, Tanner? You aren't afraid of letting someone near you anymore?" She shook her head. "Because I want to do this right. I never want to rush into anything again. I have paid that price, and I won't do it again. It is too steep."

"Corinna. I am a cautious man—too cautious, but when it comes to you, I want to lose my head, my hand, and my heart. In fact, I already gave it to you. I'm a lost cause."

"In that case, I think I love you too."

He chuckled and kissed the tops of her hands, pulling her even closer. "I *know* I love you more. I know it with the certainty of all that I am. I love you, Corinna."

"And I love you, Tanner Sterling," she whispered. "I love you with a fierceness that frightens me."

He bent to press his lips to hers when a throat clearing sent her leaping back and him pulling his gun.

"We've got him." Jude Thorpe announced. "Billy the Butcher's reign of terror is at an end, and the head of the Roberts crime family is in the wagon."

CHAPTER 23

*C*orinna nestled in a blanket beside the roaring fireplace in Victoria House's parlor with a cup of bracing tea between her hands with Winnifred beside her as Tanner paced back and forth, the grandfather clock sounding twelve times. Two guards stood at the parlor door and two more stood at each entrance and exit. While the Roberts family had fled, the police had kept the servants from fleeing without being questioned, which was already underway. The front door creaked, and the pair looked at each other as Winnifred pushed herself to her feet to greet her husband.

Detective Thorpe paused in the parlor

doorway, looking bone weary, but a soft smile on his lips for his wife as he softly chided her for leaving the house at this hour.

"I couldn't stay away! Not with Corinna running off to see to Tanner's safety and then hearing about the arrests from my father. He assured me it was safe enough."

"Your father and I are going to have a little discussion about what is good for an expecting mother of twins to hear, no matter how much I respect her opinion on cases." Detective Thorpe helped her to sit and turned to Corinna. "I have news. And it will not be easy for you to hear. Are you ready for it tonight? Or do you wish to rest?"

"I've waited too long for the truth as it is," she replied, thankful for Tanner slipping his hand in hers as he stood by her wing-back chair. "Tell me everything."

"Naturally, with Billy the Butcher's capture and identities confirmed, your name is cleared, and your assets unfrozen. The restaurants will return to you, and your home is yours once more."

She sagged back into the cushions and closed her eyes against the rush of tears. She had waited so long to be free, and now, she finally was. She looked to Tanner, but the grim line hadn't erased itself from his forehead yet.

"And?" Tanner prompted.

"There's more?" She whispered, facing the detective once more.

"We have gathered that this is not the first time Mr. Roberts attempted to woo a woman in order to steal her fortune." Detective Thorpe squeezed his wife's hand. "It was as you feared, Winnie. He was an H. H. Holmes imitator."

Corinna blinked. "What do you mean?"

"Billy Roberts was attempting to build his own empire after his uncle basically kicked him out of the family business nearly ten years ago. . . if you can call a crime ring a family business." Detective Thorpe shook his head. "Anyway, the connection is similar because of bigamy and the serial nature of his murders. Billy the Butcher, also known as William Roberts, was first married in

1889 to a Mrs. Bethel, a wealthy widow in St. Louis."

Corinna's grip tightened on Tanner's hand. "Was ours truly not a legal marriage then? He said it was a forgery, but I didn't dare to fully hope that he spoke the truth."

"I'm having the certificate analyzed and looked into now, but knowing that Billy the Butcher is related by marriage and is the third cousin to Bobby Roberts, who is a notorious forger, I would say that you can be nearly certain it was the truth." Detective Thorpe flipped open his notepad, running his finger along a line of notes.

"Billy's first wife died in an accident a year later. In 1892, he eloped with a young heiress of seventeen in Denver. She possessed a substantial fortune that legally became Billy's after their marriage. She died in childbirth the following year. He returned the child to her grandfather, effectively abandoning her. And then, in November 1897, he, of course, married you, Corinna. You were supposed to be his biggest catch yet, and when you didn't receive your fortune directly, he most likely would have killed you, if not for the clause in your inheritance that awaited your father's death before your funds were written over to you."

"And the fact that the psychopath had a warped sense of affection for you," Winnifred added.

Corinna pressed her hand to her heart at the fate she narrowly avoided. "And the tip? Who sent it?"

Jude frowned. "The source was unknown."

Tanner clenched his fist. "We know Billy will pay for his crimes. But, what of his uncle, Bud Roberts? We all know he's the leader, but do you have any evidence against him to prove a crime at last? The Roberts know how to craft a story and buy their way out of anything, and circumstantial evidence will not hold him, and I fear that he will have it out for Corinna since she threw him out of her home and made a fool of them all."

Detective Thorpe sighed. "Trespassing is all we have at the moment. Miss Corinna can, of course, witness that he attempted to take her fortune by falsifying his testimony that brought about the warrant."

Tanner squeezed her hand. "I do not want you to stand as witness, Corinna. The Roberts will have you killed for standing up to them."

Detective Thorpe nodded. "Which is a substantial hurdle with her wishing to return to her home and Chicago restaurant. For her safety, I would recommend that Miss Corinna leave the city until everything can be handled *without* her testimony."

"But with my testimony? What can happen?" She twisted her hands in her lap.

"With your testimony, the leader of the family can be put away for a long time, and the streets of Chicago will be all the better for it. But I cannot advise you to stay. It is too risky when the same thing can be accomplished given time and the right pressure applied to a family member who wants a deal to shorten his, or her, prison time."

"I know it must be a great loss to leave your home for so long," Winnifred offered her a sympathetic smile.

Corinna shook her head. "My house is

nothing without someone in it. I have no one left to love me in here. If I need to leave my city until it is safe, I will build my father's empire elsewhere. I only wish I could see William's whole family in jail after everything they have done."

Detective Thorpe rose. "I know, but the best I can do is to have you witness the eviction of the remaining servants under the Robert's rule. After they have all departed, I can allow you time to pack what you wish to take with you before putting you in hiding. Now, I know it's late, but evictions like this are best handled at once before the guilty can disappear with your property."

She nodded, and Detective Thorpe rapped on the parlor's glass and the sound of the door opening followed by a swarm of boots in the foyer filled the house. She glanced out the window to find more of his men in brass buttons lining gates that blocked the sidewalk from the stone steps to keep anyone from exiting.

She was thankful she did not need to be alone to retake her home. The police assured her that most of the Roberts clan had disappeared into the woodwork after the gunfight. The whole eviction took less than an hour, and it gave her no small amount of pleasure to throw open each door of her childhood home and flush out the remaining ghosts, in the form of anything having to do with the Roberts, that had taken up residence there.

She caught one of the maids attempting to sneak out with a figurine of a mermaid. She plucked it from the woman's pocket and insisted she go through the woman's trunks and see if anything was there that belonged to her, finding an ornate mantle clock, a pair of silver candlesticks, and three gold forks.

Tanner stayed by her side through all of it, offering her strength. At last, the house was empty, and it was hers again . . . for a few hours before it was time to draw the shutters and drape the furniture in white shrouds.

Detective Thorpe closed the door behind the final policeman exiting the house. "While the Roberts and their followers may be gone, I saw the look in the servants' eyes.

They are not happy, and until those locks are changed, I think we need to have the estate surrounded. And, as you are a witness in this case against the Roberts gang, Inspector Wylde has backed my decision to have the grounds and, if you should choose to stay, you, watched for the next few weeks until the trial concludes. But I again must warn you, Miss Corinna, you are in danger in Chicago. Even with Billy the Butcher and his father behind bars, there will be orders to have you harmed. I strongly advise you to leave."

"I-I suppose I could stay with Lorna . . . if she'll have me."

"She will have you." Tanner assured her and took her hand. "And if she doesn't, you will move in with me."

"Excuse me?" Her brows rose.

Detective Thorpe sent Tanner a glare. "I will give you the benefit of the doubt enough to leave you to choose your words more carefully, friend, but I assure you, as a gentleman, I will be following up with you on *that* statement."

"Tanner, I can't move back out to the

Sanctuary with you, not when I have a proper place to stay and money to put me up if I do not." Yes, she had stayed with the brothers before, but that had been as a prisoner, but now, as a free woman, it was beyond improper.

"Proper? Who cares about proper after everything we have been through." He grasped her hand and tugged her into a corner of the parlor, away from Jude's hearing.

Was he really this naïve? He had declared that he loved her and that created a need for boundaries. "*I* care," she whispered. "And besides, everyone there has their place, a job to do. I like to keep busy."

"There is a job for you, a very important one."

She narrowed her gaze. "I do not consider doing the dishes a reasonable enough purpose to risk scandal."

"I'm attempting to be romantic in drawing out my proposal."

"Proposal?" Her smile slowly spread as she squeezed his hands in anticipation. "Which has nothing to do with the dishes?"

He nodded. "Besides, there are rules for dishes, you know that better than anyone." He lifted her hand and kissed the top. "The position I offer is that of being my wife."

She glanced about. "Why, there's not a steak in sight and I haven't cooked for you in a while."

He closed the distance between them, wrapping his hand about her waist. "I mean it, Corinna. I don't know what I would do if anyone harmed you. I couldn't live with myself."

"That is no reason to ask someone to marry them." She shook her head. "I should know. One should never rush into a marriage."

"We are not rushing." He laughed. "Far from it." He gritted his teeth. "Unless you don't want to marry me? I want you to be mine, but I know I do not have much to offer, only my love and protection."

"You have everything a woman could ever dream of in a husband. You are loyal, gentle, kind, and possess a strength of character that is rare."

"Then what is it?" Tanner whispered.

"We've known each other for weeks and not always with this pull between us."

Her brows rose. "I remember quite well what happened at the kissing booth." She leaned toward him. "There was plenty of *pull*, but then, the pull seemed to have turned to animosity when you decided to take me prisoner. How do we know the pull is back and that it is not simply our opinions being at war with one another once more?"

"Oh, I can prove there is pull." He opened his wallet and withdrew a little red ticket, holding it between two fingers. "I still have one kiss to claim yet."

"You kept a ticket?" She reached for it, but he lifted it out of reach.

"I did. But I only want you to take it if you are willing that it will be the last kiss you wish to give me before you become my wife." He twirled it between his fingers. "What do you say? A ticket for a Harvey Girl bride?"

Corinna stared at the little red ticket between his fingers. She longed to snatch it from the air and kiss him senseless. But she had wed before on the wings of love—or thoughts of love. She had to know for certain. "How do you *know* you want to marry me?"

He tenderly held her cheeks between his hands. "I've long seen your kind spirit, your gentleness towards my brothers, and your ability to push past uncomfortable situations to do your job well. You work with your whole heart and when you dedicate yourself to something, or someone, you love with your whole heart too. You have taken my heart from one of an enemy and captured me, body and soul, and I want none other than you to be by my side." He tilted his head and amended, "*And* my six brothers. We still haven't picked our prank against them, and that will be our first order of business when we return home. Then, we will get them all married and settled into cabins of their own on the property."

She laughed and slowly reached for the ticket, plucking it from his grasp. "Then you better kiss me, Tanner Sterling, because I don't plan on being anywhere else but with you for the rest of my days."

He gathered her in his arms, with one hand at her waist and the other at her neck, he slowly drew her to him. His lips captured hers with a fierceness that excited her and made her knees weak all at once as the room spun about them and there was only her and him and that kiss.

At last, he slowly pulled back and whispered, "And that, my sweetheart, makes four."

EPILOGUE

"Finally! We are home." Tanner grinned, grabbing her hand, and helping her to standing as the train rolled to a stop in Las Vegas. "I've never been so anxious to get back to this dusty town in all my life. Sitting next to you in that wedding gown for the past hour has been torture! It should be against the law to be as beautiful as you."

She laughed and gathered her mother's wedding veil that was already fixed atop her low coiffure and draped it over her arm as she peered out the window. "And it seems as if the whole town is ready for your return as well! I suppose there will be a great mourning from the ladies in town. No one expected the Angel of Justice to take a bride so soon after retiring."

"Which is why I suggested a wedding in Chicago. But, as you refused, the crowd is here for us." He winked. "But I would wait years if it meant I could marry you, Corinna Victoria."

"Fine words for a man who is about to marry in a quarter of an hour." She leaned into his arm and rested her head against his shoulder, grateful for his ever willingness to please her. Tanner had requested they marry at once in Chicago, but Corinna did not want another rushed wedding. Besides, if she were going to live in the mountains with her six new brothers, she wanted them to witness the happy occasion.

So, Tanner wired his brothers to meet them at the chapel in a week's time, during which time, she sold the mansion to a family of ecstatic parvenus and with her assets returned to her, she promptly sent a handsome sum, along with one of Chicago's finest lawyers, to Texas where the lawyer settled the matter of the stolen stallion once and for all.

For the business, she called an emergency meeting with the board members. She retained the majority of shares of ninety percent and announced that her godfather would be overseeing the branches while she would be taking the company West to a little town called Glorieta that wasn't too far from the ranch, but far enough from the Harvey Houses so as not to cause competition. But for now, that dream would wait its turn behind the most lovely dream of all.

Corinna stood on the train's platform and clutched Tanner's arm as the crowd cheered. She could hardly believe that her dream of becoming a wife and, hopefully one day a mother, was happening. The town ushered them straight to the pretty blue chapel where Preacher Martin and the Sterling brothers awaited them within.

At the church doors, Dolly rushed up to her, giving her a hug and lifted something that sparkled in the sunlight—the beautiful heart shaped diamond bracelet. "Don't forget this! Pernilla found it and said it might be yours." Dolly clasped it on her wrist and hurried inside.

Found or returned? She shook her head. Pernilla was no longer her problem, and she had enough of the law's involvement to last a lifetime.

Lorna trotted up the stairs and handed her a bouquet of wildflowers and kissed her cheek. "I leave on my honeymoon, and you go and find yourself a groom for an early Christmas present."

"Isn't that the Harvey Girl promise? A groom by Christmas?" She giggled and lifted the bouquet to her nose.

Tanner grasped her hand and tugged her to him. Lorna conveniently twirled away, leaving them on the steps of the chapel.

"Aren't you supposed to be waiting for me by the preacher?" Corinna giggled. "You aren't going to run are you?"

"Not a chance. I never dared to hope to call a woman like you, mine." He lifted her hands to his lips, kissing them. "Are you happy?"

She rose on her tip toes and wrapped

her hands about his neck. "Happier than I've ever been in my life. You make my heart sing, Tanner Sterling. And I cannot wait to be married to you so I can have all the kisses I've ever wanted."

"No kissing booth required."

Author's Note

Dear Reader, thank you so much for reading Book Four in the Aprons & Veils series! If this is your first time reading about the Harvey Girls, know that they did indeed exist. In the 1890s, there were not many respectable jobs for women, so when Englishman Fred Harvey created his chain of fine dining restaurants along the Atchison, Topeka, and Santa Fe railroads, single women without an education, or in need of earning their own way, were given a chance to earn an honest wage without the speculation that they offered anything else but food as a service.

With Mr. Harvey's strict rules about the waitress's code of conduct, the women were given their independence while still maintaining their good name and place in society under the protective, fatherly arm of Fred Harvey. These extraordinary, brave women became known as the Harvey Girls, the ladies who tamed the Wild West with fine china, good pie, and exceptional service with complete propriety.

For the purpose of my story, I did take some small liberties with the Castañeda, such as the opening date of the hotel. Sources claim different years, so I decided to begin this series the year the Castañeda was built. I also changed the hotel's dining room floor appearance. I did attempt to stay as accurate as possible with the Fred Harvey system and layout of both Harvey buildings based on the historical pictures and references available. The Castañeda Harvey House is one of the few still standing and has been fully restored to operate once more and you can stay as a guest in the Hotel Castañeda, today.

The scene where Silver enters the dining room is inspired by true events! Before Fred Harvey had "Harvey Girls" running his restaurant, the guests occasionally were less mannered, and one even rode his horse into the dining room. As a result, a staff member suggested Fred Harvey bring on females to wait on the tables, and therefore, ensure that the men would act in a more gentlemanly fashion. Fred Harvey agreed, and the *Harvey Girls* were created!

As for the horned toad in the coffee cup scene, that too was inspired from a *real* event. I spun it into a fictional scene as it was just too good not to include.

Kissing booths were first documented in newspaper articles in the early 1900's, which surprised me as it seemed rather scandalous for the time, buuuuut what fun it was to use it as the catalyst for Corinna's story! Kissing can get one into all sorts of predicaments.

Want to know more about Winnie and Jude Thorpe and how they helped capture H.H. Holmes? Check out their forbidden love story in *Miss Wylde in the White City*!

If you enjoyed *The Vanishing of Miss Victoria*, I would love if you could please take a moment and leave a review, or rating. Happy reading, friends!

Grace Hitchcock is the award-winning author of multiple historical novels and novellas, including the American Royalty, Best Laid Plans, and Aprons & Veils series. She holds a Master's in Creative Writing and a Bachelor of Arts in English with a minor in History. Grace lives in South Louisiana with her husband, Dakota, sons, and daughter in a farmhouse that is always filled with the sounds of sweet little footsteps running at full speed. When not writing, chasing her toddlers, or tending to her chickens and golden and labrador retrievers, she's baking something delightful and can usually be found with a book clutched in her fist.

APRONS & VEILS
BOOK FIVE

The Courting of
Miss Cady

GRACE HITCHCOCK

VALMONT

CHAPTER ONE

*N*ew York City
December 1898

JANE CADY SQUINTED through the tulle of her wedding veil as she waited in the foyer of the church on Fifth Avenue. Her pulse pounded in her ears as the organist began the first notes of the Wedding March. Jane glanced about for her father, her heart sinking. He was always flighty and had his head in the clouds with each new business venture that absorbed his every thought until it was followed through, but this—this was a new level even for him.

She pushed the double doors leading into the sanctuary open a crack. The pews were filled, the lovely chapeaus of the elite society ladies creating a meadow of fake blooms that basked in the morning light streaming in from the stained glassed windows. Reverend Hall stood at the top of the aisle, between the massive flower arrangements featuring orange blossoms, speaking with—she averted her gaze, even as her heart skipped a beat at the sight of her handsome groom. She didn't want to see Graham Bank until the very moment she was to be his wife.

The church bells sounded ten times, announcing to all of New York City that she was about to be wed. Outside the front doors, the crowd gathered cheered for her. She danced from side to side, trying not to pick at the orange blossoms of her enormous bouquet. *Where is Father? He reads the news sheets, and the time was printed on every single one!* The guests were waiting for her. Could she walk down the aisle without him? No. It would cause nearly as much scandal as her being late to her own wedding.

The front doors of the church burst open, shouts and sounds of the city spilling inside for a moment as the doors shut. Father ran to her, panting in his wedding suit. "Daughter, we must speak. There has been a development with my ships from the—"

"Father! Thank goodness you are here." She seized his arm and straightened Father's silk top hat and patted down his graying beard. He was disheveled, but at least he was here. "There is no time to waste, Father. The bells have already sounded the hour, and we are already late."

"But, Janey, you see, that is why I was tardy. You need to know—"

She placed her hands atop Father's shoulders and steered him to the doors. "We can speak *after* the ceremony. Nothing—I repeat, *nothing* is as important as my marrying Graham at this very moment." She nodded to the footmen who pulled open the double doors, the blasting notes of the organ vibrating through her and sending anticipation humming to her very fingertips. After years of waiting for the right man, being judged for waiting until she was nearly four and twenty to accept a suitor, she would be Mrs. Graham Bank.

With her head held high and the demure smile that Graham liked so much, Jane attempted to glide up the aisle, but her father's steps were gratingly slow, as if he were dragging his feet. *What is he waiting for? He's not the one getting married, and I certainly know that he isn't mourning my loss.* She pulled against his arm, ever so slightly, urging him forward. *Please, please don't make a scene for once, Father. Please, let me have this moment.* She smiled at the snobby Miss Carol and the Montgomery sisters—*Wait, is Kitty Montgomery dressed in mourning over Graham?* She stuffed down her ire. No, not even the presence of her social enemies at her wedding would stifle her joy.

"Janey, I must speak with you," he whispered. "It is of the utmost importance and relevance."

She forced herself not to cringe. To everyone else, they would likely imagine his murmurs as sweet reassurance instead of his barely veiled panic. "Father, you know I love you," she returned through her pretty smile. "Please, wait to deliver this message. Don't ruin this for me."

He patted her arm and muttered something about the groom maybe not hearing the news. "Still there. That's a good sign. Perhaps it will be well."

She ignored Father's nonsensical mutterings. He often talked to himself, mentioning only fragments of sentences on his mind, making it nearly impossible to understand him most days. Behind her, she heard the heavy sanctuary doors scrape open again, but she didn't turn to see who could be entering so late and rudely interrupting her procession. Nothing could bother her today, though. She lifted her lashes and focused on Graham. Her handsome soon-to-be husband stood well over six feet, and his golden hair was brushed into a dashing pompadour. She could hardly believe that Graham was to be *hers*.

He had been named New York's bachelor of the year, and she had caught him. Certainly, her inheritance was enough to draw nearly every suitor to her door, but none had captured her attention like Graham Bank. From his deep, baritone laughter to his intense gaze never leaving her face as they conversed, Graham was a dream come true. He found her lovely and interesting and not silly at all. And his heart was hers.

From the corner of her eye, she spied a man in a simple brown suit with a bowler hat atop his hair, racing along the side of the church, as if he were trying to sit in the front. *Is he family?* But he did not stop at the front pew. He hurried straight up to Graham. Her heart pounded and her steps faltered. Was someone ill? His mother hadn't been able to make it this morning to the ceremony. Surely, she didn't pass? *No, not dear Mother Bank.* She had been so kind to Jane—far more tender than even her own mother had been.

"Oh dear. Oh dear. No, no, no—" Her father's pace slowed. "It's happened."

She tugged Father forward but nearly stumbled to a halt all together when alarm flitted across Graham's face and his eyes met hers.

Whatever it is, my darling, we will bear it together. She silently sent him the message from her heart to his. As in love as they were with one another, she was confident he would understand.

Graham staggered down the step that separated them. His large, smooth hand grasped her gloved hand. "My darling, did you know?" He bent and whispered in her ear.

"Know? Know what? Graham?" She returned, squeezing his hand. "What's wrong? Tell me."

Graham shook his head. "I-I cannot do this."

"Is it your mother, Graham?" Her chest tightened. "Is she worse?"

"No. It is other news . . . from Mother."

A *message* from Mother Banks? Surely, she would have wished the news to wait until after they were wed. *Unless it is truly terrible news?* Would Graham insist on pausing the ceremony, or would he wed her, since it was all arranged and leaving her at the altar could hardly be less than a scandal?

"Mother is fine."

"Thank goodness." She moved to press her hand to her heart but then remembered her bouquet.

His gaze landed on her father with a scowl. "But I cannot say the same for us."

Us? Her heart sped and the room seemed to shrink, every curious eye scalding her skin. "What do you mean? I don't understand, Graham."

Father's face reddened. "At least, have the courtesy to tell her in private, Bank."

"Something *you* should have done." Graham cradled her hand and slid it through his arm, pulling her back down the aisle, keeping his gaze firmly on the exit.

From the corner of her eye, she caught the flurry of black tulle as Kitty lifted her mourning veil, hope in her features. The already curious guests erupted in murmurs as Graham practically dragged Jane to the foyer, shoving the double doors closed behind them. Her groom released her the moment the doors closed behind them.

"Graham! What is going on?" She flung the veil away from her face—desperate to see Graham—to understand. She adjusted the chocolate curls framing her face and ran her fingers down the front of her exquisite wedding gown with its ornate pearl beading and diamond clusters.

He paused in his pacing, his frown softening for a moment. "You look stunning, Jane. I always loved it when your cheeks blushed." He sighed.

"T-thank you, but couldn't you have waited to tell me after the ceremony? Father was so insistent to tell me something too, but I made him wait." She refrained from twisting her hands. Graham hated it when she fidgeted. It was a horribly difficult habit to give up—fidgeting. "What happened?"

"There isn't going to be a ceremony, Jane." His gentle voice pierced her heart.

His words sent her staggering, as if he had struck her. "W-what? What do you mean? Everything is arranged. My things are awaiting me at our new home on Madison Avenue." She gestured to the closed doors. "The New York Four Hundred are seated inside as we speak and the rest of New York is awaiting our departure from the church just outside. The streets are lined with well-wishers. Surely, whatever it is isn't important enough to delay our ceremony. It will take a half an hour, and we will be wed and then, you can deal with whatever it is that needs your attention." She grasped his hand. "My dearest, please do not delay our wedding any further. I can only imagine the gossip that is spreading—"

"It is not a delay that I am seeking." He moved away from her touch, crossing his arms. "I cannot marry you. We are no longer *compatible* as our values do not align."

Compatible? "Did the messenger carry a false tale about me? I have been true only to you, Graham. I vow it. I've never even kissed anyone before you proposed to me." Her cheeks burned at the thought that *he* could not claim the same. But she had forgiven him for his momentary lapse in kissing Kitty Montgomery the very hour before requesting to court Jane. "What could that man have possibly said that would see you break my heart in front of the New York Four Hundred?"

"For that, I apologize. I would have avoided your humiliation if I had known." He shoved his hands into his pockets, remorse filling his gaze. "My mother sent the messenger. She said that if I go through with the wedding, she will disinherit me, and I will lose everything."

She gripped her stomach, her fingers rolling over the pearls sewn in patterns of orange blossoms. She couldn't breathe. Why couldn't she draw a full breath? "B-but Mother Bank was the one who championed our union. This makes no sense. And if her withdrawal of funds is stopping you, then I have more than enough to see us through."

Graham lifted a finger and pointed at the sanctuary doors. "See, there is where your father is a liar. My mother just read in the papers that your father is *ruined*."

She rested her hand on the wall, holding herself up as the room spun. *No. It can't be.* Was Graham breaking it off with her? Or simply informing and secretly desiring her to plead? She had pride, but this—this beautiful first hope of love being torn away from her because of her father's investments was something her pride could never come back from. The bouquet tumbled from her grasp as she folded her hands to her chest. "Graham, please don't do this. I'm begging you. Surely, there has been some kind of mistake—"

"No, there hasn't been a mistake." Graham raked his fingers through his hair, ruffling his perfect pompadour. "In fact, at this very moment, all your assets have been seized to pay for the debts Mr. Cady acquired for this latest venture. No doubt, they will be requiring even your wedding gown to pay back his debts."

Did Graham not know of her trust fund? A single butterfly of hope flapped its wings in her belly. "I have millions in my trust fund, Graham. Millions of dollars do not simply evaporate." She reached out to him. "There is no need to call off—"

"Not anymore. Your father had access to your funds and sank *everything* into a venture that would have seen your family the wealthiest in America. But the diamond ships sank, his venture failed, and you are without funds." He grasped her hand. "I'm sorry, Jane. I truly am. I was fond of you."

"Fond?" His once endearing touch that she had craved felt cold and a hint clammy even through her glove. "You said you loved me, Graham Bank."

He shoved his hands in his pockets and rocked back on his heels. "Love is such a funny word—it can mean so many different things. For instance, I love chocolate and horse riding."

"It is not a funny word," she ground out, her anger melting into a broken heart. Tears spilled down her cheeks. "It is a most sacred word when used by a man who wishes to wed."

"Well, whatever it is, I, in fact, do *not* love you, Jane Cady." He cleared his throat. "I wish things were different, but I must, based on my mother's message, step away from our commitment. I wish you luck."

Her knees buckled and she sank into a cloud of white as her world faded into blessed nothingness.

Murmurs filled the corridor. She could feel the cold stone seeping through her pretty silk stockings. Her head hurt. Why hadn't Graham caught her? Why hadn't he at least carried her out to the awaiting carriage and away from all the shame while she was unconscious? She didn't dare open her eyes to see how many people were staring at her, memorizing her humiliation to spill over high tea and rejoice over the great parvenus Cady family being brought low once again.

"We are ruined, Mildred." Father's voice came from her side. "There is nothing left for us here now."

"What do you mean, Benjamin?" Mother replied with a nervous laugh, as if trying to cover up her husband's troubling words and hide the fact that their world was imploding in front of the New York Four Hundred. "You aren't making any sense. Darling, can you see what is keeping Graham?" She pitched her voice to carry to the nearest guests who might spread her words, "Surely, he is fetching the doctor for our daughter, whom Graham knows so well that he anticipated her faint, which is why he pulled her from the altar!"

Poor Mother. She hated not being in control of a situation.

"Can we please leave, Mother? Everyone is staring. Father, can you lift her?" At twelve, Jane's sister Theodora was at least bold enough to tell her father what everyone else would not.

Father placed his hand under Jane's shoulder and lifted but dropped her immediately, her head thudding against the stones. She swallowed back a grunt at the sore spot being struck again. If it hadn't been for her ornate coiffure, she surely would have been concussed. She was going to have to open her eyes, wasn't she? She was going to have to face everyone as she fled the church.

Another, gentler, hand grasped her own. She nearly sagged in relief. Meg was there. Her best friend would see Jane out of this situation.

"Mr. Bank, there you are!" Meg called out to him. "Did you find the doctor?"

"No . . . ?"

"Then we must see her home to be attended to by her physician. Please, help our dear Jane to the carriage," Meg instructed.

A pair of strong arms lifted her and the sound of the large front doors swinging open were no sweeter than a choir of angels at this moment. Cool air kissed her scalding cheeks. The crowd outside cheered and faltered, no doubt at the sight of her supposedly unconscious form. They murmured and cried out, but she blocked the crowd out. She had only to survive until she was alone and then, and only then, could she fall apart. She felt herself gently deposited on a tufted leather seat.

"Just because I can't marry you, doesn't mean I wish you ill, Jane Cady. I did love you in my own way," Graham whispered.

So, she hadn't fooled him. She opened her eyes and glared at him through her long, dark lashes. "And yet, you have caused me the greatest pain of my three and twenty years, Graham. You are right, love *is* a funny word if this is what you think it means." She sat up and shoved him out of the carriage and slammed the door, rapping her fists on the ceiling. Her family could take the other carriage home. She had to get out of here. "Take me home, Oswald."

New York City blurred through her unshed tears for the short drive home and not even the sight of Central Park brought her peace as nature usually did. Nothing but further humiliation kept her tears at bay until she could be truly alone. As soon as the carriage rocked to a stop in front of her four-storied stone home, she gathered up her voluminous tulle and silk skirts and bolted out the carriage and up the steps into her home.

Men in bowler hats and dusty jackets paused to stare at her. She whirled, but they swarmed her estate, each bearing some sort of treasured collection from her home tucked in their arm, and all had notepads and pencils out.

The butler gasped and rushed to her side, his eyes wide at her sudden appearance when she was supposed to be getting married, but in his kind fashion, Smithy didn't question her. "I couldn't keep them out, Miss Cady," Smithy whispered. "The debt collectors had the police let them in—they had a warrant. There was nothing I could do. They haven't gone up—"

She nodded through her tears. She avoided eye contact with the strange men who scattered out of her path, like cockroaches being frightened by a lantern. Jane kept her head down as she raced upstairs to her room, tossing the veil over the side of the railing as she ran, sobbing for the life that had been promised to her—for the man who she thought was her dream. Father was right. She was ruined, and there was nothing left for the family in New York except humiliation.

THANKFULLY, her family did not seek her out after they returned from the church. With Mother's wailing filling the house and Father's shouted promises for a brighter future, even little Theo kept herself hidden away, so Jane allowed herself to wallow. She rested her cheek on the Parisian carpet beside her bed with her small wooden memory box next to her, the letters that Graham had written to her during their courtship spread about her feet like a fan. She had searched his letters for some sort of indication that he had not loved her . . . he had said all the right things.

Her door pushed open.

She couldn't let the servants see her like this. She sighed and pushed herself up to sit back on her heels as her dearest friend in the world poked her head inside.

"Janey?" Meg crossed the room in her bridesmaid's gown and knelt beside Jane, pushing aside the mountain of Jane's wedding tulle to sit. "I came as soon as I could, but I only just managed to keep the Montgomery ladies from calling upon you." She shivered. "The pair of them are still as spoiled and rude as they were when we were young girls." She grasped Jane's hand. "I am so sorry."

Her tears rose once more. "I'm sorry too. My father convinced yours to invest in the prospect as well."

"Yes, but he only gambled a half a million." Meg retrieved her handkerchief and gently dabbed away Jane's tears. "My dress budget will only suffer for a season, maybe two, but that matters not one whit to me. I only care about you and the fact that Graham treated you like . . . like—"

"Like a business deal gone poorly?" Jane lifted her favorite of all of Graham's letters —the very first he had sent her. She pointed to his little sketch of her at the ballroom when he first beheld her. She looked radiant in the sketch. She thought it captured how he viewed her. She felt special that the most desired bachelor of the season had singled her out. If her father's venture had been successful, their family's wealth would have surpassed even the Astor's and Vanderbilt's. "I thought he loved me."

Meg squeezed her hands. "You will find true love again, Jane. I know it." She shook her head. "Though, I highly suspect that Graham never truly loved you. And to be honest, I always thought him undeserving of you."

Jane released a short laugh. "I am inclined to agree. But what do I do now? How will I find a real love? No gentleman in this city will ever look at me again, much less wish to court me without money to my name."

Meg sighed. "I wish I could disagree, but you and I both know the types of people our set belongs to. For the majority, we fix our gazes on obtaining more and more wealth. I believe in another city, though, you may have your knight in shining armor awaiting you."

Jane released a short laugh, laced with the bitterness of the day. "What other city? Are you spiriting me away on a Grand Tour?"

Meg shook her head. "I wish that I could, dear friend. I wish that my money belonged to me and not to my father until I wed because I'd give it *all* to you, dearest Jane. I could beseech Papa, and he *might* say yes, but he is quite put out with your father at the moment. But I was referring to the message from one of your wedding guests that your father received while I was downstairs and—"

The door burst open once more, and Mother pointed to Jane on the floor. "You see? This is what your risk did for our family, Benjamin. And you expect me to abandon everything to move *West* in a matter of days? West!"

Theo's pale face appeared in the doorway, her body poised as if ready to run, if necessary, but curiosity over their fate, no doubt, compelled her little sister to listen as it did to Jane.

"We have no other choice, Mildred. And we have a week. Thankfully, I know the bank owner."

"Well, thank goodness for small mercies," Mother retorted. "A week to say farewell to a lifetime of friends? To my family?"

"They won't miss us that much for it is your parents who will not give me another dime."

"Because that portion of the family fortune belongs to my elder brother. You had my inheritance of millions, and you *gambled* it all away, Benjamin." She pressed her lips into a thin line.

"It was supposed to be a sure thing, not a gamble. How was I supposed to know that the diamond mines that I just purchased would dry up and that the diamonds I did manage to collect would sink along the coast?"

"But why did you have to send *all* the merchant vessels on this speculation? You should not have invested so heavily, Benjamin." Mother clenched her fists, her curls trembling in her effort to remain calm. "You even took the trusts that I set aside for our daughters. How did you even manage to access the funds without my signature?"

"I forged it, as I have done for years, but what is done is done. We are moving and that is final." Father nodded to Meg and had the decency to appear chastened, no doubt for what he had done to her family as well. "Please apologize to your father, Meg. I did not plan on this going so poorly." He turned to Jane, determination hardening his expression. "Plan on saying your goodbyes to your friends this week, Jane, but first, give me the ring."

Her eyes widened as he impatiently wiggled his fingers at her. "M-my ring?"

"Yes, the engagement ring. Because

Graham broke off the engagement, the ring is ours to sell, and we desperately need the funds for travel."

Meg gasped but she remained silent with her gaze on Jane, as if asking Jane if she would relinquish the one thing that could see her future secure.

Jane twisted the lovely pear cut sapphire with tiny pearls surrounding the gem in the light. It had given her such joy and pride when Graham had presented it to her. She almost protested that she wished to give it back to Graham, but what was the use of fighting her father when he had that gleam in his eyes? Years of experience dictated no other opinion would win but his. Numb, she slipped it from her finger and dropped it into her father's awaiting palm.

"There's a good girl. Tomorrow, sift through your things and pack whatever you can fit into two trunks. The creditors agreed to that much, as well as one heir-loom jewel each and the possession of our oldest horse. The rest of our belongings and stock will have to be sold off. We leave in one week."

The knot in her chest eased that at least her old gelding, Phantom, would not be taken from her too. "Can we leave sooner?" Her cheeks burned at the thought of being in New York that long—receiving guests and well-wishers and gossip mongers alike. *Lord, help me bear it.*

"I wish we could leave at once, but in order to get the best price for our things, I need to set up an auction," Father patted her awkwardly atop the head. "You must be brave for a little longer, Janey."

Meg pulled Jane to her feet and embraced her as Mother and Father departed as soon as they appeared, slamming the door behind them. "You see?" Meg whispered, her voice trembling. "It could be the new beginning you need, dear friend. Maybe you will find a life away from your father after all."

"A new life." Jane pulled away and ran her finger over Graham's miniature picture. "I was going to have it with Graham."

Meg rested her hand atop Jane's, covering the miniature. "I know this is not what you want, but perhaps the Lord is sparing you from a life with a man who values money more than his bride." Her gaze flitted to the door.

Like my parents. She lowered Graham's picture into the box, packing away his letters and tokens of affection, her tears smearing the ink on the final letter—the one where he admitted his intentions. Her heart grew too heavy, and she leaned into her friend's arms once more. If this was what a man's love was like, she wanted nothing to do with it ever again.

Sign Up for Grace's Newsletter!

Keep up to date with Grace's news on book releases and giveaways by signing up for her email list at GraceHitchcock.com

FREE from Grace Hitchcock

New Orleans, 1895

Colette Olivier, a young widow who married out of obligation, finds herself at the end of her mourning period and besieged with suitors out for her inheritance. With her pick of any man, she is drawn to an unlikely choice.

The Widow of St. Charles Avenue by Grace Hitchcock a Second Chance Brides Novella
GraceHitchcock.com

Scan to Claim Your FREE Novella

More in your favorite series . . .

Forced into a betrothal with a widower twice her age, Charleston socialite, Sophia Fairfield is desperate for an escape. Much to her dismay, Sophia finds herself falling in love with the wrong gentleman—a man society would never allow her to marry, given Sophia was supposed to be his new stepmother. The only way to save Carver from ruin is to run away, leaving him and all else behind to become a Harvey Girl waitress at the Castañeda Hotel in New Mexico.

The Finding of Miss Fairfield by Grace Hitchcock
Aprons & Veils #1
A Friends-to-Lovers Runaway Bride RomCom

With a hope for belonging, Belle Parish leaves her position as a maid in Charleston to travel to New Mexico to become a mail-order bride. Colt Lawson's letters hold great promise, but something does not add up. Belle flees straight into the Castañeda Hotel Harvey House. Giving up the prospect of marrying, she focuses on her role as a Harvey Girl waitress until a strong Texas Ranger rides into her life.

The Pursuit of Miss Parish by Grace Hitchcock
Aprons & Veils #2
A Mail-Order Bride RomCom

When former New York socialite turned Harvey Girl, Jane Cady, spots her ex-fiancé at the Castañeda Hotel, she panics—and kisses unsuspecting rancher Wade Sterling, claiming they're happily courting. Wade agrees to play along, but the longer their fake romance goes on, the more he wants it to be real. Wade determines to prove he's the man of her dreams—she just doesn't know it yet.

The Courting of Miss Cady by Grace Hitchcock
Aprons & Veils #5
A Fake-Dating RomCom